FOR LOVE

BOOK 3 OF THE BLESSED BE SERIES

ROBIN REARDON

IAM Books
www.robinreardon.com

FOR LOVE
Book 3 of the BLESSED BE series

ISBN: 978-1-7340569-8-3

Praise for the works of Robin Reardon

"Whether it's sexuality, gender identity, or religion, author Robin Reardon's impressive body of work exquisitely and profoundly examines an individual's journey of self-discovery. With *For Love of Self*, the author has crafted another unforgettable, thought-provoking tale."
— Christopher Verleger, Edge Media Network

"Featuring a broad cast of characters, the author makes everyone feel unique… will keep readers engaged and entertained."
— Kirkus Reviews

"Thanks for bringing alive the gay faith experience at such a dramatic time and place!"
— Kittredge Cherry: Founder/publisher, Q Spirit

"Reardon's prose is gorgeous. She always surprises with her originality and her emotional writing. I anxiously await whatever she writes."
— Amos Lassen Reviews

"Show me how to love in the darkest dark."
Ruth Moody, The Wailin' Jenny

"Nothing dies of too much love."
Paul Simon

FOREWORD

BY CHRISTOPHER CROUCHER

Writing about a subject as intimate as religion can be a daunting undertaking. Throughout the *Blessed Be* series, Robin Reardon touches on not just one but several faith groups, committing to both honest and compassionate representations along the way. For me, reading the series with a critical eye from the intersectional perspective of a Pagan practitioner and gay man, I have been fascinated and truly touched by the interplay of religious calling and personal discovery that Reardon has illuminated in her work.

Paganism is a broad umbrella. I've heard it said that if you ask ten Pagans what their beliefs are, you'll receive at least as many answers, if not more. My own expertise comes from over twenty-five years learning, practicing and teaching as an eclectic Pagan, some on my own and some within communities, as is often the way with Pagans. It gives me a bit of a chuckle to say that some of Reardon's descriptions of the Pagan characters in *For Love of God* and *For Love* may seem a bit exaggerated, dancing naked in the woods and having all-night bonfires in the middle of winter. Many of us may even enjoy that they seem that way. I laugh, though, because I can tell you from personal experience that it is not an exaggeration at all.

While it could never represent even a fraction of the vast range of Pagan practitioners and practices, I was stunned to read the accuracy with which The Forest and its inhabitants are portrayed. From a solo communion with Nature by dancing in erotic bliss to an open and friendly connection between communities around a maypole, the truths that are shared within this narrative are very much real. There are numerous modern-day communities that practice together, celebrating and supporting one another and sharing their love of and belief in the magic of Nature. We are lucky enough that most don't have to hide in forested communes these days but are instead open, welcoming and deeply engaged with the interfaith community around the world.

That is not to say that prejudice is gone. It most certainly is not. The shared though varied experience of queer people like Spencer, Donald, Marshall, Adam, Vanessa and the new character Kira is very similar in that way to what many Pagan people have endured both decades ago and today. The secrecy and isolation of the Forest Dwellers may seem a bit much, but many of us, both queer people and Pagans, still feel it necessary to hide our identities when we are in public or meeting people until we are more certain of our personal safety. There is a real and too-often-realized danger of losing employment, being isolated from family and friends, suffering harassment and even being misrepresented in court if one is "out of the broom closet" (as some Pagans lovingly call it).

That is why this series is so relevant today. Though we are technically decades removed from the events of this story, they are perennially relatable. Being gay or queer is a biological, physical, mental and personal truth that we cannot deny. Being drawn to a faith that fills our souls is equally an undeniable calling. As a Pagan who participates in and holds space for spiritual practices within communities, and as a gay man who has felt the personal struggle of self-discovery and the love and loss that goes along with being that authentic self, the *Blessed Be* series has been a pleasure to experience. I learned a lot. I may possibly have shed a tear (or several). Most importantly, I have appreciated the way that this story is told. May it be a blessing for you as well!

Christopher Croucher
Pagan Practitioner and Teacher
Leominster, Massachusetts
2024

PREFACE

ON THE ISSUE OF TRANSGENDER

The entire *Blessed Be* series takes place in the 1980s. *For Love* takes place in 1988. At that time, there was less understanding than we have today about many things, including the phenomenon of transgender.

In *For Love*, readers will meet a transgender teen. In the then current edition of the DSM (*Diagnostic and Statistical Manual of Mental Disorders-III-R*, pub. 1987), this phenomenon was referred to as transsexualism (see section 302.50 of that manual).

The DSM-III-R, which I refer to in *For Love*, describes "transsexualism" in ways that will seem prejudicial and even primitive, compared to how transgender is viewed by the medical and psychiatric community in 2024, the year of publication of *For Love*.

Individuals who are transgender, and their advocates, continue to work toward acceptance. There has been progress since the 1980s, but much more progress must be made. As an advocate myself, my own belief—which readers will see played out in *For Love*—is that each individual knows who they are better than anyone else.

CONTENTS

Note that while reading all three of the *Blessed Be* books in order will take you on Spencer Hill's journey with him—his first love, his successes and failures, and the maturity he gains along the way —each book can be read and enjoyed individually.

CHAPTER 1

My darling Bettina,

That's how the letter opened. In my entire life, up until my father died, I don't think I'd ever heard him use the word "darling." Not in any context.

The letter went on.

When you left the room, the light went with you. It was not unexpected, for this phenomenon occurs each time you leave my presence. And yet the smile you cast over your shoulder to me fairly made the air sparkle, and some of that remained long enough to ignite my hopes for seeing you again.

I had to set the letter down. Closing my eyes and pinching the bridge of my nose didn't help bring me back to reality.

Father had written these words? *My* father? Bettina had been my mother's name, so at least I could picture the intended recipient. I think, from what my late parents had told me, they had met when my father had gone with another Catholic priest to perform the monastic consecration service of two women in the convent where my mother, along with another couple of postulants, had been assigned to serve food and drink to the visiting priests.

How the relationship had moved on from there was never clear to me. As an ordained Catholic priest, Father would not have been with Mother unaccompanied, so it was quite beyond me how he would have known her well enough to write letters professing the kinds of feelings the word "darling" carried with it.

I picked up the letter again.

Many hours I have spent in prayer, as my sore knees can attest, to banish thoughts of you, images of you, the phantom warmth of you encircled by my arms. As I know I must, I reach for guilt, for shame. Sometimes these appear faintly, along the edge of a feather that would be remorse and repentance if it turned. But as if with a breath, they are gone. And I am left with wanting you.

How on earth... how in *heaven* would my mother have responded to this missive, this outpouring of a passion I never suspected?

As I read these letters I was in New York City, in the commercial storage room where I had stowed so many of the things from the townhouse where I had grown up—a property I had sold just last year. From my perch on a sealed crate I reached again into the wooden box where the letter had lain for decades. The box was a simple thing, maple or perhaps birch, maybe eighteen inches long, six inches deep and eight inches wide. Once it would have had a sheen. Now, it appeared almost dingy. There were no markings on it, as though to fool someone who came upon it into thinking it held nothing important. It had no lock.

My hand grasped a different pile of letters. The letter to my mother had been in a pile tied with a satin ribbon of faded blue. The ribbon on this other pile was yellow, faded almost to cream. A quick glance told me these were letters Mother had written in response, so I looked for one with a date close to the one I had been reading from Father to her.

Joshua, my earthly angel,

Angel? *Father?* I shook my head in confusion. There was no doubt in my mind that my parents had loved each other. But my experience with Father had never once hinted at anything angelic. He'd been righteous if not Draconian, firm almost to the point of being rigid, and he'd expressed himself with a conviction that brooked no argument from me. And Mother had always bowed to his will, at least in every way I witnessed.

She had written:

I, too, struggle with the conflict of what I believe I should feel and what my heart's longing puts before me so undeniably. That heart knows it should be in a debtor's prison, having sworn itself to the service of Jesus Christ and fealty to His people, and yet the convent's walls prove inadequate to the task of imprisonment. I dare not tell you what my fondest hopes would have happen between us.

Tenderly, almost ashamed of having violated the private lives of the people responsible for my existence, I restored the letters to their faded ties and set them back into the box.

I had come to the city, taking a few days during the week away from my ministry in Vermont, to sort through the material remnants of my youthful life, and to visit my parents' graves. Father had died when I was at Columbia, and Mother had died during my first year at General Theological Seminary. The memory of her, wrapped in a dark green shearling coat—a luxury unlike almost anything she had ever allowed herself—as she dashed across Fifth Avenue in an attempt to prevent a young girl from straying into traffic, will haunt me for the rest of my life. Helpless, disbelieving what I was seeing, I had been unable to stop her.

I had buried her in that green coat.

Mother had been my source of love, of caring, of comfort. Her sweet face, her submissive behavior that hid a spine of steel, were attributes I could imagine any straight man falling in love with. Only now, reading these letters, did I have a sense of how in love with Father she must have been.

Neither of my parents had known I was gay. Or, if they did, it was never spoken of. I truly doubt Father knew. Mother, if she had known, would have said nothing unless I did. And I did not.

As for the box.... Should I leave it here in storage? Should I take it home with me?

I held it in both my hands and looked at it, allowing my vision to blur a little, leaving myself open to a message from the Universe.

No message came. Or, nothing I recognized as a message.

I took the box with me.

~

"So, Spencer, how's the archeological dig going?"

I would not have guessed that David Foster and I would become close friends. Assisi, Vermont, where we were both ministers, was barely large enough to support one Catholic church, one Unitarian Universalist (mine), and a third that could be classified as vaguely Protestant. David was the minister there. He knew I'd been to the city, and why.

I set my coffee cup down and regarded David across the Formica table, taking amused pleasure in the way his sandy blond hair did its best to stand out from his head in a way he almost certainly didn't intend.

We met here frequently, in the only diner the tiny town of Assisi had to offer. Sometimes, when we had more serious ministerial topics to discuss, one of us would go to the other's home. Usually it was mine, in case we wanted to talk about something private enough that his wife or his young son should not overhear. But today, Thursday, it was casual.

In answer to his question, I told him, "It's quite a process." His face registered understanding, knowing I meant it was just this side of hell. "I don't know what to do with things I don't want to keep." I waved a hand. "Oh, some of it can be put to use somewhere. Clothing, for example. But things like the few stuffed animals I had as a child give me pause. One can't donate those. But can one merely chuck them away?"

I considered telling him about the letters. But—no. They were intimate, containing material it wasn't mine to reveal.

He said, "Forgive me if this is too personal, or too—oh, I don't know, too lame-brained. Can you see yourself having a child who might want them?"

I grinned at him. David knew I was gay. "Even if I did, one look at them and you'd know that no child would want them now."

We sipped our coffee and nibbled on our respective doughnuts for a moment. Then David asked, "Have you had a heads-up yet for what tricks your parishioners might play on you this weekend?"

I gave him an arch look. "You should be asking me what *my* plans are for an April Fool's trick on *them.*"

He laughed. "All right. What tricks do you have in mind?"

April first, that year, 1988, would fall on a Friday, but I'd been warned to expect something foolish to happen on Sunday, the third. One aspect of Unitarian Universalism that I found simply delightful was the sense of humor that runs all though that tradition. We take our commitment to each other and to the betterment of life on earth very seriously, but we don't take ourselves so seriously that we lose our sense of humor. I had long ago lost count of how many jokes UU members themselves have created and told about our tradition. My favorite was that we begin prayers with "To Whom It May Concern."

I said, "You know how UU congregations don't join in right away singing a hymn they're not familiar with?"

I waited for David to nod. He said, "They want to read through the text first to see if they agree with it."

"Exactly. So Sunday, my secretary, Deena Cunningham, will have put an insert into each program. It's for a special springtime-oriented call-and-response, where I make a statement and they respond. Only there are several different versions of those inserts. They don't all have the same response for any of my statements. So everyone will be saying different things, only not because they decided to."

David chuckled. "But are you sure they'll even notice?"

I hesitated, just for a second, and then laughed. He was right;

UU members are quite accustomed to doing their own individual things their own individual ways. "You're absolutely right to wonder! I'll let you know how it goes."

❧

Back home, I fastened a leash onto Klondike, the Great Pyrenees dog I had adopted from my predecessor at church. Vanessa Doyle had been the UU minister for many years, until her failing health forced her to turn the pulpit over to someone else—me. And when her health failed further last winter, Loraine Fuller and her two cats had moved in to care for Vanessa, and the interaction between Klondike and the felines left doubts as to which flying fur came from which animal. Klondike and I had already developed a healthy friendship, so he came to live with me. I wasn't sure, but I suspected that this one act—the adoption, and the fact that as I walked Klondike I encountered many people who lived in this rural town—helped me gain acceptance as the UU pastor, despite my young age of twenty-eight.

When she had been still able, Vanessa had instructed me in the best way to walk Klondike.

"His is a willful breed," she'd told me. "You need to maintain a firm leadership position, or he'll take advantage. And he almost outweighs you."

This was an exaggeration. Even so, as I walked beside this white creature, nearly the size of a small pony with a long, thick, white coat and golden tips on his ears, I made sure he didn't walk ahead of me, and that the lease was short but relaxed. Vanessa had taught me some tricks to distract him in the event he seemed to be too focused on something, and mostly they worked. But despite my own height of six-foot-two-inches, sometimes he won.

Vanessa had also told me Klondike was a great dog to hike with, and she'd been right. At those times, I let him roam, running around without guidance from me, because he always came back when he heard the sound of the whistle Vanessa had given me.

That afternoon I walked Klondike to Vanessa's for a short visit. With the help of her home-care worker Sheila Johnson, she was able to come out into the mild, early spring afternoon for a few minutes, though it was challenging to keep Klondike from jumping joyfully onto her.

Loraine, whom Vanessa had married in a ceremony on January first—officiated by me—was at work. Sheila, who sported a slight Irish accent and a prim, white apron, brought out three mugs of hot tea and some cookies, and we all sat in lawn chairs in the back yard and chatted until Vanessa's energy faded.

As she was helping Vanessa inside, Sheila asked me, "Can you stay for a few minutes, Reverend? There's something I'd like to ask you about."

When she came back outside, she brought a pot of hot tea and refilled our mugs. "Vanessa is settling into a nap, and I don't think this will take long."

"Is there something I can help you with?"

She sipped from her mug, a vessel so thickly covered with painted flowers I couldn't discern the color of the thick ceramic beneath them. She gazed at me over the rim, her heavy, dark eyebrows contrasting with the almost-grey of her hair. "I want to know more about the fire."

Ah, yes. The fire. *The* fire. Sheila had moved here from Newport, about forty-five minutes away, to take this job. She didn't know a lot about the history of this region.

I asked, "How much do you already know?"

"Just that something you did last fall got everyone all stirred up, and now there's a lot of general talk about it. But no one will talk to *me* about it."

"Really? I don't know why not. It isn't a secret, as far as I know. Even Vanessa and Loraine won't discuss it?"

"Vanessa just tells me to ask you. I don't see a lot of Loraine, and when we talk it's mostly about how Vanessa is doing."

"Okay. Well, I'll try to make a long story a little shorter. There's an area just east of here called The Forest. The original settlers came in the eighteenth century, mostly people who'd been accused of witchcraft. Then in a kind of accident of fate, another group of people took refuge there, people who had been in a group called Perfectionists. I won't go into a lot of detail about *their* traditions, other than to say they were unorthodox. For whatever reason, these folks all got along, and the settlement thrived."

Sheila interrupted. "So are they still there?"

I shook my head. "Not exactly. But around the turn of the last century, a family in Little Boundary—a town a little north of here —a family by the name of Burgos, whose land was adjacent to The Forest, accused the settlers of taking over some Burgos land and absconding with some livestock. There was an attack on The Forest, and many homes were burned. Several people died."

"Good God in heaven."

"It seems someone from The Forest thought he recognized a man from Assisi as one of the perpetrators, and that rumor took hold to the point that Assisi got blamed for the attack. After that, there was a lot of enmity between The Forest and Assisi."

I stopped to sip some tea, and Sheila asked, "So what was it you did?"

"No one here ever spoke of it in my hearing out of a profound sense of shame. And then, completely by accident, I stumbled upon the story, and with the help of David Foster at the Protestant church, and Milton Bryant at the Catholic church, and Ben Marks the police chief, we figured out that the recognition had been in error, and no one from Assisi had been involved at all."

Sheila scowled. "That's—I don't know what that is. So did the Perfectionists get over it?"

"Well, as far as I know, there hasn't been anyone still calling themself a Perfectionist there for many years. The people who live there now are Pagans. And, no, I wouldn't say they've gotten over it, though they now understand that Assisi wasn't involved. I'm on good terms with them, as are a few others here in Assisi, but we're still learning how to mix with each other."

She shook her head. "I confess I don't understand who those

people are. My church in Newport would have had nothing good to say about Pagans."

I chuckled. "Well, now that warmer weather is creeping up on us, there might be some opportunities for you to get to know a few of them. They're quite friendly."

"They don't have a bunch of weird rituals? Things like that?"

"I wouldn't call them weird, no."

"No infant sacrifices?"

I did my best not to laugh; that scene was very far from what I knew about the Forest Dwellers. "No. Not even any animal sacrifices. They grow most of their own food, they have their own livestock, and their children come to the town high school when they're old enough. They have their own grammar school."

"Devil worship?"

"Satan, the devil, is essentially an invention of the early Christian church. As such, it's a Christian concept. So for the most part, if someone isn't coming in some way from a Christian point of view, there's no devil to worship." I wasn't about to go into the Islamic view of evil, and I was pretty sure that Satanists would take issue with at least some of my explanation, but I thought it would serve to draw a sharp line between Paganism and devil worship. And never mind that there were devilish persona in other religious traditions. It's unlikely Sheila would have seen images from the *Tibetan Book of the Dead*.

"Hmmm." Sheila seemed unconvinced. "Do they run around naked, or anything?"

I had to hide my involuntary smile with a long drink of tea as I shook my head.

Adam. Adam Cooper. That Forest Dweller had, in fact, been "running around naked" the first time I'd seen him, though I'd never known the other Forest Dwellers to do so. I still didn't know how much of an anomaly that scene had been.

It had been my first walk in the woods around Assisi, not long after I'd moved here last September from New York. I had been communing with Nature, feeling very at one with the universe as

I'd approached a small pond, when I'd seen him. He stood naked, near the water's edge, his beautiful body worthy of being a template for a Greek sculpture. He had seemed unaware of me as I watched him go through the motions of a kind of dance, ending in a sunlit orgasm that arched into the water before him. I won't deny it had aroused me to watch. I also won't deny that I'd brought the scene to mind many times in the following weeks.

And now we were lovers. At least, after a fashion. In recognition of my genuine interest in their community, I'd been invited to participate in their winter Solstice celebrations last December. Adam had driven me home, and after kissing me, he'd told me he'd never love me. He'd said I would be foolish to love him. And he'd said that wanting was something else entirely.

So we had—well, wanted, and partaken of each other many times since then. He was creative and fearless in life as well as in bed, and I had barely managed to avoid falling in love with him.

I shared none of this with Sheila. But I finally managed to say, "I've found them to be wonderful neighbors. They keep largely to themselves, wanting to maintain their way of life without disturbance, but I always enjoy any interactions with them."

She tilted her head, a look of skepticism on her face. "I'll take your word for it."

Sunday was a wonderful day for fools. I hadn't known what to expect from my congregation, and their prank caught me by surprise. Somehow they had organized themselves well enough that if anyone wasn't in the know about what to do, it wasn't obvious to me.

Playing on the typical habit of waiting to join in with an unfamiliar hymn until they'd read through the text to see if they agreed with it, when it was time for the first hymn of the service, Violet Verette at the piano played through the music for the first verse as usual, and then—again as usual—I began to sing, lifting my voice into the arched ceiling overhead, expecting some would join with me, and then others as they chose. But no one else sang! Violet kept playing as though nothing was amiss. My own strong baritone began to falter as I realized mine was the only voice, and then laughter took over.

At this point, everyone was laughing. I gave it a moment and then said to them, "You got me."

My prank on them, with their varied responses to my statements, took them a few minutes to catch on to. Again the whole thing collapsed as laughter rose to that ceiling and danced there.

It didn't matter that the day was cool and drizzly. It was a terrific day, and not for the first time I felt grateful that I'd been assigned to what had, at first, seemed to me like a remote outpost.

Later that afternoon, I walked Klondike, toweling off his thick coat when we got back to the small, cozy house the church owned and allowed me to live in. I stood in the kitchen, contemplating whether to make something for dinner or reheat a casserole given to me by a parishioner, when the phone rang. I picked it up, hoping ungenerously that there was no problem that required my attention that evening.

"Spencer Hill here," I said, and waited through a few seconds of silence.

Then, "Hi."

I knew that voice. One word was all I needed.

Donald Rainey.

CHAPTER 2

"Sorry to take you by surprise." Donald didn't sound sorry. He sounded like his old self, the mercurial, playful, teasing Donald I'd fallen in love with over four years ago, the Donald he'd been before he was swallowed whole by a cult known as Risen Christ.

"Yeah," I said, doing my best to sound unsurprised, "I was never one for surprises. But it's good to hear from you."

"Maybe you'd like to *see* me as well?"

I held the phone in front of my face, blinking stupidly at it as though I wasn't sure what it was trying to tell me. Finally I managed, "Is this an invitation to visit the city?"

"Nope. This time, I'm coming north. Well, that is, *we* are coming north."

We. Right. I had tried to forget that Donald was now seeing someone seriously, a man named Jonathan. My mind raced; how could I respond to this news?

"Oh?" I said, stalling for time. "Springtime in Vermont, or something?"

Donald chuckled, and I told myself he sounded a little nervous. "Not exactly. Jonathan is on a mission. He wants to save gay kids."

I shook my head as though Donald could see me. "I'm gonna need a little more than that."

"Okay, well, how about if we all talk about it when we're together in person? We're driving up Wednesday. I thought about asking you for a hotel reference in Assisi, but Jonathan wanted someplace a little bigger. So we're staying at this inn in Little Boundary, just up the road. Pinewood B&B, it's called."

I tried to speak and failed. Little Boundary held so many different feelings for me. Some good, but more not so good. But would I prefer to have Donald and his new boyfriend stay in Assisi? I would not.

"I know that place. I often stop in the restaurant there for hot chocolate after hiking in the area."

There was a slight pause. "You hike?"

"I do. Klondike and I hike together."

"Um, Spence…?"

I laughed. "Klondike is my dog. A Great Pyrenees. You'll meet him at some point, I'm sure. So, Wednesday, you say?"

"Yeah. We'll be there at least a week, so we're planning to come hear you preach on Sunday. Um, Jonathan is Jewish. Jews are welcome at UU services, right?"

"Of course. Everyone is welcome." I did my best not to react to the idea of both of them hearing me preach. Bad enough that Donald, the actor who had insisted that his was a craft I would need in my vocation, might gauge how good a student I had been. But now Jonathan, too? This hardly seemed fair; he would get to assess me, judge me, while he sat there and made mental notes. "So… does Jonathan know anything about me? About us?"

"He knows enough. He's not the jealous type. And anyway, I've told him you have someone gorgeous warming your bed for you these days. Maybe we can all have dinner together?"

I hoped Donald did not hear my sharp intake of breath. "Possibly. Why don't you give me a call when you're settled."

∼

There was so much flotsam floating around my brain after that call that I hardly saw anything right in front of me. I managed to heat up a portion of tuna casserole that Andrea Beale, one of the lay ministers at my church, had sent over with her teenage son Duncan at his piano lesson last week. I threw a handful of lettuce into a bowl, set it next to my plate, and sat down at the breakfast nook that overlooked the back yard. I stared out the window for a few minutes, not even seeing how the setting sun had lightened all the soft greenery of spring, showing off its new life. I barely noticed Klondike when he came to sit at the end of the bench and looked at me, clearly puzzled.

Then, "Oh, Klondike! I'm sorry, boy. I didn't feed you, did I?" I got up and prepared the dog's dinner, babbling to him about how much Donald's phone call had garbled my brain.

Back in front of my own plate, I made an effort to eat. The casserole was fine; Andrea was a pretty good cook. But my thoughts would not settle.

Jonathan wants to save gay kids.

Jonathan is not the jealous type.

Donald and Jonathan will be staying at the inn Marshall Savage had introduced me to. In Little Boundary. The town from where, eighty-plus years ago, the Burgos family had launched a cruel, barbaric, fiery attack on the settlement now known as The Forest.

Little Boundary, Assisi's closest neighbor, despite the enmity that began before the turn of the century, even before the attack on The Forest. Gold was discovered on land between the towns, land that hadn't yet been claimed. Both towns vied for ownership in a conflict that nearly turned violent. Little Boundary won the battle, but they lost any goodwill Assisi might have had for them. The gold didn't last long, but the rancor between the towns remained. Little Boundary, also home to Alan Jermin, pastor of the Assembly of God church. A most unpleasant man. He had refused my offer of friendship. "Get thee behind me." "Sodomizer." Even when I, along with Adam and his housemate, Myra Langtree, had rescued not only his two children but also his three pure white horses from his barn after his young son had set the place afire, the man had been as boorish and offensive as ever. "Get off my land!"

Pinewood B&B, where Marshall and I had stopped with Klondike after hiking.

Marshall.

Oh, Marshall! How I wished I knew where he was. He had disappeared completely, left Assisi without a look back (unless you count that painfully beautiful note he'd left me). He had loved me. And I had almost loved him, a truly gentle soul, but fragile in many ways. Still, he'd had the backbone to leave under his own steam when it was clear he could no longer stay in Assisi. I don't think Donald knew about Marshall.

But Donald already knew something about Adam. In January Donald had called to wish me a Happy New Year, and to tell me about Jonathan. And when he'd asked about my love life, it was just after Adam and I had—gosh, had what? It wasn't quite correct to say he was my lover. Nor was he my boyfriend. One term that could describe our sexual encounters was "fuck buddies," but that was no fitting description for the sublime yet overwhelming sense of the ethereal, the otherworldly, that came over me each time we were intimate.

I should never have mentioned Adam during that phone call, except that Donald had just told me about Jonathan and I was—all right, I admit it, just a tiny bit jealous. And I didn't want to say, "Well, yeah, I was with someone until a few weeks ago, a really sweet guy, but he got fired from his teaching job when this asshole of a pastor in Little Boundary sent proselytizers over to Assisi to scout out whatever nasty things he could find about me, and they accidentally discovered that my lover was teaching high school English, and when they reported him as gay to the vice principal, he got fired and had to leave town."

I also hadn't wanted to say, "No one right now, no."

So I'd said, "A very beautiful man, as it happens. A sculptor." I had *not* added, "He's pansexual, and Pagan, and almost engaged to a woman who knows about us and who lives in the same house with him and a couple of other people in this settlement outside of town called The Forest. We're in lust."

Klondike had finished his dinner several minutes ago, and now he sat beside me, watching me closely as though worried, while I leaned my elbows on the table and my head in my hands, at least half of my dinner still in front of me.

I sat back, dropped my hands to my lap, and looked at Klondike. "What's your advice, boy? How am I going to handle this meeting?" I leaned my head back against the wall behind me and barked out a humorless laugh. "A dinner. With Donald, and Jonathan, and me, and Adam. Ha! That ain't happenin'."

Klondike lifted a paw and set it gently on the bench beside me. "What's that? You'll go with me instead, as my date?" I ruffled the fur on his head. "That's more likely than anything else."

David's phone call Tuesday afternoon was a welcome distraction from thoughts of Donald's arrival the next day. He asked if he could stop by, which I assumed meant there was a ministerial matter to discuss. I was right.

"It's about a young boy in my parish," he opened. We sat in my small living room, made noticeably smaller by the presence of the black baby grand piano I'd had moved north last fall. I had never been without it, my whole life, until I'd put it into storage to take up my Assisi assignment at the end of last summer. Even though I knew it was too big for this space, and even though I knew its voice was less impressive here than it had been in the large music room in my parents' townhouse, I wanted it with me. I needed it with me.

I asked, "Is he in some kind of trouble?"

"I suspect that he's suicidal, actually. He loves to sing. Or, he used to. He's always been involved in anything that included music—pageants, choir, solos, everything. But now that he's sixteen, the sweet soprano voice is gone."

"Ah, yes. I love singing, myself. I recall how embarrassing it was when my voice changed. But I kind of like where it ended up. So he doesn't sing anymore; that's too bad. And that might change. But—suicidal?"

David scrunched his face as though trying to squeeze unwilling words out. "I'm far from positive, or I'd be taking more assertive steps. It just seems as if he's lost himself. Not just that he's stopped singing. It's more. He's pulled into himself so far that he's nearly disappeared."

"Not physically, though? I mean, you still see him in church?"

"He does come to services, or at least his body is there, sitting with his sister between his parents. But when my eyes fall on him, I can tell he's not there mentally, or emotionally, or spiritually… it's hard for me to put a finger on it."

"What can I do to help?"

David gave me an inscrutable glance. "I suspect he might be gay."

Involuntarily, I sat back a little in my chair. "I see." We gazed at each other for a moment. "Have you spoken with his parents at all?"

"I did try. I didn't feel I could just come out and say something direct, so although they were happy enough to chat, that's all they thought the meeting was about. At least, as far as I could tell."

I wasn't sure what to say. The awkwardness of this situation was apparent: a boy in David's Protestant congregation had a problem he hadn't voiced, a problem that might or might not mean that I had something important in common with him, and David had presented me with this situation as though I'd know what to do. I didn't. But I did have one idea.

I asked, "How familiar are you with Teens for Truth?"

"You've referred to it a few times. I confess, though, that I have only a vague notion of what it is."

"Marshall Savage and I started it last fall. He and Jenny Pratt, one of my lay ministers, were the leaders. At first there were just a few kids from the high school, but it grew, and even a few kids from The Forest joined. When Marshall left, Myra Langtree—a teacher at the grammar school in The Forest—joined Jenny. So it's more or less under the auspices of my UU church, but not all the kids are in my congregation."

David asked, "What's the purpose?"

"They call it Teens for Truth because it's a safe place where they can express themselves pretty much however they need or want to, within certain parameters and with guidance from the leaders, of course. They talk, they write, they put on skits, they paint or draw or sculpt, and they sing and play instruments. I've attended some sessions, though they've been clear they don't really want 'the minister' to spend a lot of time there. Some of the discussions I've heard have impressed me with their candor, and with the depth of personal experience they bring to the group."

"You're thinking this boy might like to join?"

"It's worth a question. At least you can see what he knows about it, tell him a little something, and see what happens. They meet every Tuesday at four, in the UU function hall."

"Do you know whether any of them are gay?"

I shook my head. "No idea. Jenny or Myra might know, but they would never mention it to me. They wouldn't 'out' someone." I added, "If he's interested, he can either just show up, or Jenny or Myra could contact him and ease him in."

We left it that David would let me know how his conversation with the boy went.

I watched from my open front door as David walked to his car, waving good-bye as he drove away. Then I stood there for several seconds until Klondike nuzzled the back of my leg. I'd been planning to work for a while at the piano, an attempt to avoid thinking about Donald's arrival. But I fetched the leash.

Klondike and I headed, almost by spoken agreement, toward the high school where Marshall used to teach English. One of my first impressions of him had come from how well he'd handled his students as they'd studied Shakespeare's *MacBeth*. He'd managed to inspire their interest in something most school kids found to be obscure and maybe even ridiculous.

As I headed for the wooded path that left from the school's parking lot, I recalled that it had been on this path that Marshall had told me how he felt about me. I hadn't been completely surprised, but it had taken me a while—weeks, really—to figure out how I felt about him. I still cringed inwardly whenever I recalled how much more attached he'd ended up being to me than I'd been to him. I missed him, yes. I'd been very fond of him. But the note he'd left me had made it clear that it had been much harder for him to leave me behind than it had been for me to have him go.

I'd been on the path for maybe ten minutes when I saw a tall figure coming toward me. He looked for all the world like some kind of slender lumberjack, with a blue and brown plaid flannel shirt, baggy pants of some color that would defy even an artist to identify, and scuffed workbooks the color of dirt.

Adam. Odd; I hadn't seen his green truck in the school parking lot, but it must have been there. My preoccupation must have made me oblivious.

I smiled and waved. He lifted his chin in greeting, his arms fully engaged in balancing a large log on one shoulder. A sheathed hatchet swung from his belt. As we got close, he set the log down, one end on the ground, and grinned.

I said, "Taking the trees home one at a time, are we?"

"Take a look at this specimen." He glanced down, but I watched him, not the log. As usual, his auburn hair was tied back with a leather thong, falling down almost to his waist. I knew that beneath the flannel shirt was a muscled chest, nearly hairless, that responded beautifully to my touch.

"What's special about it? Sorry. I can't tell."

He shook his head. "Philistine. It's sugar maple, but not just plain maple. Sometimes a maple tree grows in a certain way, and the grain takes on a wavy, striped pattern. Tiger maple."

Now I did look at the log. The bark had been removed, probably by Adam, as it looked freshly done, exposing a four-inch line of raw, wooden flesh, still bleeding a little sap. The log was maybe two feet long and eight or nine inches in diameter. Adam bent over it and followed the waves with a finger. Then he pointed to the round cut end. "You can see the waves in the cross cut as well."

"So, you cut down a maple tree just to see if the grain was wavy?" This seemed unlike Adam or, really, anyone from The Forest, where the respect their tradition had for all of nature made it unlikely they'd destroy a tree just to see what was inside.

"You know better than that. The tree this came from was recently damaged. I came across it last week, after that windstorm, so today I went back to see what I could salvage. There's more, too; I'll have to go back with a horse to drag the rest of it out."

I imagined him, the sculptor, paring away anything that didn't look like what he wanted to create. "What will you do with it?"

"I'll wait for the wood to tell me." He tilted his head slightly. "Your energy seems odd. Everything okay?"

I chuckled. So many of these Forest Dwellers apparently had a way of sensing things that eluded me. One of their leaders, Erik Stillman, could read auras. The woman Adam might or might not end up marrying—Myra Langtree—could find someone in a crowd by following whatever it was she perceived as their energy. Aside from the depth of his sensuality, Adam had not revealed to me any special powers other than the intimate relationship he had with wood (and perhaps the intimate relationship he had with my body), but it didn't surprise me that he sensed how out of sorts I was. He was right.

I said, "Nothing earth-shattering. I've told you about the man I knew when I lived in New York."

"Donald."

"Yeah. He and his—I guess his lover, really—will be here

Wednesday. Tomorrow. Donald was a little vague about the reason. Something about how Jonathan is on a mission to save gay kids."

"What does that even mean?"

I shook my head. "No idea. Anyway, they're staying in Little Boundary. At the Pinewood. For about a week, if I understood correctly."

Adam looked at me from under his eyebrows. "Will they come to your church Sunday?"

"That's the threat."

He laughed. "Threat? You don't want them there?"

I let out a long breath. "I'm being a little histrionic."

"Not *you*." He grinned.

"Sarcasm does not become you," I said, my tone teasing. Then, "I've never met Jonathan."

"And you've never gotten over Donald."

We locked eyes. Seconds passed. Finally, "Not completely." Both of us regarded Klondike for a moment. The dog seemed ready to continue our walk, but I wasn't. I added, "Donald thinks you and I are an item."

I thought Adam would laugh at that. I was sure he definitely did not see us that way, and neither did I. But he said, "Where did he get that idea?"

"From me, I'm afraid. I mentioned you in a moment of weakness last January, when he called and told me about Jonathan. He asked if I was seeing someone."

Adam nodded. "And you said me."

"I did."

"You need to set him straight."

"I will. He said we should all have dinner together, and I will make it clear that isn't going to happen, and why."

"Okay. Good." I looked down at Klondike, embarrassed. I felt Adam's eyes on me. He added, "Because I don't want to have to change our relationship, which I would need to do if your feelings are too different from mine."

I looked up and smiled at him. "They aren't. I love my time with you. I love our friendship. Nothing has changed for me."

He nodded, stooped, and hefted the log back onto his shoulder, grunting just a little with the effort. "I'll come to you tonight, if that's okay. Then I won't see you until after their visit."

"Perfect."

I wanted to watch him walk away, to see the confident strides of that lean body, to imagine the swells of muscle beneath his clothing. But Klondike was restive.

"All right, boy. Come on. Let's walk a little while longer."

CHAPTER 3

Wednesday morning, my body was still thrumming from the pleasures of Adam's attentions the night before—a good way to feel anytime, but especially as I waited to hear from Donald. I suspected Adam had known that.

Of course, as a minister, I couldn't just sit around and wait. There was the couple, Jeff and Linda Lawrence, who had just suffered a miscarriage, their third. I would do what I could to help them know they were not alone and to support them as they considered adoption. There was the meeting with someone who might be my new lay minister, Boyd Harper, recently transplanted to Assisi from Boston to care for his mother, whose health was failing. And there was next Sunday's sermon to plot out. I had a theme already: the kind of love that connects us all, that's independent of physical or even spiritual attraction, the kind of love that as Unitarian Universalists we strive to share with the world. It wasn't by any means an attempt to dampen the kind of lust many people feel this time of year; I merely wanted to put it into context.

Oh, all right. I also wanted to make sure my own head, and Donald's, and Jonathan's, were focused on something other than carnality.

~

When I had moved to Assisi last August, four lay ministers had been in place; I hadn't had the luxury of recruiting anyone. And when Marshall had relinquished his role so he could spend time getting Teens for Truth underway, the other lay ministers hadn't felt as though there was a particular need to replace him. But recently there'd been another resignation; Loraine Fuller, Vanessa Doyle's wife, needed to devote more of her time to taking care of Vanessa, who had chosen not to fight her third bout with cancer.

Assisi is a small, rural town. As I've said, it's a little surprising that it could support three churches. I hope I'm not boasting when I say the UU congregation is the largest. It was already a good size when I was assigned here, and it has since grown a little larger. A few people even travel from Little Boundary now, where there is no UU church.

So, sure, we got along for a while with only three lay ministers (Loraine, Andrea Beale, and Jenny Pratt). But it had come to the point where three had been cutting it just a little short, and then Loraine had resigned.

Then in early March, when Boyd had told his UU Boston minister he was moving to Assisi, she had contacted me.

"Meghan March here," she'd said when I'd answered the phone. "I lead the All Souls Fellowship UU in Boston."

The call had been a surprise. I'd done my best to sound unfazed. "Pastor March. Good to hear from you. Something I can help with?"

"Meghan, please. Yes, I think there is. I hope so, anyway." Her voice was devoid of the accent of eastern Massachusetts, though it was clipped—not unfriendly, but implying that it was business first. "One of my lay ministers needs to move to Assisi. His mother lives there, and she is not well."

"She's in the UU congregation here? What's her name?"

"No. Actually she's Catholic. Theresa Harper. Her son, Boyd, will move in with her. He'll be in Assisi as of the first week of

April. But Boyd is UU. I'm wondering whether there might be a place for him with you. I mean, as a lay minister."

My ability to feign nonchalance failed me, and I was lost for words.

She added, "I'm sorry. This must seem highly irregular. But I did hear through church channels that you'd had a recent resignation."

"We did." Again, words wouldn't come. This discussion seemed highly irregular to me.

"Look, if this is out of the question, I'll understand. Perhaps you already have a replacement lined up? It's just that I think Boyd will need something to give him purpose beyond caring for his mother. He's led a fairly active life here, and although he doesn't say so, I believe the change is weighing on him. He's been an excellent lay minster here, although—like anyone—he has his quirks."

"Quirks? Can you be a little more specific?"

She chuckled. "Sure. He turned his back on his Catholic upbringing and now calls himself an atheist. I suspect that's an overreaction, but it's not my place to tell him that. His personality —his style—is a little assertive, but he's learned to soften his approach in his role."

"I see." Another pause.

"Also—and I understand this would not be an issue for your congregation—he's gay and out. He knows I'm telling you."

I stopped short of revealing my own orientation; it shouldn't matter. "Is there a particular reason you're telling me?"

"No. No, but he volunteered his permission, so I thought I'd mention it."

"Okay, well it's true we could use another lay minister. Of course, I would want to talk with him, have him attend services for a while and meet a few people. I might even see if I could meet his mother. I know Father Bryant, the Catholic priest here, so I might speak with him as well."

"Of course. Of course. I won't give Boyd too sunny a prognosis. But I will tell him there's a possibility, if that's all right."

～

And now, just two days after moving in with his mother, Boyd had agreed to come to the church to meet with me. As I walked over on the afternoon Donald was expected, conflicting thoughts plagued me. Marshall had been a lay minister when I'd arrived. After he'd resigned his post to establish Teens for Truth, we'd begun our relationship in earnest. I needed to think of Boyd as a potential replacement for Loraine, not for Marshall.

Also, while I could of course decide against Boyd assuming this role, it felt as though yet again I'd have little say in who was a lay minister in my own parish.

The role of lay minister was not intended to be a substitute for me, for the minister; it was to support the pastor's approach, and lay ministers needed to fit in with the congregation. They provided spiritual and, to some extent, emotional support as needed to members of the congregation. They were volunteers. They were not therapists. They were not even counselors. This meant that personality counted for a lot.

It was unusual, at best, for someone to become a lay minister if they hadn't already been a member of the congregation for some time. The only reasons I was even considering Boyd were because he'd been in a UU congregation, he'd had the role already, and Meghan had sung his praises.

That, and the fact that we really needed another lay minister, and I couldn't for the life of me come up with someone else in our congregation who had the time and the aptitude.

～

Boyd was already in the church, sitting in one of the front pews, when I entered. Early; so far, so good. He stood when he heard me enter and watched as I made my way to the front.

He was not especially tall, so I had a distinct height advantage. In my head, I told myself, *That shouldn't matter, Spencer; if it does, this isn't going to work.* Boyd's blond hair was cut very short, but it had a distinct style. The colors on his cotton sweater, ornate cables that snaked horizontally, put me in mind of the serpent in Paradise. I had to stifle a chuckle; unlike that snake, this man was unlikely to teach me any more about duality than I knew already. I focused on his face. It had a kind of rugged look, nothing soft or pretty about it, but his grey-blue eyes drew mine with an intensity that matched the assertiveness Meghan had mentioned.

I was ready with a polite greeting, but he spoke first. "Reverend Hill. Thanks for meeting with me." He held his right hand out, and his grip on mine was a little firmer than necessary.

"Spencer, please. Welcome to Assisi, and welcome to our UU congregation. Shall we sit here?" I beckoned to the pew he had occupied. He sat, and I moved to the pew behind him. He had to turn to face me—a slight disadvantage for him—but the barrier would, I hoped, allow him to settle into a less forward attitude. I needed to know whether he was able to moderate his personal style, to relax somewhat. Plus he appeared to be at least a little older than my twenty-eight years.

His grin told me he understood what this seating arrangement meant. "Sorry if I'm coming on a little strong. Nerves, I guess."

I doubted that. At least, I wasn't sensing nerves. "I understand from Meghan March that you're here to care for your mother. Don't share anything you'd rather not, but can you tell me how ill she is?"

His face told me this was not where he'd thought my questions would go. Perhaps he'd expected to discuss the lay minister role immediately. But first I wanted to know a little more about him.

"Not that ill, really." He shrugged slightly. "She's eighty-six, and her mild dementia isn't quite as mild any longer. She left the stove on a couple of months ago. She wasn't hurt, and the house didn't catch on fire, but the fire department had to come. Now the kitchen is in need of work, and there's no one to oversee it. And with the kitchen only partially functional, the authorities are threatening to remove her. Besides, I know the people in her congregation are getting a little tired of stopping by to check on her, bring her food, that sort of thing. She can't afford in-home care, and neither can I."

This tracked well with what Milton Bryant, her Catholic priest, had told me. "I'm sorry to hear about the fire," I said. "Will you be looking for work, or will your mother's care be full-time?"

"I write novels. Romance novels. My pen name is Rosalie Malone." He gave me an arch look, one eyebrow raised. "Every read any of my books?"

I chuckled. "Can't say that I have. So, other than the dementia, is your mother's health good?"

"Oh, I think she'll be around for quite a while."

I nodded; I wanted to be sure Boyd wasn't likely to disappear if his mother passed on anytime soon. I let a beat go by. I was about to change the subject, but also I wanted to see if Boyd could tolerate a brief pause or if he'd feel a need to fill it. He waited; a good sign.

I said, "Tell me a little about your Boston congregation."

"Like—anything in particular?"

"Whatever comes to mind."

Clearly, he knew this was a kind of test. One side of his mouth lifted in a wry smile. He seemed to settle into his position on the pew a little more.

"I won't be coy," he said, which made me wonder if he was implying that I had been. "I know this is unusual, that I'm hoping for a role in your congregation I haven't earned. So I'll tell you about my experience in the role in Boston."

Boyd talked for maybe ten minutes. I didn't interrupt him; I wanted to give him free reign to say whatever he wanted to say. He told me about some of his interactions with his parishioners. He related a few of his favorite jokes about the UU tradition, which

I felt was in his favor. He talked about his relationship with Meghan March. He also, to his credit, talked about ways in which he felt the church's practices could have been improved, how he had presented these ideas to Meghan, and how she had decided against most of them. He didn't sound resentful—maybe a little surprised—about her decisions.

"I hope," he finished, "that if I have ideas about the Assisi practices, I can come to you with them, whether or not I'm a lay minister here."

I smiled. "It wouldn't be a true UU congregation, in my opinion at least, if you couldn't."

Before I could come up with another question or a comment about what he'd told me, he asked, "What can you tell me about The Forest?"

I did my best to hide my surprise; don't know how well I succeeded. "How do you happen to know about it?"

He lifted a shoulder and dropped it. "Not sure. I think my mother mentioned it."

"The Forest," I opened, not convinced by his response and determined to keep my description to bare essentials, "is the name of a settlement—a community, really—somewhat east of Assisi. The people there refer to themselves as Forest Dwellers. They follow a neo-Pagan tradition of life, which guides their spirituality and their daily lives. They grow much of their own food, and they have their own livestock."

"Do you have much interaction with them?"

Here, I dissembled. I wasn't about to refer to my relationship with Adam. I also wasn't going to reveal that they considered me a kind of ambassador between them and Assisi. "They mostly keep to themselves, though our congregation has a friendly relationship with them."

"But not other congregations? Not the Catholic one?"

"I'm not aware of anything negative." I pitched my tone to let him know he wasn't going to hear anything more about The Forest from me. At least, not at this point.

I noted mentally that although he'd asked about The Forest, he had not asked anything about my congregation. So I took the initiative to give him a general description of us, and then he did ask a few questions that seemed pertinent and appropriate.

I couldn't tell whether he was disappointed or surprised that I did not broach the topic of whether he might be considered for the role of lay minister. And rather than give him a chance to bring it up, I did not ask if he had any more questions. I brought the meeting to an end by standing and holding my hand out.

As he stood and we shook hands, I said, "It's been a pleasure to meet with you, Boyd. We'll talk again soon. I look forward to seeing you Sunday."

Ministerial duties for the day done, I was back home by four. There was no message from Donald to say he and Jonathan had arrived, and I didn't want to sit around waiting for a phone call. It had started to rain, but no heavier than the occasional slap of a drop against the window, so I took Klondike for a long walk through town. I didn't expect to see a lot of folks, but I was open to distraction. Klondike always drew attention. He was huge, and gorgeous, and very friendly. After about forty-five minutes and several short conversations, I headed home.

There was a car in front of my house. I didn't recognize it. Two men sat inside. I didn't need to look at them; I knew who they were.

Donald saw me and got out of the car. Even from ten yards away, I could see the change in him, a change so much for the better over the last time I'd seen him. That had been at his sister Ruth's wedding last October. At the time, he'd been with a man named Bruce Cobb, a dominating, boorish fellow who'd kept Donald on a short leash and had been profoundly suspicious of me as Donald's previous lover. Donald had seemed cowed, submissive, lacking the spirit of the impish fellow I'd known him to be.

Before we'd become involved, I'd seen him play the character Puck in Shakespeare's *A Midsummer Night's Dream*. As Ruth had once declared, it had been a terrific example of typecasting. Bruce had smothered all the feistiness, the playfulness, the life within the Donald I had known. And it seemed Jonathan had recovered it.

Hands on hips, a mock-annoyed expression on his adorable face, Donald stood by the car as bits of water spit down upon him from the sky, leaving dark spots on his light blue jacket. His dark blond hair, which had been quite short the last time I'd seen him, now fell nicely into a longer style, just long enough to frame his face without overwhelming its delicate features.

I stopped walking, a tension in my chest that was part thrill, part grief. Klondike looked up at me as if to ask what was happening, and that prompted me to move forward again.

Donald kept his eyes on mine, ignoring the dog, until we were mere feet apart. *How could I have forgotten about the stunning lashes that framed his hazel eyes?*

He looked at Klondike. "Is he friendly?"

"Very."

"He won't bite?"

"Not if you behave yourself."

Donald raised his head and stepped toward me, arms open for a hug.

I couldn't breathe. I think my heart stopped, just for a moment. Without realizing it, I dropped Klondike's leash to wrap my own arms around Donald, my Puck, my imp. Despite the years since I had held him, his body felt heart-achingly familiar.

He pushed away, wiping his eyes with one hand and laughing quietly. I think it was at this point that Jonathan stepped out of the car and came toward me, right arm extended.

Jonathan was almost as tall as I was. His full, dark brown beard hid the contours of his face, but his dark eyes sparkled with pleasure. As he took my hand, he said, "You're every bit has handsome as I've heard."

Flattered, but having no idea how to respond to that, all I said was, "I thought you might call. But never mind; will you come inside?"

Donald picked up Klondike's leash. "He's very well behaved." Ruffling the dog's ears, he said, "Good boy, Klondike."

"Just so you know," Jonathan said as we made our way inside, "we aren't expecting you to feed us. We got to our inn a little early and called, but there was no answer. Perhaps we should have left a message. Anyway, we drove around Little Boundary for a bit and then headed over to you. I hope we're not intruding."

"No, no. Not at all. It's true I don't have a meal ready, but I can offer you some refreshment. Why don't you—"

"Oh. My. God!" Donald stood just inside the front door, eyes on the piano. "I remember this thing!" He turned toward me. "It does have a presence here, doesn't it? I mean—that is—"

I laughed. "I couldn't leave it in storage. I needed it with me more than I needed a living room."

Jonathan grinned. "There's still room for us to sit."

"And why don't you make yourselves as comfortable as possible while I prepare a few things in the kitchen."

I turned, straining my brain to think what I had in the refrigerator, and I was all the way into the kitchen before I realized that Donald had followed me. He leaned against the doorframe, arms crossed, while I rummaged through my cupboards for wine glasses and plates and searched for crackers to go with the cheeses I had bought recently.

"So you're a bone fide minister now. You made it."

"I was a minister last time I saw you."

"Yeah, but I wasn't taking a lot in at that time. I think you know why."

I stopped what I was doing and turned to him. "Is there any way you can tell me how you ended up with Bruce Cobb?"

He shrugged and crumpled his face, making me think of a piece of paper one might mangle to hide what was written there. "Oh, I could tell you *that*. What I can't tell you is why I was still with him at Ruth's wedding, after several months of him lording it over me."

I bit my tongue as I turned back to my task, not knowing why I had asked my question, not really wanting Donald to answer it. From the living room, I heard a few chords played on my piano. "Jonathan plays?"

Donald didn't answer right away, so I looked at him. Head tilted, he said, "Not as well as you."

CHAPTER 4

I liked Jonathan. I couldn't help it. His laugh was easy and genuine, he seemed to adore Donald, and he asked me questions that were more creative, or intuitive, than most people would probably ask in his place ("What would you say is the biggest difference between the Episcopal Church and UU?" and "Do you get more sermon ideas from reading or from interactions with people?"). But the most interesting thing about him was the reason for this trip north.

"As you probably know," he told me when I asked why he was here, "New York is a magnet for all kinds of people. In particular, it seems to attract young people in trouble. I've been working for the past three years as a guidance counselor at Stuyvesant High School, in lower Manhattan. Do you know it?"

I shook my head. Donald, beside Jonathan on the couch, poked an elbow into Jonathan's ribs. "Spencer wouldn't have gone to a public high school." He looked at me. "Loyola, wasn't it, Spence?"

"It was." I kept my tone dry; I didn't like to draw attention to my family's wealth.

"Anyway," Jonathan continued, "it has bothered me more and more to see how many young people are on the street, taking money for sex, rejected by their families or merely victims of financial deprivation. I started visiting some of the places where they might find a bed for the night. And it seemed to me that so many of these kids—the boys especially, or perhaps I just noticed them more—were gay. Their families turned them away because of it, and they have no resources."

As a minister, I was not only moved by what Jonathan had seen and done, but I was also a little ashamed that I had no first-hand knowledge of this tragedy. I didn't know how to respond.

Donald saved me from having to think of something to say. "Jonathan wants to help these kids. Wait till you hear how."

Jonathan's face registered fond impatience, and he smiled at Donald. "What I discovered is that a troubling number of these kids had been in what's known as conversion therapy. Are you familiar with that?"

"Enough to know what you refer to, yes." Conversion. A terrible word for what happened to teens placed into those facilities. Marshall had been a victim of such a place. It had caused him to try and take his own life. "My impression of them is that teens get the message that God has made them something God can't love, and it's up to them to fix it."

Jonathan's face lit up, and he leaned forward slightly. "Exactly! That's exactly what they do. Most of them are religious in nature. Anyway, in New York I heard from several of these kids that they had either escaped or been turned out from a couple of these places that are just over the Canadian border from here. And what I want to do is set up a kind of group home, or halfway house— still working out the details—far enough north so these kids find my facility instead of heading down to the city to prostitute themselves." He sat back and let out a deep breath.

Donald, still beaming, looked from Jonathan to me. "What do you think?"

"What *can* I think? It sounds amazing. And wonderful. How far along are you in terms of financing this effort?"

Donald grinned. "Jonathan's family is like yours was. Money."

This time Jonathan's look of impatience was not quite so fond, and I understood that. He said, "I do have seed money, and I have a list of people who have expressed interest in contributing. I've set up a tax structure for a non-profit and opened a couple of accounts dedicated to various parts of the effort. I've started the licensing process. I'm up here," and he glanced at Donald, "*we* are up here scouting for a good location and, possibly, existing real estate that could be transformed."

"So you're not particularly looking for that here in Assisi."

"I doubt there's enough opportunity here. It's too small. Kids tend to gravitate toward cities."

"Newport, then?"

"Newport might be ideal. But I also want to explore something a little more rural, like Little Boundary. What can you tell me about it?"

What could I tell him.... I could tell him some things that would discourage him from considering it, but I wasn't sure my limited experience would be fair to the town.

"I don't know it well, though I have driven through it a number of times on my way to hiking trails. I know the proprietor of the inn where you're staying, and I have... um... made the acquaintance of the pastor at the Assembly of God church there."

The look on Jonathan's face stopped me from continuing. "There's an Assembly of God?"

"There is. It seems you know something about them." Assembly of God. The church Marshall had grown up in, the belief system that had sent him into the prison of conversion therapy.

Jonathan's face was dark. "I've heard nothing good. I believe I'm not offending you by saying that."

"You are not. I know nothing about them that doesn't make me furious."

Donald asked, "Why? What do they do?"

I tried to read his face. How much, I wondered, did Jonathan know about the cult that had pulled Donald into its clutches a few years ago? The Risen Christ Church had several things in common with the Assembly of God.

I told him, "They consider the resurrection to be physical, and the return of Jesus will be physical as well; he will appear in person. They believe life must be lived without sin, or serious atonement is necessary. And one sin to be avoided at all costs is that of homosexuality."

I turned to Jonathan. "Do you think there are enough conversion therapy escapees to warrant the kind of facility you describe?"

"I think that once word gets out, it won't be just those kids who come to us. We'll also get kids whose families rejected them without taking the trouble to send them anywhere in particular."

At my front door, as my guests were about to head out to their car, I shook hands with Jonathan. Donald said to him, "I just need a sec. Be right out." And he stepped back inside, leaving the door open.

"What do you think?" he asked, his face turned up toward mine, something like hopeful anticipation in his eyes.

I smiled. "I like him. I hope you stay together as long as you want to."

He hugged me, and again I felt that bittersweet wrench.

He fairly danced out to the car, turning to wave before getting in. "I'll call you about dinner with you and your sculptor."

Sculptor, Adam was; mine, he was not.

By Sunday, I hadn't heard anything more from David about the boy in his congregation. It was probably unrealistic to hope he might attend Tuesday's Teens for Truth meeting.

During the service that morning, Boyd Harper sat one pew back from the front, off to the side. I made a mental note to speak with him later.

True to his word, Donald was in the congregation, Jonathan

beside him. I opened my address by taking a page from Dr. Elaine Stein, pastor at the UU church in Manhattan, where Donald's sister Ruth had taken me while I was still conflicted about the Episcopal priesthood as a vocation.

"Welcome," I opened, filling the space with my deepest, warmest voice. "Welcome Muslims. Welcome Pagans. Welcome Jews. Welcome women. Welcome men. Welcome children and grandparents and aunts and uncles. Welcome gays and lesbians. Welcome Buddhists. Welcome atheists. Welcome Zoroastrians. Welcome agnostics."

I beamed a warm smile at the congregation. Then I chuckled. "Oh, dear. I almost forgot. Welcome Christians."

The quiet, friendly laughter that rippled through the building warmed my heart. Yes; these were my people.

After the service, Boyd relieved me of the need to seek him out. He approached me and waited patiently as I introduced Donald and Jonathan to Vanessa Doyle and Loraine Fuller.

Loraine, whom no one would call shy, told them, "Spencer married us. Just last January." She beamed at Vanessa, who was in the wheelchair she seldom left these days.

Jonathan looked at me, clearly puzzled. I told him, "Unitarian Universalist ministers have been presiding over the marriages of gay couples for quite a while now. One day the government will catch up with us." I watched for an interchange between him and Donald; were they so far along in their relationship that such a step was under consideration? But I saw nothing. I tried not to feel relief.

I was about to turn to Boyd when Donald said, "Would tonight be a good time for our dinner? I'm dying to meet—"

I interrupted him before he could say anything someone might recognize. "I'd be delighted to have dinner with you both, but it will be just me, I'm afraid. Excuse me a moment."

Quickly I turned to Boyd, extending an arm toward him. "Boyd Harper, I'd like you to meet my predecessor here, Vanessa Doyle, and her wife, Loraine Fuller." As they shook hands, I explained briefly to them how Boyd had come to be here, and what his role had been in Boston. I did not reveal his hopes regarding the Assisi church.

Loraine, still uninhibited, said, "So you were a lay minister there? We could use a new one here. Interested?"

Vanessa, bless her, laid a gentle hand on Loraine's arm. "I'm sure that's something he will discuss with Spencer if the possibility exists. I'm feeling rather tired, now. Home?"

I asked Donald and Jonathan if they could wait for a moment while I spoke to Boyd. I walked a few feet away, and Boyd followed.

"I'm happy to see you here," I told him. "I hope you found the service to be something along the lines of what you might have hoped."

"Oh, more than that. Yes. You did a great job of highlighting the role of our community in its relationship to the world." He chuckled. "And I loved the amusing reference to a different kind of love, the kind many of us feel in springtime."

"I'm glad that came through. There are so many different kinds of love."

"And I thought it was brilliant to use them as all parts of the one love we strive for."

I didn't need any more flattery. "How is your mother today? Was she well enough to go to her own church?"

"Yes. There are people who take turns coming to get her." He glanced at his watch. "She's at their social hour now. I should probably go so I can take her home."

"I'll look forward to seeing you here next week, if we don't run into each other before then." I smiled and turned away, relieved that he'd said nothing about the lay minister role.

Donald and Jonathan were slowly making their way to their car when I caught up with them. Donald turned to me, hands on hips.

"What's this about no sculptor joining us for dinner?"

I glanced around to be sure no one was hovering, waiting to speak to me, or close enough to overhear. Adam's sculpting was not a secret. "Our relationship is a very casual one. It would feel odd to both of us to appear as though it were something it isn't."

"So you're not madly in love?"

I laughed. "No. That would ruin everything. Did you have someplace in mind for dinner? If not, there is a decent restaurant a mile or so outside of Little Boundary."

"Do you mean Plating?" Jonathan asked. "We were there Thursday. We could certainly go there again, I think." He looked at Donald for his agreement.

I said, "It's a little embarrassing how few places like that there are around here. We could of course go into Newport."

Donald lifted an expectant face to Jonathan, who said, "I do have another suggestion, though it might be forward of me to mention it."

"Please. Go ahead."

"I wouldn't ask you to cook for us, but I really enjoy cooking. What if we have dinner at your house, but I prepare the meal?"

"He's really very good," Donald assured me. "And he does love it. What do you say?"

"Oh. Well. I, um, just give me a little time to put the kitchen to rights, and then I suppose we could do that."

"Excellent. Donald and I will leave now and go shopping."

"If you, um, think you'll need any specialty tools or pans or whatever, you should know my supply of kitchen items is pretty rudimentary."

"I'll keep that in mind. See you around six so I'll have time for prep?"

And just like that, I was having guests for dinner. I wasn't entirely sure how I felt about it, but it was true that our conversation could be less stilted, less restrained than a restaurant setting would allow. And I wasn't sure how I felt about that, either.

~

As soon as I got back from walking Klondike that afternoon, my phone rang. It was David Foster.

"Spencer, I know this isn't your problem, but I could really use your support right now."

"What's going on?"

Through the phone line, I heard the deep breath he took. "I'm sure you remember that boy I told you about."

"Yes. And?"

"He did what I was afraid he'd do."

"He—what?"

"He's in the hospital in Newport. His mother found him in his room, nearly strangled. He'd hung something from the upper part of his bedroom window frame, wrapped it around his neck, and leaned forward."

"My God." It was all I could say. I almost said it again. "What can I do?"

"I'm going to drive out to see him. Leaving in about an hour. Would you be willing to come with me?"

Willing.... Would his parents want a gay man, a minister notwithstanding, visiting their suicidal son? "You said you thought he might be gay. Does his action today have anything to do with that?"

"That's not what he told his parents after church."

"Which was what?"

"That he's not a he. That he's really a girl."

There was silence on both ends of the line for perhaps ten seconds. Finally I said, "If you think his parents won't mind, I will come with you. But, David, I'm by no means prepared to address this issue."

"Can you read in the car?"

"Um, read what, exactly?"

"I have a copy of the DSM-III-R."

"Which is... what?"

"The Diagnostic and Statistical Manual of Mental Disorders. Section three-oh-two dot five covers transsexualism."

I had never heard of the DSM. "Where did you get that?"

"My wife is a doctor, remember? Martha?" His tone was teasing. "You remember her, yes?"

I nodded as though he could see me. "Very funny. Well... all right, I'll come. But David, I can't promise I'll be helpful. And his parents...."

"They don't need to know you're gay."

"Is it likely they wouldn't already know?"

That gave him pause, but he said, "It's irrelevant here. And they might not even still be with him when we get there."

"Jesus. I would hope they'd stay with him."

"They, um, let's just say they weren't happy."

Christ. What was I getting myself into? Maybe nothing. Maybe everything.

I left a message at the Pinewood for Donald and Jonathan, apologizing profusely and giving them permission to use the key hidden in my back yard to go in and cook for themselves; what else were they going to do with the groceries they'd purchased? And with a slight but nagging feeling that I might be taking advantage of her status as a single person, I called Jenny Pratt and asked her to walk Klondike and feed him. I was in David's car by three forty-five, ready and not ready for the forty-five minute drive to support my friend in something I didn't understand.

David had photocopied the pages from the DSM he wanted me to read, and as I read I looked up occasionally to clear my eyes and to clear my brain. This was a challenging read, more because of my emotional reaction to it than of how technical it was.

I read that a medical diagnosis of the "disorder" of transsexualism is made only during or after puberty, and then only after at least two years of the individual having "persistent discomfort and sense of inappropriateness about one's assigned sex." Well, yeah, if I had been born into a female body, I'd have a real problem with that; I'm not female. And maybe the *diagnosis* is puberty or later, but surely there were youngsters who suffered with this confusion.

I read that these individuals are often repulsed by their own genitalia. I looked up and stared sightlessly at the houses and trees and whatever we were passing. I'd never really thought about it. Were my genitals repulsive? I admitted that they were no garden of beauty. That said, though, I was certainly able to admire the genitalia of other men, so….

I read that there were psychiatric, hormonal, and surgical sex reassignment treatments, but that the long-term outcome was unclear. Apparently, there were cases of "spontaneous remission." What would that even mean? Might a boy like the one we were going to see opt for surgical removal of his "repulsive" genitalia only to feel regret when he's older? That idea made me shudder.

I read that there was a distinct difference between cross-dressing and transsexualism. Well, duh.

I read that depression and suicide are common. Again, duh.

I read that some males mutilate their genitals. Another shudder overcame me.

All of that was disturbing. Maybe the worst, though, in terms of what this boy was going through, was this: "Transsexualism seems usually to develop within the context of a disturbed relationship with one or both parents." This might leave room for a transexual kid to have sympathetic parents who wanted to understand and maybe even help, but it also implied that the disorder *resulted* from a dysfunctional family situation, rather than from something inherent to the individual in question.

"David, you've read this, yes?"

"Of course."

"Did you make note of this statement that implies a cause? Dysfunctional relationship with parents?"

"I did. Yes."

"And is this family dysfunctional?"

"I wouldn't have said so. No."

"Then—what the fuck?"

"Well, either I don't know them as well as I thought, or that presumption is wrong."

"Or both." I leaned back in my seat and stared forward. "Look, I'm no psychiatrist. But—my God." I struggled to collect my thoughts. "It's like saying I'm gay because my mother was domineering and my father was distant. My mother was anything *but* domineering, and my father was… well, he was a little distant at times, but he was a definite presence in my life. I can't help thinking this DSM stuff is bullshit!"

David nodded. "I hear you. Like you, I have no psychology in my background beyond the few courses I took for my Master of Divinity. But something about that statement feels… I don't know, maybe misguided. I'll just say misguided."

We drove in silence for several minutes. Then he told me something his wife Martha had related to him.

"She said there was a case in Canada, different from this one in some ways. In nineteen sixty-five, an infant boy's penis was severely damaged during a botched surgical procedure. Later the parents took him to a psychologist at Johns Hopkins in Maryland, who recommended that the boy be raised as a girl, under the belief that nature would bow to nurture. So the baby Bruce Reimer became Brenda Reimer. He was about two when he underwent surgery to remove his testicles and create a vagina. They even gave him estrogen when he hit puberty. But Brenda was always more boyish than a girl, and at age thirteen or so he became suicidal. His parents told him the truth, and not long after that he had a double mastectomy to remove the breasts the estrogen had caused to grow, and he had more surgery to reconstruct male genitalia. He began living as a male, having chosen the name David for himself."

"I can't begin to imagine…."

"I know. I feel the same."

"How is David today?"

"No idea. I imagine he wanted to be out of the spotlight."

"And this boy? Today? What's his name?"

"He was given the name Ralph. Ralph Blake. After his grandfather."

"And now?"

"Kira."

My brain did a flip. "So should I have asked what *her* name is?"

"I wish I knew."

CHAPTER 5

R alph, or Kira, was alone in his—I guess I mean her—hospital room, in the psych ward. I didn't know whether the suicide attempt or the transsexual aspect was the reason for this ward, though I supposed it could have been both. David and I were allowed in only by virtue of our religious profession.

We stood for a moment in the doorway, not sure what lay behind the youth's closed eyes. I made a sudden and definitive decision to think of this person as the girl, Kira, and to address her as such. If Kira changed her mind, she could do that; meanwhile, she was Kira.

Kira's body took up only a fraction of the bed's surface. She lay in semi-fetal position, and I could see some kind of bandage around her neck. Her hair was an improbable shade of pink, short enough to be considered a boy's cut. I moved forward a couple of steps. The flesh around her eyes appeared puffy and almost grey. Her features struck me as androgynous, neither especially masculine or feminine.

"Kira?" I asked, tentatively.

The eyelids lifted to reveal two pools of deep brown. "Who are you?"

David stepped in beside me and followed my lead. "Hello,

Kira. I hope you don't mind that I'm here, or that I brought Reverend Hill with me."

We waited. I watched as tears filled Kira's eyes. Her lip quivered, but she managed to say, "Thank you."

I knew the thanks were for addressing her as Kira rather than for bringing me along. I asked, "May we come in and sit with you for a while?"

Kira let out a long, very shaky breath, and something seemed to soften in her body. Until I saw that, I hadn't noticed how very tense she had seemed. "If you call me by my right name, and if you don't tell me who I'm not, then yes."

David pulled a chair close to the bed, and I decided to pull the other one beside him rather than on the opposite side of the bed; I didn't want Kira to feel surrounded.

David spoke first. "Your parents told me what happened."

The softness disappeared for a moment, and Kira said, "They told you their side of what happened."

"I mean, they told me why you're here."

I said, "Kira, would you like to tell us your side of what happened?"

After another shaky breath, she said, "They won't see me for who I am. They won't listen to me. They want me to be someone I'm not." Her fists clenched, gripping bits of sheet. "They hate me!"

David shook his head. "I'm sure they don't hate you."

"Why?" I asked. "Why do they hate you?"

David gave me a hard stare, but I felt sure Kira was tired of people telling her what was and wasn't true.

She looked at me, not at him. "They want me to be a boy. They already have a daughter. They want a son, named after Dad's father. I didn't even like my grandfather! And they think just because they call me Ralph and make me wear boys' clothes and give me trucks and plastic guns for presents, that will make it so. But I'm not a boy! I'm not!"

David looked at me as though he didn't know what to do with

that. I wasn't sure, either, but I took a chance. "Can you tell me how it is you know you're not a boy?"

"I just know it!"

David's voice was soft, even tender as he said, "You look like a boy to them."

Kira's eyes spilled tears onto her face. "Don't you think I know that? Don't you think I know I look like a boy? I don't know what went wrong! I don't know what I did to make this happen!"

"Oh, Kira." I shook my head. "You did nothing. You did nothing wrong. I wish I could tell you how this happened, but I *can* tell you it has happened to other people as well."

Kira blinked several times. "What did you say?"

"You're not alone."

Kira made an effort to sit up and failed. David stood and adjusted the bed's controls to raise the head of the mattress, and Kira settled back.

A voice, sounding almost disembodied, as though it came from the air itself, said, "Say that again."

I cleared my throat. I knew I was wading into waters foreign to me, addressing an extremely sensitive topic I knew nothing about. I worded what I said next with extreme care.

"There is a word the medical community has for people who are convinced they're in the wrong body. It's called transsexualism. There are people in girls' bodies who tell us they're boys, and people like you in a boy's body who tell us they're girls."

Kira's body stiffened again. "I'm not *telling* you I'm a girl. I *am* a girl."

"I hear you." As soon as my words were spoken, I realized that there was, indeed, a gap between what I was saying and what I believed. It wasn't that I doubted Kira, exactly. I just didn't under-stand how this could happen. "My point is that you're not the only one who feels like this."

Kira relaxed just a bit. "My parents think I'm insane."

David sat forward slightly. "Did they tell you that?"

"More than once!"

"So it isn't something they said only after they found you in your room today?"

Kira released an exasperated breath. "Look, I don't know why you're here. I don't know what you want. All I can tell you is I told my folks last night, right after they started yelling at me for *this*." Her hand went to the bright pink hair. "The yelling went on and on. Hours of it."

Kira did her best to imitate first one parent and then another, generally sounding more like a man than a woman. "'Why would you do such a thing?' 'It's so hideous! You're an attractive young man.' 'You march yourself upstairs right this minute, young man, and wash that hair until it's normal again.' 'Stand up straight, can't you? Hold yourself like a man!' 'Why do you have to act like that? You're not a faggot, for God's sake.' 'Don't be insane!'"

The room went silent except for an occasional, stifled sob from Kira. She snuffled a few times and wiped her eyes with the hand that didn't have an IV needle in it. "Somewhere in all that yelling, I told them I wasn't a boy. I told them who I really am. I told them the name I'd chosen for myself. So they just found even more horrible things to yell at me."

I felt an almost irresistible urge to wrap this tortured child in my arms and whisper to her how brave she was to be honest, how things felt horrible right now but that they wouldn't always be this bad. Almost. But despite David's presence in the room, despite how well he knew me and how he would know my action came from spiritual love and not physical attraction, I was wary of doing anything in an environment where no one knew me, and where—as a gay man—my motives could easily be misinterpreted. This would be bad for me, and it would do Kira no good at all.

David, bless his heart, did reach out and wrap Kira's free hand in both of his. "We will work together, Kira. I'll speak with your family, and I will do everything I can to help all of you return to a peaceful time again."

Kira's eyes on David appeared both bottomless and full of

despair. "It wasn't peaceful before. Some people just thought it was."

All David could do, I guess, all I could have done, was to nod. He patted Kira's hand and withdrew his. "Is there anything I can do for you right now, before I leave to go and speak with your family?"

Her voice strained, she pleaded, "Call me by my name once more?"

David smiled, stood, and planted a light kiss on her forehead. "Good-bye for now, Kira. I'll see you again soon."

I searched my brain for something comforting to add and came up empty.

We drove in silence for at least fifteen minutes on our way back to Assisi. Then David struck the steering wheel hard with a hand.

"What the fuck am I going to say to his parents?"

"Her parents."

"Christ. Yes. *Her* parents. Spencer, what would you say in my place?"

I had no answer. Instead, I said, "I've been thinking about the DSM. But not about what it says. More about what it doesn't say."

"Meaning?"

"Martha would have a professional's understanding of what the DSM is, what it's used for, and so on. But nothing in what you gave me points toward Kira having a psychological problem. I mean, it never says people with transsexualism are suffering some kind of mental breakdown, or psychosis. It doesn't recommend commitment to an institution, or even psychiatric care."

"And so...?"

"A diagnosis of psychosis implies that whatever the patient is experiencing is not real, that it's not actually happening. So without that diagnosis, the implication is that transsexualism is real. That people experiencing it are not deluded. This would suggest that Kira is in her right mind, that she is correct."

David said, "In a way, I suppose there are similarities with David Reimer. I mean, he was deliberately shoved in the wrong direction, whereas with Kira no one knew until now."

"No one knew until she did."

"Right.

I spent a few quiet minutes placing David Reimer and Kira Blake side by side in my mind, trying to make connections, to identify similarities. One common factor kept rising to the top.

"The thing David and Kira have in common, as I see it, is that each of them knows who they are better than their families, better than anyone else."

I saw David nod and then he said, "I think that's true of anyone."

"Agreed." We gave that some space. Then I added, "I wouldn't say that I doubted Kira as she was talking to us about who she is. But the concept is so foreign to me that I was having trouble looking directly at it, seeing it for what it is. Because I didn't know what it is."

David chuckled. "And now you do?"

"All right, you got me. No, I can't say I understand it. But I can look directly at this phenomenon, instead of looking aside, or over it, as though it were an embarrassing relative who's a raving lunatic spouting nonsense and running from imaginary enemies."

"Her enemies are real."

I slapped my thigh for emphasis. "Exactly. And she's in her right mind. Somehow her body got a different message."

David heaved a worried sigh. "And I need to do something to help her parents see that."

I took a minute to imagine how I would have wanted someone to talk to my parents if I had come out to them, and if they had reacted badly.

I said, "Not knowing these people, all I can think of is to assure them that taking what Kira is telling them seriously is the only way forward. Whether they believe her or not, she is convinced. She has shown phenomenal courage in telling them her truth. The harder they push against it, the more rigid her resistance will be. But if they accept her as she presents herself, if they just say, 'Thank you for telling us, Kira; it's an important thing for us to know,' then in the event there is any doubt in Kira's mind, they will have left space for it. If they believe she's wrong and that she'll change her mind, she'll be more likely to do that if she isn't forced to dig her heels in too deeply."

"That might give them false hope that she will. Change her mind, I mean."

"If that gets them through the next couple of years, then I say let them have it. After that, Kira will be old enough to be on her own. And maybe, just maybe by that time, her family will have become inured, even if they don't actively accept it."

I half-turned in my seat. "In any case, I think they should find a therapist for Kira to talk to, someone who also won't push her into resistance. She needs someone to just let her be. She's— what, sixteen? She barely knows who she is, *outside* of the question of gender. Who knows where she'll go from here? I think the best approach would be to leave all avenues open for her. Don't you?"

He shook his head, not in disagreement; it was more in frustration. "I don't even know how I'm going to get them to call her Kira."

After another few minutes of silence, I said, "I guess it will depend on how much they don't want her to try this again."

There was barely room for David's car in front of my house, there were so many other vehicles. I saw the black car Donald and Jonathan had been driving. I saw Jenny's white Subaru station wagon. I saw my own dark green Jeep, penned in by the other vehicles. And I saw another white vehicle I didn't recognize.

David pulled over, engine still running. "Quite a crowd at your place tonight, eh?"

"Guess I'd better go find out what's going on." I stepped out and glanced at David before I shut the door. "Just so you know, if I mention anything at all about where I've been, I won't name names."

David nodded and drove off.

Laughter greeted me as I opened my front door. Everyone seemed to be in the kitchen, so I headed that way. The small room was full to overflowing.

Donald saw me first. "Spencer! At last! I hope you don't mind us constellating in your absence."

I saw Jonathan's head nearly snap in Donald's direction, but I didn't have room in my brain to ponder what it might mean. It was enough that I picked up on "constellating," which told me that Donald was up to his old tricks. When we'd been together before, I had sometimes been delighted and sometimes annoyed at his penchant for coming up with words I'd never heard anyone else use. I was sure that when he'd been with Bruce Cobb, dominated and beaten down emotionally as he'd been, Donald's vocabulary would have been as deprived of vitality and joy as his life had been. Was that over? Was he back to his old self? I smiled at him.

"Constellate away," I said. "Jenny, thanks for standing in for me with these raucous people."

I missed her response because the next thing I noticed was the presence of Boyd Harper. He had been leaning over in his chair to fondle Klondike's ears where the dog lay on the floor at his feet, and as he sat up he grinned at me.

"Hope you don't mind my joining the circus."

So that was Boyd's car in front, the one I hadn't recognized. I smiled back, not trusting myself not to say that I wasn't entirely sure it was appropriate for him to be here. We weren't friends. Not yet, certainly. And he hadn't been invited.

This time I heard Jenny's words. "I was walking Klondike, and when I got back to your house Boyd was sitting on the front steps. We chatted for a bit about the lay minster role here, and then your New York friends showed up, and—well, one thing led to another."

Donald jumped up and pulled a wooden chair I didn't recognize away from the wall. He positioned it facing the table, between Jonathan and Jenny. "For you," he said. "Jenny fetched it herself when we realized you were one short."

I nodded to Jenny. "Very thoughtful." Silently, my thoughts were more about how I wouldn't be "one short" if Boyd weren't here.

My next thoughts were more along the line of, *Why do I find this man so annoying?* I resolved to be more generous, to accept him until and unless he proved himself unworthy.

I took the offered seat, noticing that the table was littered with various cheeses and condiments, mixed nuts, sliced vegetables and some kind of dip. I looked at Jonathan. "Did you buy all this?"

He smiled and shrugged. "You said we could bring food. We brought food."

"Wait till you taste Jonathan's roast chicken!" Donald's voice seemed not quite his own. There was a ring of something like anxiety in it. And suddenly it hit me that this wasn't the first time I'd heard that tone since he and Jonathan had arrived in town. I didn't know what it meant. Maybe it meant nothing more than Donald's slight discomfort at being with both me and Jonathan in the same space.

I helped myself to some cheese and a few dipped vegetable pieces, suddenly feeling ravenous. The tantalizing aroma of roasting chicken made it worse.

Jenny leaned toward me. "Everything okay? Anything I can do?"

I heaved a sigh and reached for more cheese. "It's not an easy thing to talk about, especially with everyone here being so jovial and lighthearted."

That caught Jonathan's attention. "I, for one, would love to know anything you feel you can share."

The room was silent other than Klondikes paws hitting the floor as he pawed and chewed some toy. Everyone's eyes were on me. And Jenny deserved an explanation.

"Very well," I said, "as long as you'll allow me to munch as I talk."

I gave them a very abbreviated version of what had happened. I didn't mention the suicide attempt, but I described a situation in which a young person's parents had reacted in a way that was quite painful to their child, who was apparently—and rather suddenly, at least to the family—transsexual. I almost missed Boyd's silent reaction because of Jonathan's. Almost. Boyd's back straightened suddenly.

Jonathan leaned forward, elbows on the table. "I've been thinking we should expand the shelter to include transsexual youth as well, not just gay and lesbian kids. This is almost like a sign that I should go ahead with this idea."

Boyd's voice was terse, almost irritated. "They're not the same thing at all."

Jonathan seemed taken aback by the pointedness of Boyd's tone. "Oh, to be sure. But transsexual kids are just as likely— maybe even more likely—to be disowned by their families." He paused, but Boyd said nothing, just watched Jonathan's face. "When I visited the shelters in New York, I wouldn't even have known whether any of the kids there was transsexual. I just knew they needed help. And that's what I want my home to do."

Jenny turned to Boyd. "What can you tell us about the difference? Would you say that a boy who thinks he's a girl isn't just a gay boy who's, you know, very gay? Very effeminate?"

Boyd's head shook hard enough to make me sit back a little. "No. Sexual orientation and gender identity are two different things. Someone can be a male-to-female transsexual and be attracted to men, or they might be attracted to women. It's not who you sleep *with*. It's who you sleep *as*."

Jenny was about to ask another question, but I interrupted. "You sound as though you have some experience with people who find themselves in that situation."

He nodded. "I do. There were two transsexual people in my Boston parish. My minister thought that because I'm gay, I would know how to relate to them. She was wrong in one way, but right in another. I have no idea what it must feel like to be in the wrong body. As you know, I'm an author. I write romance stories. There's a lot of sex in them, in one way or another."

Boyd waved a hand dismissively as though to begin again. "What I'm trying to say is that I have a good imagination. And I can't imagine what it would be like to have to live in a female body. To have people insist that my name is—I don't know, Betty. That as a girl I should want dolls and tea sets and clothes with pink ruffles. How would I convince anyone who I really was? Like I said, I can't imagine what that would be like. Seems to me the only advantage is that you get to choose your own name."

Jenny chuckled. "It kind of sounds like you might have some idea. So that's how your minister was wrong. In what way was she right?"

"When someone tells me—however they let me know, which is not usually in so many words—that they're straight, they expect me to believe them. But when I tell people I'm gay… I can see it on their faces. They don't quite believe me. Or at least they don't accept it. And sometimes they say it aloud."

Just as Kira had changed her voice, Boyd did the same. "'He just hasn't met the right girl.' 'He's just rebelling against society.' 'This is his parents' fault.' 'He just needs a good therapist, or maybe a good doctor.' 'He'll figure it out eventually.' In other words, they don't believe me. They think it has to make sense *to them*. And it doesn't. It can't."

Jenny turned to me, concern on her face. "Is this how it is for you?" Instantly, she covered her mouth with both hands. "I'm so sorry!"

I knew she was concerned that she'd revealed my sexual orientation to Boyd, who might not have known about it.

I smiled at her. "Not to worry. But no, it doesn't happen so much here. But Boyd is not wrong. And, really, even here, I do get the sense sometimes that people—some people, anyway—are half-hearted about their acceptance. It's like I've said, 'I'm gay,' and they respond, 'I hear what you say.' But the acceptance goes only so deep, as though they're thinking what Boyd just said."

I glanced at Boyd to see if he was surprised by my revelation. He did not seem to be.

Dinner conversation moved away from these serious topics, at least for a while. Somewhere between the chicken (which was amazing; Donald had been right) and the ice cream, with fudge sauce Jonathan had made, Jonathan turned to me.

"So, Spencer, I'm hoping you'll tell us a little more about this Pagan community."

Instantly, I was on guard, though I couldn't have said why. "Like what? What about it?"

Donald said, "Jenny told us what you did. How you found out who really started that fire so long ago, and how that exonerated Assisi."

I was fast reaching the point where I was bored with this story, having been asked about it by many people. And I didn't enjoy being in the spotlight about it, having anyone think I'd done something remarkable. I had done what I believed I needed to do. I didn't do it alone. And I didn't enjoy fame. Even more, I didn't like holding The Forest up for scrutiny; they kept to themselves, and they wanted it that way.

I said, "I'm not sure I can tell you anything Jenny hasn't. She works with someone from The Forest, herself, in our youth group."

Her voice quiet, Jenny said, "I've never been there."

I looked at her, surprised. "Myra hasn't invited you?" Jenny shook her head. "Have you asked to go?"

Jenny shrugged. "I didn't want to seem forward."

That made me laugh out loud. "Oh, Jenny, how do you think I got an invitation?"

She shrugged. "I know. You asked for one. More than once."

"More than twice!" I smiled at her. "Let's talk later." I would get Jenny her invitation. But I didn't want anyone else to think it could include them. It wasn't up to me anyway, but I certainly didn't want to invite a crowd.

Boyd had been watching me. "I'd kind of like to see the place, myself."

"Yeah," I said, "the thing is, they're very sensitive to being put on display, like some kind of circus act."

"That's not—"

"It's how they feel about it. They were very clear with me."

"Then how did you get invited?"

"I earned it." I waved a hand. "Never mind. I'll just say it's not my place to introduce anyone to The Forest, and I respect their preference to be left largely alone."

Boyd didn't want to drop it. "Are they afraid?"

The look I gave him from under my brow was nearly a glare. "They've been burned. Literally. But no, they aren't afraid. Just very selective."

"Okay, so what does it mean to be Pagan?"

This was firmer ground for me, based not only on my interactions with the Forest Dwellers, but also with some research I'd done last fall after Vanessa had told me about The Forest.

"Paganism—Neopaganism, really—is a loosely-structured, earth-based belief system. If you encounter a Pagan who seems to be worshipping something, like a tree, or a butterfly, or whatever, they're actually acknowledging the god-spirit they find there. Someone paying reverence to a tree is someone who feels an affinity for trees, or for a particular tree, and for that person the tree is like a doorway to the ultimate Spirit, capital S. Some Pagans see that spirit as a god, some as a goddess, some as just spirit, or life force. There is no dogma. If they have a doctrine, it's that no action should be taken until you've done your best to be sure it won't hurt anyone."

Into the quiet that followed my speech, Donald said, "That sounds wonderful."

Jenny said, "I like it, too. And the thing about being earth-based means that when it comes to spirituality, and God, or whatever, they start from where they are."

Jonathan wanted to know, "What does that mean? As opposed to what?"

Jenny's chin rose just a little. "As opposed to expecting people to start from where they're supposed to want to be."

I knew a little something about Jenny's background. Coming from a Catholic family, she had rebelled in her teens, and after college had moved far away from her Ohio home. Now, in the UU tradition, she had a very different way to approach God.

Jonathan frowned, more in confusion than challenge. "Explain?"

She seemed happy to oblige. "Some religions insist that if you don't act and even think in line with some kind of perfection, there's something wrong with you. You're a sinner. Like at heart, you're some kind of evil creature in need of absolution."

Jonathan wasn't convinced. "Aren't we all in need of improvement?"

"Of course. But not because our starting point is evil."

Boyd wanted to know, "So why aren't you a Pagan?"

"How do you know I'm not? UU welcomes Pagans."

He laughed. "Touché."

CHAPTER 6

We had almost too many hands willing to help with after-dinner cleanup. I finally sent Jenny home, promising to return her chair tomorrow, and ushered Jonathan and Donald after her.

"Thank you," I said as I shook Jonathan's hand. "You're reputation as an excellent cook is well-deserved."

Donald hugged me briefly when I offered him my hand. Into my ear, he whispered, "I want to meet them. The Forest." He released me, clearly not expecting a response, and followed Jonathan to the car.

I had almost forgotten about Boyd, but when I turned back to the kitchen, there he was, up to his elbows in sudsy water.

"Thanks," I said. "You should go home, too."

"Actually, I want to talk to you about something, now that the others have left."

I steeled myself, sure he was going to talk about being a lay minister. "Oh?"

"It's that child. The transsexual." He lifted his hands from the sink, shook the suds off them, and wiped them on a towel. "I want to help."

"You—what do you mean?"

"I know how to talk to them. Girl? Boy?"

"Girl now, according to what she's saying."

"You don't believe her?"

I thought back to what I'd said to David on the drive home. I'd meant all of it. I believed all of it. Even so, I had to admit, "I don't know what to believe." I sat back down on Jenny's chair, and Boyd sat on another. I asked, "How much do you know about this, really?"

"In Boston, like I said, I worked with two trans kids. One of them was suicidal. By being there for him, listening to him, *believing* him, I helped him stay alive." He grinned. "Sorry if that sounds like self-aggrandizement. But I feel pretty sure that he wouldn't still be around if I hadn't been there for him. Perhaps because no one else was, except Meghan."

I regarded him closely. "Do you see this work as some kind of mission for yourself?"

He shook his head. "I'm not prepared to say that. But I think I can help. I also worked with the parents, helping them to see what it took for their child to tell them the truth about who they are."

"Is it like that, though? Truth, I mean? Isn't it possible the child could be misguided, or misinformed, or exploring who they might be, rather than actually being in the wrong body?"

"Sure. That happens. But with the two kids I worked with, it was real. Obviously I don't know about the kid you were with today. But it's only by listening to them, taking them seriously, that we help them figure that out. And, Spencer," he tilted his head, "they are the ones who have to figure that out. It's not our job to do that. All we can do is make space for that to happen."

We watched each other's eyes for a moment, a spark like some kind of simpatico dancing between us. Finally I said, "So what would you recommend at this point?"

"I'd like to meet her. Just that, to start. Maybe she won't want to talk to me. But I'd like to try."

I glanced at my watch: not quite ten o'clock. "Give me a minute."

I went into the living room and called David. "Look, I don't know whether this is a good idea or not, but I have a new parishioner who was a lay minister in Boston until recently. He worked with transsexual kids in his parish there, and he thinks he might be able to help Kira. I don't even know what that means, but I'll do anything to help keep her alive. What do you think?"

"God. Really? Let me think." I waited in silence for maybe a minute. Then, "Kira isn't due to be released until Tuesday morning. I'd need her parents' permission, of course; it's one thing for me to bring another minister in, someone I know well. It's quite something else to introduce this new person. Let me get back to you."

I let Boyd know the question was being pursued and sent him home. I needed time to think.

At some point it occurred to me that I didn't know why Boyd had been sitting on my steps when Jenny had returned with Klondike.

~

Unsurprisingly, I found it hard to fall asleep that night. My thoughts and feelings were in turmoil.

I tried imagining Adam here with me, but even the release I got from that fantasy did nothing to bring on the pleasant lull one can feel in the afterglow. It probably didn't help that my thoughts strayed from Adam and veered, despite my efforts to stop them, toward Donald.

Sometime after three I awoke suddenly from a troubled sleep and sat upright in bed with a grunt that startled Klondike, on his bed in the corner. Almost as though it had been seared into the insides of my eyelids, I could still see what my dream had shown me: A small plane, flying in swirls and loops, smoke behind it spelling out the name Bettina.

Since returning from New York, I hadn't allowed myself to dwell on the letters I'd discovered in the storage room. I rubbed my hair, digging my fingers into the scalp to try and get my brain to focus.

Bettina.

Some of the phrases from my father's letter were still in my head. *...the phantom warmth of you encircled by my arms...guilt... shame...appear faintly on the edge of a feather that would be remorse and repentance if it turned...I am left wanting you.*

Father had loved music and poetry and, really, all the arts. So his phrasing wasn't what surprised me. What I couldn't wrap my mind around was the feeling behind his words.

Even while I had never doubted that Father had loved me, I don't remember ever feeling it. I had felt as though Mother had a pretty good idea who I was, sexual orientation aside. But Father? I had always been convinced he didn't know me. Not really. And my conviction hadn't changed since his death.

If my mother had known I was gay, I suspect she would have felt sad for me, believing that I was headed for a life with unfair challenges that wouldn't have existed for a straight man. But if Father had known?

I threw myself back down onto the mattress, staring at the dark ceiling, and tried to imagine a scene in which I told him.

I'd become convinced I was gay at around the age of sixteen—Kira's age now, though I suspected she'd known her truth for some time. What if, at sixteen, I had said, "Father, I'm gay"?

My entire body jerked with the emotional shock that went through it, as though to distract me from even considering such a scene. But I forced my mind back to it.

Here's the scene. It's a year past my epiphany at sixteen so I feel secure in my conclusion.

"Father, I need to tell you something. Something important."

He sits in his wing chair in the music room, a floor lamp behind him lighting the book he's reading. Soft grey light coming through the tall windows seems darker in contrast to the cone of brightness around Father. I am in shadow.

He reads for another several seconds, expecting me to understand that he is reading until he comes to a good stopping point before looking up at me, standing before him, his seventeen-year-old son, terrified and yet determined.

He closes the book, a finger remaining to mark his place; closing the book completely would imply he had more time for me than he intended to take away from his reading. "What is it, Spencer?"

My chest is so tight I'm not sure I'm breathing. I'm pretty sure I can't. I try anyway and fail.

"Spencer?"

"I'm gay." It comes out almost like a small explosion.

"I beg your pardon?" His voice is calm, pitched to leave room for doubt: Did he not understand the words? Did he not understand the meaning? Did he understand what I said but wants me to see in that question the opportunity to retract?

"I'm gay, Father. I've known for a while now."

His mouth compresses just enough for me to see it happen. He glares at me from under his brows as he opens the book. "Don't be absurd." His eyes are back on the book as if to dismiss me.

But, like Kira, I will not be dismissed.

"I'm serious, Father." I wait, but it's another few seconds before he looks up again, book open. "I thought you'd want to know."

"Why?"

"Why am I gay?"

"Why would I want to know?"

At this point, in my dark Assisi bedroom, I shake my head. In that imaginary scene I was putting words into his part of the script that he would almost certainly not have said. Calling my assertion absurd, that made sense; it was entirely possible he'd have said that. But as for why he'd want to know—he wouldn't have said that. So I was indulging in a pettiness that sprang from my belief that he hadn't known me, taking it to a bizarre level where he hadn't wanted to. I would not allow myself to go into sulky child territory.

And then I sat up again. It wasn't only that *he* hadn't really known *me*. I hadn't known him. And my surprise at what I'd read in those letters confirmed it.

~

Monday, early afternoon, found me back in David's car, with Boyd in the back seat. Kira's father had told David he didn't care who talked with his "son" about anything, because the only thing that was going to happen was that Ralph would come home and be Ralph. He'd added that if anyone wanted to help, they should get that through the boy's head. Mrs. Blake, as David saw it, had been less rigid, but she hadn't seemed willing to say anything that contradicted her husband.

David had spent roughly twenty minutes talking with Boyd and me, no doubt to be sure that at least, Boyd wasn't going to make things worse. And, of course, Boyd now needed to know why Kira was in the hospital, that she had attempted suicide.

In the hospital bed, Kira was again—still?—curled into a ball, this time facing away from the door. She didn't move when David called her name. We stood, waiting, and eventually heard a muffled, "What do you want?"

Boyd gently touched David's arm. He said, "The question, Kira, is what do *you* want?"

She shifted in the bed, turning her head enough to see us. "Who the fuck are you?"

"My name's Boyd." He chuckled. "I guess that's a pretty piss-poor name in your ears right now, isn't it?"

Kira turned enough to sit up, this time adjusting the bed frame herself to raise the head. "You got that right. Why are you here?"

"I heard you were having kind of a hard time getting through to people. Is it okay if I sit?" Kira lifted a shoulder and dropped it, and Boyd pulled a chair close to the bed. "I'm here to listen to you."

Kira scowled. "Whaddya want me to say?"

"Well, how about you tell me how you chose the name Kira? It's unusual. I like it."

Kira pulled her knees toward her chest and wrapped her arms around them. "It's from a book I read. Kira Megalos. She's a warrior, even though everyone around her says she should just do what women are supposed to do."

"Megalos. That's Greek, right? Doesn't it mean something like big? Or great?"

"I dunno."

"So is it just the name that appealed to you, or are you a warrior, too?"

"I have to be. I have to fight."

"For what?"

"For myself."

"Because—?"

"Don't you get it?" Kira sat up a little. "I have to fight everyone who's trying to tell me who I am."

"Who are you?"

"Duh. I'm me. I'm a girl."

"Yeah, but who are you?"

That seemed to confuse Kira. "Well… I like to make things."

"What things?"

"Jewelry. Dresses. Hats."

Boyd nodded. "How many people know this about you?"

She glanced up at David, then at me, and then back at Boyd. "What are you gonna tell my folks?"

"I don't plan to tell them anything. I've never even met them."

"Cuz they don't know. About any of that. I was going to tell them, but they were so horrible when I told them about me, I couldn't say anything else. Now I don't want them to know. I don't want them to know anything." She crossed her arms over her chest and sat back.

Boyd nodded again. "I know how you feel."

"No you don't."

"I was seventeen when I told my folks I was gay. My father told me to straighten up—funny, huh?—or else I was on my own." He shrugged. "I've been on my own ever since."

I wanted to ask about his mother; surely, she knew he was gay, and he was very much a part of her life. But this wasn't the time.

Kira's voice and face changed from challenging to sulky. She waved an arm dismissively. "Yeah, well, I'm not seventeen."

"You will be. And then you'll be eighteen, and pretty soon you'll be able to take charge of your life in a way you can't, just yet. But you'll get there."

"I don't want to get there if I have to pretend to be a boy the whole time."

Boyd drew a deep breath and let it out slowly. "It's not easy, is it? Not being something your parents want you to be." They regarded each other for a minute, and then Boyd said, "How long have you known you weren't a boy?"

Kira seemed to relax, just a little. "For sure? A long time. Maybe a couple of years. Though I think I knew, somehow, all along."

"Was it a difficult thing for you to understand?"

"Duh."

"So your folks just found out." He paused, clearly waiting to see if his implication would dawn on Kira. He must have given up, because he added, "They must think it's hard to understand, too. Don't you think?"

Again he paused. This time, I think Kira began to get his point, but she wasn't about to give ground.

"Kira, you've been thinking about this, trying to figure it out, trying to come to the truth for at least two years, maybe longer. They've just found out." Kira turned a furious face toward him, but he held up his hand. "I know, I know. That's no excuse to say mean things, or to threaten you, or whatever else happened Sunday. I'm just saying that with a little more time, they could calm down. In their minds, this is a huge adjustment, and it's come up very suddenly for them. Maybe, just maybe keeping that in mind will help make things a little smoother when you go home tomorrow."

Kira crossed her arms over her chest again and turned her face away. "You're taking their side."

Boyd shook his head very slowly. "Truth is, Kira, I'm not especially concerned with them. I'm concerned with you. If things calm down for them, they'll calm down for you. That's what I care about."

Kira's face took on a stubborn look. "They still call me Ralph."

"Yeah, that sucks. I know. It's just how they've always known you. It's not a change they're going to be able to make quickly."

"No matter what you say, I still have to go back and live with people who call me by the wrong name. They try to make me do things that are wrong for me. They won't let me be who I *am*."

At this point, I thought Boyd would be stumped. He nodded, and took a minute to think. Then, "Life sucks sometimes, Kira. And it's not fair that you've had to hide who you are, and act like someone you're not. This is something you've been doing, though, so you know how to do it. Your parents don't yet know how to treat you like a girl. I guess what I'm saying is I hope you'll be able to find ways to be your true self quietly for now."

"You want me to lie? Is that what you're saying?"

"Not exactly. I'm saying that sometimes a frontal assault won't get you what you want. Sometimes we need to use guerrilla warfare. Sometimes we need to be sneaky. When they call you Ralph, you'll know the truth."

David, standing next to me, had a question. "Kira, what about your sister, Molly? She's two years younger than you, I think. How is she responding to you now?"

"I don't know."

David fished something out of his pocket. "I went to your house early, before your dad went to work. Before Molly left for school. She left before I did. When I went out to my car, there was a note on the windshield, in a sealed envelope with the words 'from Molly to Kira' on it." He held it toward Kira. "Would you like to open it?"

Kira's eyes revealed both fear and hope as she held her hand out. She stared for a moment at the envelope, perhaps relishing that she saw "Kira" there. Inside was a scrap of paper, large enough for only a few words. Kira read them silently and her face crumpled. She dropped the paper and hung her head, and she sobbed.

Boyd, closest to her, asked, "May I read this?" Kira nodded. Aloud, Boyd read, "I always wanted a sister."

My throat tightened, and tears filled my eyes. I knew I wasn't the only one who felt that joy, mingled as it was with pain.

So Kira had an ally. She grudgingly agreed to follow Boyd's advice and, essentially, keep her head down, at least for the near future. She would give her folks some time. But only some. It was all she would give, so we had to accept that.

Boyd gave her his phone number and address, which Kira wrote on the back of Molly's note. She put the scrap back into the envelope and folded it several times. Apparently not feeling my sense of impropriety, Boyd gave Kira a long hug before we left.

On the ride back, David told us why he'd waited to give Kira the note. "I wanted to gauge her reaction to you, Boyd. I had to hope that what Molly had written on the envelope—'to Kira'—was a good sign, and I wanted her to see that at the right time."

Boyd said, "I think you chose well. Um, is there any way I could talk with her folks?"

I glanced at David, ready to offer an opinion if he wanted one. He shook his head, which would have been my response. "Not for now, at least. I really liked the point you made about how sudden this is for them, which of course had a lot to do with how they reacted. I'm prepared to talk to them myself about that, to make a case for everyone to give each other some time and space. Thanks for the offer. If I think it's a good next step at some point, I'll certainly reach out to you."

"Got it. It's huge, what Molly wrote." I think he was about to go on, but David spoke first.

"Agreed. Though I don't plan to reveal Molly's position to her parents. It's up to her whether to let them know."

Boyd nodded. "I was going to say that. I agree."

David drove first to Boyd's mother's house to drop him off, even though it would have been faster to go to mine first. David thanked Boyd, and we watched him walk toward the house before pulling back onto the road.

"Your new lay minister is quite the personality."

"He's not a lay minister here. Not yet, anyway. I'm still assessing."

"Do you think he might be a little too assertive?"

I let out a breath. "He might be. But Loraine Fuller was assertive, and everyone loved her. Well, almost everyone. But she didn't have any enemies I knew about."

David added, "It was always clear that Loraine's heart was in the right place. I'm not saying Boyd's isn't. It just seems a little less obvious."

I chuckled. "I know what you mean. His Boston minister spoke very highly of him. Even so, I'm planning to see how my parishioners—and my other lay ministers—respond to him before making a decision. That's going to take time. He might be a little impatient, but that's not my concern."

Adam's green pickup truck was in front of my house when David dropped me off. David said, "Isn't that man in the truck one of the Forest Dwellers?"

"He is."

"Odd."

I glanced at David. "Not really. They are friendly, you know, and I do have a relationship with them."

"Still."

I grinned. "I guess there are some differences after all, between Christianity and UU. We seem to be more comfortable with the idea of Paganism."

I watched David drive off before turning to Adam, who was now standing next to the truck, relaxed, arms crossed.

"You've been busy," he greeted me.

I nodded. "I have. Have you been trying to reach me?"

"Not urgently. But now I have another reason." He followed me to the door and into my living room.

"Another reason?"

"Besides this one." He pushed the door shut and pressed his body to mine, his tongue searching my mouth before I could react. But, yeah, I reacted. In kind. And I decided against pointing out that this reason had, um, arisen before Donald and Jonathan's departure, despite what Adam had told me would be the case.

Lying in bed after a quick but thorough coupling, I asked, "So what was the other reason?"

He propped himself up on an elbow. "I hear you have a trans kid."

I sat up. "She's not mine. She's in David Foster's parish." I headed to the bathroom for cleanup; it was the middle of the day, and there were parish duties. There were also parishioners, any one of whom might drop by unannounced.

Adam followed me. "You said 'she' because that's who she really is, or is she really a boy?"

"I'm not sure I can parse that. She's biologically male."

"Well then, good for you, referring to her that way."

I stood still and stared at him. "That sounded patronizing."

He shook his head. "Sorry; you're right. I didn't mean it like that. Not exactly."

"What the—"

He chuckled. "It's just that accepting someone like that isn't always the way most of society would react." He pulled one of my earlobes. "Should have known you'd be different."

I was only partly mollified. "Well…. How do you know about her, anyway?"

"Myra heard it from Jenny. By the way, did you tell Jenny she should invite herself to visit us?"

I headed back to the bedroom to dress. "Not in so many words. But I think she's earned it. Don't you?" I heard no response, so I turned to look at Adam. "Did Myra refuse?"

"No. Not outright."

"What does that mean?"

"She'll need to talk with Erik, and maybe Elaine as well." Erik Stillman had an authority in The Forest I wasn't entirely clear about. I was pretty sure Elaine Gault was the community's primary elder, inasmuch as there was any hierarchy there. I was going to protest, but he held up a hand. "You were a special case. You started with Erik."

"I was a special case because I kept asking to come."

"You were a special case because you proved you understood the relationship between how you live and how we live. You understood what faith means to us."

"Hasn't Jenny done that? She and Myra have been working together with the teens for months. There are Forest Dweller kids in that group, more now than ever."

"Look, I'm not saying we won't agree to a visit. I think it's likely we will. But we have to go about it in a way that doesn't look like an open invitation to just anyone. You know how easy it would be for us to be treated like a curiosity."

"I do. But consider that if you were a little less aloof, less mysterious, the curiosity would decrease."

"You and your UU people don't represent everyone."

"This might be a good time to remind you that the Protestant minister, the Catholic priest, and the chief of police all helped get to the truth about the fire. Even some folks in Little Boundary helped clear the air. That wasn't all me. It wasn't all 'my' people."

We regarded each other for several seconds before we resumed our task of dressing. Neither of us said anything else until we stood just inside my front door.

Adam opened the door but then didn't move. "It might be a while before you see me again."

I felt my back stiffen. "If that's true, it will only be because that's what *you* want."

He nodded and left.

I shut the door and leaned against it. Was there something going on I didn't understand? Or was Adam not quite as deep and wise as he'd led me to believe he was?

I shrugged. No one's perfect. He'll get over this, or he won't. Meanwhile, Klondike was barking from the back yard where I'd left him before going to Newport, to the hospital. He wanted a walk. So did I.

CHAPTER 7

After dinner that night I had a call from Donald.

"Jonathan's going into Newport tomorrow to talk details about a property. I assured him I'd just be in the way. Can you come get me late morning sometime? We can have lunch here at the B&B and do whatever. Talk about old times. Pay a visit to your Pagan friends. Gossip like quidnuncs about—oh, anyone we both know. Maybe you could play piano for me. What do you say?"

Tomorrow. Tuesday. Kira would be sent home from the hospital, but I didn't think there was anything else I could do for her that David couldn't. Mentally I reviewed my calendar and came up with nothing that couldn't wait, other than an appearance I wanted to make at the regular late-afternoon meeting of Teens for Truth. So the only question left was whether I wanted to do as he asked.

I did. And I didn't. It would be really good, I thought, to get to know him again, the new version of Donald: free of the cult; free of Bruce Cobb; happily ensconced in the life and the arms of an admirable man who loved him. What gave me pause was the knowledge that I was still attracted to him. Even Adam had seen that, and he'd never met Donald.

Oh, fuck it, I said to myself. "Only if you tell me what a quid-nunc is. Then, sure. Around eleven?"

"Someone who gossips. Eleven sounds great."

"Wear comfortable shoes." And I hung up before he could ask why.

~

As in the days when Marshall and I used to stop at the Pinewood after hiking, Maggie Downing still reigned over the restaurant there. Today's half-apron featured a repeated pattern of sketched flowers with raindrops falling on them. Appropriate for April, I supposed, and she did vary her aprons with the seasons.

"Reverend Hill!" she greeted me, beaming. "Haven't seen you in a bit." She glanced down toward where Klondike lay on the floor with as much of his massive bulk as possible sheltered beneath the table. "And Klondike. Hello, boy."

I heard the dog's tail thump on the wooden floor. "True. I'm waiting for better weather to go hiking. Then you'll see more of me."

Donald and I ordered and sat quietly for a moment, taking each other in visually. Then, his voice heavy with sarcasm, he said, "You come here often?"

I laughed at the silly pick-up line. "Not lately, as you heard. But there is a great hike a little farther out of town. I like to come here afterward for hot cocoa, or iced tea, or whatever seems refreshing."

"Are we going there? Is that why you made me wear ugly shoes?"

"No, not that hike. You'd need something sturdier than what you're wearing. I do have a walk in mind, but it won't be chal-lenging."

"Lovely day for it, that's for sure. Um, since when do you hike, though?" I hesitated for just a moment before deciding that, yes, this would be a good time to talk about Marshall.

"Well, for one thing, how could I not? I mean, look around you.

Mountains, hills, woods, forests, streams, ponds everywhere. They don't call this the Green Mountain State for nothing. But in fact, someone who doesn't live around here any longer got me hooked." Donald's eyes were looking for a sign that might reveal who that person had been to me. "Someone who was very important to me."

"Do tell. What was his name?"

"Marshall. He was the English teacher at the Assisi high school until last December. When I arrived here last August, he'd been one of our lay ministers. But then he resigned that post so he could devote more time to our youth group. He's very musical. Lovely voice. Has this medieval string instrument he can play."

Maggie arrived with our order. Donald assured her we were all set for the moment, watched her walk away, and said to me, "And you were in love with him."

I paused to collect my thoughts and decide what words to use. It hadn't been that simple. "He was in love with me. I was in like with him. I cared about him deeply."

"Is that why he left?"

I shook my head. "No. I was never brave enough to be honest with him. He left because—it's complicated. But it has to do with the Assembly of God church here in Little Boundary, and with the bitter, vengeful man who serves as their minister, and with the fact that the vice principle at Marshall's school hates gays and got him fired."

"Shit. So he had to leave, I guess. Nothing else for him to do here?"

"Pretty much. Yeah."

"Wow. Well, if he intends to continue in that career, I hope he has something apotropaic with him." Donald looked down at the ham sandwich on his plate as if he'd said nothing unusual.

I sat back and laughed. When he looked up, an unconvincing look of confusion on his Puckish face, I said, "So you're still at it."

"At—what?"

"What the hell does 'apotropaic' mean?"

"Oh, whatever works to ward off evil. Some kind of object, usually." He took a bite, watching me as he chewed and swallowed. "What do you mean, 'still at it?'"

I smiled and shook my head. "You know very well. Your odd vocabulary. Your penchant for collecting words most people have never heard of, and then using them to some effect I've never completely understood."

He shrugged as though to say, *Oh, that*. He took a sip of water. "Jonathan doesn't like them."

"Doesn't like what? Your odd words?"

"He eschews toploftiness." He laughed at my confused expression. "Says I'm putting on airs."

I chuckled. "And aren't you?"

"Well…. But it's fun."

"Of course it is. So, you, uh, you hold yourself back when you're with him?"

He shrugged again and took another bite of sandwich.

I didn't like what I'd just learned about Jonathan. What the hell? I'd always found Donald's little personality quirk to be more or less endearing, though of course it had its irritating moments. But I saw it as part of who Donald was, part of how he wanted to be seen, how he wanted to express himself. Who was Jonathan to tell him not to do that?

It was challenging to refrain from saying what I wanted to say. In the few moments of silence, I remembered that at Sunday dinner, Jonathan had given Donald what I now believed was a disapproving glance when Donald had used the word "constellating."

"I don't want to get you into trouble with Jonathan, but as far as I'm concerned you may use whatever words you like."

He looked at me from under his eyebrows. "Thank you. That gives me a feeling of querencia." He grinned. "Sanctuary. Safety."

～

After our early lunch, I took Donald and Klondike for a walk to McGowan Pond. The trail was mostly level with only a few rocks and roots to trip unwary hikers. The deciduous trees along the path were just beginning to show that intense, concentrated, light green where leaves were being born. We came upon one tree that seemed to have sprouted pink fur all along its branches and upper trunk.

Donald stopped suddenly and gaped at it. "What on earth is that? A gay tree?"

I laughed, and as I did it occurred to me that I hadn't laughed, really laughed, very much in the last few months. Was it spring? Or was it Donald? "That's called a redbud tree. Isn't it beautiful?"

He walked toward it and gently plucked a clump of the tiny pink blossoms from a low-hanging branch. "I suppose they don't stay very long, these blossoms."

"Probably not. This is my first spring here, but I've walked along this trail a few times, and I didn't see the pink until last week."

We continued our walk, mostly in silence, until we could see the pond through the trees. I found a certain pine tree and stood still. Klondike sat obediently at my feet.

"What?" Donald wanted to know.

"It was on this spot, last fall, that I watched as a gorgeous young man with long auburn hair stood naked on the edge of the pond there. He did a kind of dance, and then he came, shooting his cum in a graceful arc, right into the water. Then he put on clothing that was mostly leather and disappeared to the east."

Donald's eyes were huge. "Did he see you?"

"I didn't think so at the time. I found out later that he had known I was there, but he didn't see any reason why he shouldn't go ahead with what he wanted to do."

"Have you seen him since? Clothed or otherwise?"

I turned to look at Donald. "If I tell you something, will you agree not to tell another soul?"

A half-grin lifted one side of his mouth. "You didn't. You did! You devil."

"His name is Adam. He's the sculptor."

Donald leaned his head back and laughed. "Of course he is! Oh, say—is he part of that Pagan community?"

"He is."

"And does he love you more than you love him? Like with Marshall?"

"No. Nothing like that."

"So you're fuck buddies."

"I—" Was there a better term? "I guess. Although he's not very happy with me right now. I don't know when, or even if, I'll ever see his naked body again."

Donald faced the pond and spread his arms wide. "Honey, just hang out right here. He'll turn up sooner or later."

We walked forward and gazed into the water, standing where Adam had stood that day. Then we continued around the pond. At one point, Donald took my hand. Neither of us said anything, as though it were the most natural thing in the world and not something one would comment on. And maybe it was.

It was after two o'clock by the time we got back to my house. I had thought Donald and I would go to the diner for coffee and a doughnut, but he said, "Can't we stay here? I happen to know that you have some good cheese, and if I know you, there's a great selection of wines we could consider."

I gave Klondike a few treats while I thought about Donald's proposal. He was right about the cheese and the wine. I even had a pretty decent loaf of bread in the house. But was this idea a good one? It had felt awfully nice, walking with Donald, holding his hand, feeling a kind of connection I hadn't felt in a long time. He wasn't mine any longer, and if either of us was going to get hurt here, it would probably be me.

Perhaps I hesitated too long, because then he said, "I'll remind you that Jonathan is not the jealous type."

I turned to face him where he sat at my kitchen table. "I'm not entirely sure I know what that means."

He looked confused for a moment, and then he laughed. "I'm not suggesting we go upstairs or anything. Jonathan would not approve of *that*."

Any more than he approves of your unusual vocabulary, was the thought that went through my head so fast that I almost didn't avoid saying it aloud.

I couldn't see my way to declining his suggestion without implying that he might have been thinking something along those lines. "Good to know. Let me see about the wine. Why don't you get the cheese out?"

The pinot noir I chose went well with the moderately pungent cheese Donald found in my refrigerator, and we settled down for a small repast.

Donald pointed a piece of bread at me, sending my mind reeling back to our first shared meal years ago in New York City. He'd pointed a French fry at me to support a verbal point he'd been making. Today, he said, "So how did a city boy like you end up in such a rural environment? And has it turned you into a bucolic philocalist?"

I shook my head, amused. "I can't answer that until I know what it is."

"Someone who loves beauty. So a bucolic philocalist would be a lover of all things trees, and mountains, and rocks, and streams, and—"

"Okay, I get it. As to your question, I'm sure you know that ministers mostly go where we're sent. There's some negotiating room, to be sure, and the longer I'm in this vocation, the more latitude I might be given."

"And now, you hike. With this gorgeous monster of a dog. Ever go with anyone else?"

"Marshall and I used to hike sometimes."

"Not Adam?"

"There was one time when Klondike and I went with Adam and Myra Langtree, someone else from The Forest, on a winter trek through the woods. Turned out to be quite the eventful afternoon."

I recounted for Donald how Klondike had sensed danger and had led us to where a barn was on fire, and how we had rescued horses and children.

"I didn't know it at the time," I said, "but the barn turned out to be on the property of Alan Jermin, pastor at the Assembly of God church in Little Boundary."

"Oh, my! I remember what you said about them. I don't suppose he was grateful."

"Told us to get off his property. So, no."

We munched for a few minutes in silence, and then I decided to take a chance. "Is it all right if I ask you about what happened? How you got pulled into the Risen Christ group?" I stopped short of referring to it as a cult, which it most certainly was.

Donald let out a long sigh. "I was afraid you were going to ask about that." He said nothing else.

I prompted. "And?"

He sighed again. "I wish I could tell you something that makes sense. It was kind of a perfect storm. There was my background in the Lutheran Synod, which was indisputably dreadful in specific ways, but which also made me consider what it would be like to be in a more generous denomination, and also whether I could be a minister, myself. There was the connection I wanted you to see between acting and the ministry. You know?"

I nodded. "Sure. You were right. Sermons are a bit of an act, but they need to engage people's hearts and minds. The rest of the ministry, of course, is not an act at all."

"And then there was the unpromising future of a gay man— that would be me—who badly wanted children and knew that he could have the children if he gave up being gay."

We looked at each other across the table, his expression vulnerable and hopeful, mine no doubt confused and unconvinced.

He shrugged. "I told you it wouldn't make sense."

"I do recall that you once said you missed the church. I even remember you having a stray thought or two about the ministry. But, Donald, children?"

"You know, Spence, you weren't with me every minute. I don't think you even knew about the volunteer work I did at city schools, where I'd coach kids who were doing school plays, skits, that sort of thing."

I sat back, nearly stunned. "No. I didn't know that. Why didn't you tell me?"

"I don't know. It kind of felt like my secret. Not from you, particularly, but just something about me I didn't let the world in on. Something private. I can't really explain it."

I downed a good half-glass of wine, thinking about what I'd just learned, making a connection between that and Donald's difficult childhood: a fire-and-brimstone minister for a father, a weak and submissive mother, and Donald hiding for dear life the fact that he'd never be the man his father expected him to be.

I said, "Was it anything like the survival tactic of keeping a very private part of yourself hidden from your father?"

He blinked. "You're hardly my father."

"And yet I was in training for the Episcopal priesthood when we met." I stopped before saying aloud the next thought I had. While I was seeing Donald, and also after he disappeared into the cult, I had a therapist who made that connection—the one between me and Donald's father—and helped me see that it was at least in part a role Donald needed me to play, while at the same time not a role I could fill.

He waved a hand in the air as if to dismiss the entire conversation. "Well, like I said, it wasn't going to make a whole lot of sense. So I guess I can't answer your question." He glanced at the watch on his wrist. "Listen, I need to get back. I'm hoping you have time to drive me to Little Boundary. Otherwise I'll have to hitchhike."

I glanced at my watch as well, remembering that I wanted to

make it to the afternoon meeting of Teens for Truth. "Sure. Shall we leave now?"

∼

Teens for Truth was nearing the end of its meeting by the time I got there. Myra Langtree and Jenny Pratt were both singing, leading two sections of kids in a round I'd heard once before: "Sumer is icumen in." It's a springtime song in old English, and only some of the words are recognizable today. The teens were really getting into it.

Marshall and I used to sing together, sometimes while I played the piano, sometimes when only he sang and I played. Music was a place where we'd bonded powerfully. We'd sung this tune, a cappella, after Marshall had coached me on the words.

I stood in the doorway as they sang, unseen for the moment, delighted at how clearly they were all enjoying themselves. It was a rollicking tune, but for me it also held notes of sadness for how things with Marshall had ended.

He had been raised in the Assembly of God Church. What I hadn't told Donald and Jonathan was that Marshall had been subjected to the horrors of growing up gay in that denomination, which distorted rather than furthered the love that their proclaimed prophet espoused. Donald, having been raised in the Lutheran Synod where his own father was a minister, would have understood how vile that would have been for Marshall, because the two approaches had much in common. But Donald had never been sent to a conversion "therapy" camp to have the gay wrung out of him.

So when the Congregational church in Little Boundary had changed hands to become an Assembly of God, Marshall had been terrified they'd find him. In addition to the trauma of his early experiences, he hadn't believed it was safe to be gay and out even here in Assisi. He'd told me his chances of being allowed to remain in his high school teaching position were slim to none, if his true nature were discovered.

I'd been sure he was over-reacting. That is, until my efforts to discover who really launched that fiery attack on The Forest had drawn the extremely unfriendly attention of Pastor Alan Jermin—not because I'd found out the truth about the fire, but because I was gay.

I was fairly certain that it was through Jermin's investigation of me that Marshall's former church affiliation had been uncovered. All it took after that was Jermin's dropping a few words into the homophobic ear of the vice principal at Marshall's school, and Marshall was fired for "conduct unbecoming."

Of course, Marshall's history with the Assembly was almost incidental to his termination. All he had to do was be gay. But if Jermin hadn't set his ugly sights on me, Marshall would probably have been safe.

So in addition to my sadness at Marshall's leaving, there was the grief I felt because of what I saw as my own inadvertent culpability. Marshall had disappeared one night, telling no one where he was going. He'd left me a sweet, heart-wrenching note. And that, along with memories, was all I still had of the sweetest man I'd ever known.

I watched as the teens' singing ended and everyone applauded raucously. Jenny caught sight of me and her grin grew even wider.

"Reverend Hill!" she called. "Welcome! What did you think of our singing?"

At first my smile felt forced, but within seconds it was genuine. "Amazing. Truly wonderful. And I know that tune, so I know how well you all sang it."

Myra looked surprised. "Really? How do you come to know it?"

"A story for another time." I was unwilling to mention Marshall. Some of the teens in the room had been in his English class. Addressing the whole room, I said, "Don't let me interrupt.

I'm just hoping to have a few words with Ms. Langtree after today's meeting."

I sat in a chair off to the side and watched as the two women wrapped up the meeting and reminded the teens about next week's agenda. I was here to speak with Myra, but I watched Jenny. She was an excellent lay minister. She had intelligence combined with an open heart, always presuming the best of someone unless they proved themselves unworthy. I'd seen her turn regretfully away from someone who refused the spiritual love she offered, though she remained open to their possible change of heart. I valued highly her service as a support to me in furthering the UU spirit of love, acceptance, and the betterment of life for all.

Myra, also, was a welcome support, though she was a Forest Dweller—Pagan, not a part of the UU congregation, though it did seem to me as though there was little difference in our respective missions. She had stepped into this role with Teens for Truth after Marshall had disappeared, based on the increasing number of Forest Dweller teens who had joined the group—a development that had warmed me to the core. Marshall had started Teens for Truth, but Jenny and Myra were carrying it forward in the best possible way.

I waited until all the teens had left, jostling and teasing each other on their way out of the UU function hall. Jenny approached me.

"Shall I stay? Or is it just Myra you want to talk to?"

"Just Myra today, though I will tell you I'm thrilled with what a wonderful job you're doing with the group."

She grinned, said "Thanks," lifted her jacket off a chair, and left.

I positioned two chairs so they faced each other across a few feet of wooden floor. "Please," I said, gesturing to one of them as I took the other.

Myra remained silent, and I collected my thoughts before I spoke.

"I had a conversation recently with Adam," I opened, "in which he led me to believe that although I was welcome in The

Forest, others from Assisi might not be. I want to ask whether that's how you see it as well."

"If by 'others' you mean Jenny, I'm sure she will be invited. Adam mentioned that you'd talked about it. I think he just wanted you to understand that we don't want to throw the doors open indiscriminately."

"I understand that. And I wanted *him* to understand that the more… we'll say reluctant you are to mix with us, the more of a curiosity you remain."

We watched each other's faces for a moment. Then she said, "What if that 'mix,' as you put it, could take place on neutral ground?"

I scowled in mild confusion. "What do you have in mind?"

"One of our Sabbat holidays is May first, Beltane. It's a time to express gratitude for Nature's bounty, for the fertility and greening of the earth. There will be flowers, and greenery, and a maypole, and music, and singing, and dancing, and prayers for blessings. We typically celebrate Beltane the same place we celebrated Yule, which you saw when you joined us last December. What if we had a celebration someplace outside of The Forest?"

"Like, for example, a field? Or even the high school sports field?"

"Exactly. Everyone could bring food to share, and soft drinks." Her face nearly shone; I could tell this idea was unfolding even as she spoke. "Oh, there are so many things we could all do together. But—" and she stopped speaking suddenly.

"But?"

"Of course it would require Erik and Elaine to agree."

"Do they already know about Jenny's request?"

"They do. But they haven't made a decision yet, I suppose because they'd want to be clear about how it would happen."

"You're just coming up with this idea now, correct?" She nodded. I said, "As ambassador from Assisi to The Forest, I would like to come talk to Erik and Elaine, or either of them, about this idea. I really like it, Myra; it addresses so many questions."

"Good! I'll relay your request, which I'm sure they'll grant because it's you asking, and I'll let you know. By the way, as I said, Beltane is always May first. This year that's a Sunday."

"Even better. This is such a great idea. Thank you. I know it's still undecided, but I'm very hopeful."

We stood together and hugged. I was tempted to ask her whether Adam was actually angry with me, but I thought better of it. Even though she and Adam weren't engaged, at least not yet, and even though she knew that he was pansexual and that he and I were intimate, saying anything to Myra that referred directly to that intimacy felt like a step too far.

Lying in bed that night, my mind wouldn't stop racing. It had been a full day. Hell, it had been a full week. And it was only Tuesday!

Kira had been released from the hospital. I would call David tomorrow and see how she was doing.

Donald and I had spent the day together, and my feelings about him were a bit—no, they weren't a bit anything. They were roiling. It had felt so right to be with him again. And there was that niggling doubt in the back of my mind about how Jonathan treated him. Not badly; I wasn't worried about that. Jonathan was no Bruce Cobb. But I was getting a sense of confinement, or restraint, of Donald's mercurial spirit. Was Jonathan allowing him to be his enthusiastic, sometimes silly and sometimes deeply profound self? And how would I know? And what would I do about it, anyway?

Then there was Adam. It had been months since I'd felt from him anything like the antagonism I'd felt Monday afternoon. When I'd arrived in Assisi last fall, both the town and The Forest had still been under the impression that the horrible attack, decades ago, had come from Assisi. The few times I'd encountered Adam—after the pond ejaculation, that is—had been just this side of hostile. He had seemed to feel nothing but contempt for me, for what I represented, and for the town I served.

In my ignorance, not knowing about the fire at first, and then not knowing for weeks what the truth was about it, I had hoped to make a connection between my congregation and The Forest. More than once I had reached out a hand in friendship, only to feel not quite spurned, exactly, but definitely put off.

And then the truth about the fire had begun to circulate.

Finally Erik Stillman had challenged me: Could I preach a sermon to my congregation, on the Sunday of the winter solstice, during which I could prove to him that I understood what the Pagan Yule was about?

I'd met the challenge, and Adam himself had taken me to participate in their all-night celebration. I'd met Elaine Gault. Advanced in age but not in vitality, she clearly outranked Erik. She was the one who, that night, had deemed me ambassador between her community and my town, a role whose aspects were still mysterious to me. But, surely, convincing Erik and Elaine that Myra's idea was a good one was well within the purview of that office.

CHAPTER 8

Kira was home, David told me Wednesday morning when I called him, but that did not mean all was well.

"Her parents haven't exactly seen the light," he told me. "I went to see her at home, as she's not back in school yet. She's wearing a bandanna around her neck to hide the marks left by the fabric she'd used during her suicide attempt, and of course she's in boy's clothing. The hair is still pink, but I expect that won't last. She's still a he, as far as her folks are concerned, and her name is still Ralph. I called her 'Kira' once, and her mother nearly threw me out."

"I can tell by the sound of your voice that you're worried."

"I am. I'll check in as often as I can, but I have my doubts about whether that will be enough, or whether it will even help."

"Did you see Molly?"

"She was in school. I'm putting a lot of faith in her support."

I felt helpless. "I wish I could do more."

"Your—um—I guess he's not actually a lay minister yet. Boyd. He called me just before you did."

"Oh?"

"He came up with an idea, a kind of intercession. The Blakes don't know Boyd is gay. Or an atheist. He suggested that he offer himself to Kira's folks as someone who could help 'Ralph' understand what a great thing it is to be a man. Of course all the while, he'd be supporting Kira surreptitiously."

"Interesting idea." It was interesting, all right, though I was a little surprised the Blakes fell for it. Perhaps it was an indication of how desperate they were. But I wasn't happy that Boyd hadn't spoken to me first. Of course, he was a free agent, but if he wanted the role of lay minister, he wasn't going about it in quite the right way.

David said, "You disapprove."

"Oh, I don't tell Boyd what he can and can't do. I must say, though, that it's almost as though he's *your* lay minister."

"Yeah. I asked if he'd spoken to you yet. He seemed a little surprised that anyone would expect that."

"I wouldn't say 'expect.' Anyway, it's not up to me to approve or disapprove. If he can help Kira, I say he should do that. This isn't about me, or him. But how will you explain to them how Boyd even knows Kira? Or why you think she'd respond to him?" David started to reply, but I interrupted him. "What about you, David? Do you think this is a good idea, deceiving the Blakes like this?"

"I think Kira comes first. What she did doesn't strike me as a cry for help. I think she meant to die. At any rate, I must act on that likelihood. If Boyd can keep her alive until we figure out what the next steps are, and perhaps while I work on Kira's parents to help them accept her, I say he should do that. And as for an explanation about who he is...."

"Yes?"

"The truth is always best. I'll tell the Blakes that I happened to be speaking with you, that the subject of their 'son' came up, and that you mentioned someone in your congregation who had some experience working with young people like Kira. Ralph."

"Won't they assume that his 'help' would go in a direction they wouldn't like?"

"I'll need to be, um, circumspect."

"That's one word for it, I guess." The line was silent on both ends for a few seconds. Then I said, "You should probably have a plan for what happens if the Blakes figure out what's going on."

David sighed. "I agree, though I don't yet know what it would be."

~

Myra had moved quickly. She called me just before lunch.

"Can you be here tomorrow morning? Around ten, maybe? Both Erik and Elaine would like to talk with you."

"I can. Will you be there?"

"I'll be teaching." Right; she taught in the grammar school in The Forest. Then she said, "Adam will be there."

"Really? Why?"

"I'm not sure. I couldn't get a good sense of whether he liked the idea."

~

Meanwhile, today marked the end of Jonathan's and Donald's sojourn to the north. Donald had called to say they'd stop by on their way south, so I invited them to stay for lunch.

It felt odd to see them together again, as a couple. And that feeling told me I'd let myself fall too much into the way Donald and I had been, when *we* had been a couple. I resolved to shake myself out of that trap.

Jonathan had news. "I've found a place I like. It's just outside of Newport, on the road to Derby."

Donald's enthusiasm was more obvious. "It's a big old farmhouse! Rooms for days. A gorgeous view of mountains. And the property goes down to a river!"

Jonathan added, "It's going to take some work. No one's lived in it for a few years."

Donald: "The woman who lived there died in the kitchen!"

Jonathan: "It would need work even for a single family. But it'll take even more to bring it up to code for housing as many people as I intend. The kitchen will need to be expanded, and the bathrooms—"

Donald: "You should see the bathrooms, Spencer. Even more ancient than yours upstairs here."

"My" bathroom, here in the house that belonged to the UU parish, was in excellent shape. True, it still had the green and black tiles that must have been fashionable once, and the sink had separate hot and cold water faucets, but I didn't think of it as "ancient."

I looked at Jonathan. "How long do you think it will take?"

"I'm guessing the whole summer, really. Maybe longer. But that will give me time to finish the licensing and inspections, and get the news out about it, so I can start helping kids as soon as it's ready."

Donald turned to him. "Don't you mean so that *we* can start helping kids?"

"Of course."

I sensed some tension and did my best to deflect it. "Have you made an offer?"

Jonathan nodded. "It's on the low side, but the realtor feels it's reasonable. And the family are rather anxious to get rid of it. It's been on the market for nearly a year with no offers at all, so…."

"Do they know what you intend to do with it?"

Donald's head shook "no" vigorously. He said, "Like I told Jonathan, they don't need to know. And there's no point in taking the risk that they might not like it."

Jonathan leaned toward Donald and planted a kiss on his cheek. "Very wise, too. Even the realtor doesn't know the whole story, though I did let on that I'd be making a lot of changes."

After lunch I stood at my front door, Klondike by my side, and watched as they drove away. It had been good to see how much Jonathan appreciated Donald's involvement. At least, that's what I told myself.

~

When I'd gone to the Yule celebration in The Forest in December, and Erik Stillman had grilled me about my intentions toward his community, we'd met in the great room of one of the buildings there. Today's meeting was in the same room. Erik and Elaine were both there, as was Adam, and he seemed as deferential toward the other two as he had the last time I'd been there. That is, he spoke little and mostly watched. As Myra had said, it was difficult to see where he stood on the question at hand.

I removed my shoes as before. Elaine greeted me.

"Welcome, Reverend Hill. May I call you Spencer?"

"Please."

"And you may call me Elaine. Please, sit."

The massive fireplace was lit with a small fire. This far north, even mid-April days were chilly, and today was overcast with occasional drizzle. We three took the heavy, wooden chairs near the fire. Adam stood off to the side, which made me wonder whether he had requested to be present but was not considered a party to the discussion.

Elaine opened. "Myra Langtree has told us of her idea, which she says you support. Is that true?"

"It is." I felt constrained, as though there was a formality to this meeting that meant I should be succinct in my responses.

"Please. Tell me how you envision it."

"I believe Myra called it Beltane. The way she described it, I think a maypole would be involved, and although I confess I don't understand how it would be incorporated, I love the idea. I also love that the intention is to celebrate nature's bounty with flowers, and food, and there would be singing and dancing. Am I on the right track so far?"

"That's a rough sketch of our part. What would yours look like?"

Fortunately, I had given this some thought. "Mine, as you call it, would really be Assisi's. Though I haven't yet spoken to my congregation, my vision is that a Unitarian Universalist committee would connect with other congregations, as well as with the town in general. One idea I had, for the day itself, would be for Forest Dwellers to teach any townsfolk who were interested one or two of your Beltane songs or chants. And there are a number of UU hymns that would, I think, pass muster in terms of being sufficiently ecumenical, in a non-specific way, that we could sing for the crowd. I would take it upon myself to ask David Foster, the Protestant pastor, and Milton Bryant, the Catholic priest, to have their parishioners sing one or two hymns of praise as well."

I paused, but there was silence. I saw nothing concerning in their faces, so I asked, "How does that sound so far?"

Erik glanced at Elaine, who said, "Ambitious. Beltane is a little over two weeks from today."

I nodded. "True. But I'm thinking the day might lose something true to itself if things are too choreographed. And as far as food and drink, all we need to organize, really, is water and punch and soft drinks. People can bring contributions that don't require cooking or refrigeration. There are plenty of tables in church function halls that could be pressed into service."

"What if it rains?"

She had me there. "I don't know. What would you do here, celebrating as usual, if it rained?"

"We celebrate anyway. Rain is part of Nature. Rain is, in fact, essential, and we celebrate it as much as sunshine."

"Then I suppose we would do the same. Though I confess it would cut down on participation. But the way you just described it? That could be part of the general invitation."

"Where would it be held?"

"There are a few possibilities. I haven't spoken to anyone else yet, wanting to speak with you first, but I doubt that would be a problem."

"So it wouldn't be here."

I blinked. "I assumed you wouldn't want that."

"You assumed correctly."

We regarded each other for a moment, and then I asked, "Do I have your permission to send out some feelers about how this will work? I imagine you'd need to know very soon whether it's going forward."

"Yes, on condition that we are kept very well informed about progress."

An inspired thought came to me. "I think you know that one of my lay ministers, Jenny Pratt, has asked to visit The Forest." I waited for Elaine to nod. "Jenny is a remarkably organized person, and I'd like to ask her to work closely with me on this project. That would probably mean she'd need to be in touch with The Forest, as well. Would that be a problem?"

Another glance between Erik and Elaine told me they had discussed Jenny's request. Elaine said, "That would solve a problem, actually. We like the idea of welcoming Jenny, though we saw two obstacles. One was to avoid having her visit look like an open invitation. The other was how it would take place. This would be a good solution."

I smiled and nodded, and both Elaine and Erik stood; the meeting was over. We said our goodbyes, and Adam walked me out to my Jeep. He leaned against the door so I couldn't open it, his arms crossed on his chest, and he grinned.

"You've done it again."

"And what's that?"

He shook his head as his grin widened. "You've built another bridge between town and forest. Don't you see that?"

I grinned back. "I hope that's true."

He looked down for a second, and then up at me, the smile gone. "I want to apologize."

"Oh?"

"I was such a prig the other day. I mean, the way I responded to you, about our not being so mysterious."

I laughed. My understanding of that word, prig, was that it was someone who was moralistic in an antagonistic way, behaving as though they were superior. And that's pretty much the impression he'd left me with.

"Apology accepted."

He grinned again, stood away from the door and opened it for me, bowing slightly to indicate I should enter. Once in the car, I reached for the handle to close the door, but Adam held it.

"I miss you."

I chuckled. "It's only been three days."

"Ah, but I didn't know how angry you were."

I nodded, tilting my head in a manner I hoped was at least a little seductive. "Interesting. I didn't miss you at all. So I guess you don't have to worry about my, um, intentions."

He threw his head back and laughed. "Excellent." We grinned at each other for a few seconds. Then he said, "May I come to you tonight?"

"I hope you do."

I pulled my door shut, but Adam knocked on the window, so I rolled it down.

"Just wanted to say I think you missed your calling."

"My calling?"

"You really are an ambassador."

I shook my head slowly. "Silly man. That *is* my calling."

As I drove away, in my rear view mirror I saw that Adam didn't wave, but he did watch.

Jenny, whom I invited over for dessert and coffee, was thrilled at the idea of being my assistant for the May Day festivities, as well as with the promise of a visit to The Forest.

"You know," she told me, "last fall, when you started to reach out to them and everyone advised you against it, I was afraid to cheer you on. I had wanted to do something like that for a couple of years, but I never had the courage."

I waved a hand; I didn't want the implied kudos. I'd nearly

made a mess of things because of my initial ignorance about the fire.

By the time Jenny left, she'd come up with a host of ideas about what the day might look like, what supplies and other things we'd need, and how best to work with Myra to make sure our goal of kinship and learning was met. She loved the idea of singing and volunteered to look for some suitable hymns from the UU hymnal. My part of the effort included connecting with the other two parishes, as well as with the town in general, and to encourage as much overall participation as possible.

As she left, she said, "I'll talk to Myra tomorrow, and we can get started!"

∼

Adam did come to me that night. It was well past dinner, and I had been on the phone with several people to get started on the Beltane celebration. I was determined that this would be at least fun, and maybe even more than that.

I had hung up from a call to Vanessa (though she was asleep, and Loraine promised to have Vanessa call me back the next day) when I heard Adam's truck pull up.

For a few seconds, I had a flashback to when it had been Marshall who had paid me nighttime visits. His had been surreptitious, secretive, honoring his fear of what would happen if our relationship were known. I had allowed his caution, and as it had turned out, he'd been right.

Adam had no such scruples, and I knew of no reason why I should have any. I sent a silent prayer of thanks to the Universe for helping me understand that I could fulfill my calling outside the confines the Episcopal Church would have placed on me.

The forcefulness of his kiss, as soon as he was inside my living room, confirmed what he'd said. He had missed me. I grabbed the hair on either side of his head, pulled his face a little away from mine, and almost growled when I spoke.

"I'm going to fuck you silly."

And I did. I teased his tits with my teeth, nibbled my way around his penis, sucked on his balls, and then pumped my sheathed dick into his ass. I yelled, "Tell me you missed me."

"I missed you! I missed you! Oh, God, I missed you!"

I pumped until he could no longer speak, until he screamed with that mysterious duality of pain and pleasure, a duality of which mankind in Eden would have remained ignorant if not for Snake.

In the afterglow, he lay face up, breathing deeply, eyes closed, and I leaned on one elbow to watch his face. I smiled, recalling his apology.

I said, "Now we're even."

CHAPTER 9

Vanessa called me just before lunch.

"I tend to retire early these days," she told me. "Loraine unplugs the phone down here and goes into the bedroom if she wants to watch TV." She paused to take a breath, and I waited. "What can I do for you, Spencer?"

I pictured Vanessa's living room as it had to be, with her health waning. The hospital-style bed, the IV hanger and oxygen supply ready for when she'd need them, were harbingers of the inevitable. In the small cottage, they crowded out any but limited socializing.

"Actually, if you're up for it, I'd love to come for a brief visit. Is now good?"

"Bring Klondike?"

"You bet."

~

Sheila had chamomile tea ready by the time I arrived. She set a tray near my chair. "Soon it will be iced tea, eh?"

I smiled and nodded, wondering silently whether Vanessa would still be around to enjoy that.

Vanessa felt well enough to sit in a chair, and Klondike—who had learned that rambunctious behavior around his former owner was not allowed—sat quietly beside her, gazing up at her from time to time as she stroked his huge head.

Before I could give her my news about May Day, she scooped me. "I hear you're making yet another connection with The Forest." She grinned.

One side of my mouth lifted in a smile I couldn't quite keep at bay. "You do hear everything, don't you?"

She chuckled. "Not quite. I don't know how this came about, so tell me that. Then tell me how I can help."

I gave her a summary that included Jenny's request for a visit to The Forest, Myra's enthusiastic suggestion, and my visit to see Erik and Elaine.

"Did I ever tell you," I asked, "that during the Yule celebration I attended, Elaine Gault appointed me to be the ambassador from Assisi?"

Her eyes widened. "Okay, you got me. No, I hadn't heard that."

"I guess that's because I didn't tell anyone here, in town. I'm still not sure what it meant. Or what it means. But one thing is that they've taken seriously that there could be a gathering like the one Myra suggested."

"And where will this take place?"

"Now we come to why I need your help. I don't think the high school athletic field feels right. You know everybody who lives anywhere around Assisi. Do you have another suggestion?"

Her face nearly beamed. "I think you'll get a kick out of one place that comes to mind. You remember Shane and Roberta MacPherson?"

"Of course. They come to services maybe twice a month." And, I didn't add, it had been during a visit I'd paid to them last fall that I had learned Adam, their grandson, had been aware of my presence during his orgasmic dance at the pond. The MacPhersons were Forest Dwellers who had decided to move closer to town. People from The Forest had built the cabin-like home they lived in now.

Vanessa told me, "Behind their house is a very large field. I believe the Forest Dwellers have gathered there for one thing or another over the past few years. I'm surprised no one suggested it to you."

"I'll definitely inquire. Given who Roberta and Shane are, the symbolism would be very meaningful."

"If they can't or won't accommodate, talk to the Sherwoods. They have a large field as well that they use for various things, including children's activities. If you talk to them, use my name."

"I don't recognize the name. Are they UU?"

Vanessa shook her head. "Catholic."

"Thanks. I'll definitely start with the MacPhersons."

"Now, tell me about young Ralph Blake."

"Kira."

"Of course."

"So you heard about that, too." My summary of Kira's situation included mention of Boyd.

Vanessa said, "Ah, yes, the fellow from Boston. How does he strike you?"

"The jury is still out."

Vanessa was not surprised to hear how assertive Boyd had been in the few weeks since his arrival. "Do you want my advice?"

"Absolutely."

"Don't. His style might have worked well in Boston, but here?" She shook her head. "He might be valuable to you in many ways, but I believe he would come across as raw, here. Perhaps if he stays and mellows, in a few years he might work as a lay minister. But I don't think he's ready."

I gave her an assessing glance. "What have you heard?"

She grinned. "Nothing that contradicts how your description makes him seem. Now, what about your recent visitors?"

I laughed. "I don't believe you need me to tell you anything!"

"I want to know how you felt about seeing Donald."

I had confided in Vanessa last November, right after I'd gone to New York for the wedding of Donald's sister, Ruth. At the time,

Donald had been like a thrall under the influence of Bruce Cobb, whom I had detested for his generally curmudgeonly attitude, his rudeness to me, and his forceful domination of Donald.

"He's almost like the Donald I'd known. It's been a few years, so there were certain to be some differences. He's now with a man named Jonathan Ehrlich, and they seem very good together." I could have said more, but I stopped; Vanessa was not, after all, my confessor.

"And you? How did you feel?"

"I like Jonathan. He's clearly coming from money, and he's going to use it well. Do you know why he was here?"

She didn't, and I gloated for just a moment; that was another thing she hadn't known. I gave her a general picture of the property and what Jonathan, and Donald, planned to do with it.

Vanessa's eyes watered with emotion. "That is beyond commendable. I wish them all the luck they're going to need."

Sheila appeared. "Time for medication, I think."

Klondike and I bid Vanessa a fond farewell. And as soon as I got home, I called Jenny.

She loved the idea of the MacPhersons' field. "Do you want me to go with you to talk with them?"

I smiled at the phone. "This is exactly what I hoped you'd do. That is, dig right in. Yes, please." We agreed on a few possible times for a meeting, and then I phoned the MacPhersons.

Roberta answered. I barely got started describing the plans for May Day when she said, "Yes, we heard about this. It sounds… um, interesting."

Slow down, I told myself; they're not quite on board. Yet.

I avoided mentioning the field. "I'm hoping you and Shane would be open to having a conversation with me and Jenny Pratt. I believe you know her. She'll be working closely with me on the project. As parishioners with such close ties to The Forest, I think your input would be invaluable."

We agreed that Jenny and I would visit tomorrow, after church.

"We won't be in church tomorrow," Roberta said, "but if you come by around one that will be fine."

~

On the drive out to the MacPherson's, I cautioned Jenny about the lukewarm feeling I'd gotten from Roberta. "First, we need to sell them on the idea of the combination festival. If they don't warm up to it, we could still ask about using their field, but we need to be prepared for a No."

~

"You've already spoken to Elaine?" Shane seemed surprised.

"Yes, to her and to Erik."

Shane still seemed doubtful. "I knew you'd come to Yule. But now you've met Elaine?"

"Actually, I met her in December. At Yule." I had to stop myself from revealing the title, that of ambassador, Elaine had given me. Shane didn't need another reason to feel left out, which was the impression I was getting from him.

I described, in very general terms, some of the ideas Jenny and I had discussed. For her part, Jenny sat quietly and let me take the lead.

"So," I finished, "there are two reasons we wanted to speak with you." I glanced at Shane and then Roberta, who'd been silent to this point. "First, we're hoping you'll have some thoughts about the ideas we've had so far. We don't want to make this about Assisi. And if you have other ideas, we'd love to hear them."

Now Roberta asked, "Who is it you're working with in The Forest?"

"Myra Langtree is our point person."

Roberta smiled. "I like Myra. She has learned to fit in with us very well." I knew Roberta referred to the fact that Myra had moved to The Forest from Sedona a few years ago.

I glanced at Jenny and saw that she, too, had picked up on the word "us." The MacPherson's clearly still felt a part of the forest community.

Shane's question was pointed. "What's the other reason?"

I took a breath. I'd been hoping to talk more about *what* would happen before discussing *where,* but Shane expected an answer.

"The goal of this festival is an exchange of culture and traditions. The Forest Dwellers are understandably reluctant to have Assisi residents traipsing through your community, but it also seems less than ideal to meet on land that specifically represents the town. So I was hoping you'd consider allowing it to take place in the field here, on your land."

Roberta's face beamed. It was clear she loved the idea. She glanced at her husband, who had sat back a little at my statement.

I thought he might ask how I knew he had a field at all, but perhaps he figured Myra had mentioned it. That's what I hoped.

Shane drew in a long breath and let it out slowly. "I understand your request. I'll need to speak with Erik and get back to you."

"Thank you," I said. "I appreciate your consideration. I need to point out, though, that May Day is only two weeks away."

He nodded. "I'll speak with Erik tonight. Now, if you'll excuse me, I have some things to attend to."

Jenny and I stood as he left the room, ready to leave, but Roberta stopped us. "Let me give you a quick tour, shall I?"

We went outside through the kitchen door, which led into a moderate-sized garden surrounded by a waist-high rock wall, the ground here evidently recently readied for spring. Protected as it was, the feeling was almost as though it were a secret garden.

"Flowers over here," Roberta pointed, "and vegetables over there. We can't garden as much as we'd like. Getting on in years, you know."

Jenny smiled. "I think it will be lovely." She lifted her head and gazed forward, through a stand of trees, some evergreen and some showing the beginnings of bright green leaves. "Is that the field?"

"Yes." Roberta led through an opening in the rock wall and

along a path strewn with pine needles to an opening much larger than I would have imagined. "It used to be a horse pasture. Not ours; we never had horses."

My jaw dropped at the size. There was a slight rolling effect in places where the land rose gently and flowed down again, but most of it was fairly flat. Grass grew everywhere, bright green from spring showers and peppered with dots of color where wildflowers had taken hold. As if someone had planted them deliberately, trees marked the borders all around the field. Beyond them, more of the greening of spring was evident on mountains in the distance, new leaves catching sunlight as if laughing at the dowdy evergreens that grew among them. The word idyllic came to mind.

"This would be—oh, my goodness. This would be perfect." I turned to Roberta. "Where would people park?"

Roberta pointed to the far left side of the field. "There's a dirt road leading to a part of the field we've used before, as a parking area for Forest Dwellers. They built our house, you know."

I nodded. "I remember." I turned to her. "Mrs. MacPherson—"

"Roberta, please."

"This would be absolutely perfect. I do hope Shane feels comfortable after speaking with Erik."

Roberta glanced at me out of the corners of her eyes. "You leave Shane to me. If he has doubts after talking to Erik, I'll remove them. I truly love this idea." She glanced at Jenny and back at me. "May I tell you something in confidence?"

Jenny and I said "Of course" almost simultaneously.

"We've felt a little isolated here. It has felt radically different, after being in The Forest, in that tight-knit community. The idea of bringing the town and The Forest together like this?" She opened her arms wide toward the field. "I love it."

I felt I had found an ally. "I've wanted there to be more connection since I arrived in Assisi."

Roberta sighed. "Yes. I know. Erik was so resistant. He lost his mother in the fire, you know."

"Yes. He told me. If only that fire hadn't happened."

"And if only we hadn't blamed Assisi."

I shook my head. "It must have been so hard to understand what was happening, and why, at the time. A mistaken identity is not surprising."

She watched my face for a moment. "May I say, I find you to be a very generous spirit. I was quite fond of Vanessa, but I'm glad you're now our minister."

Our. She'd said "our minister." I felt a glow fill my chest and threaten to cause my eyes to tear up. The MacPhersons were like an elision of town and forest; when they said "us" or "our," they might be referring to either community, and they were a focal point for both.

"Thank you, Roberta, so much, for saying that. I'm very glad to be here."

And I was.

CHAPTER 10

Shane's conversation with Erik must have gone well, and if Roberta's influence had been necessary it had done the trick. Shane called me Sunday evening and agreed to hold Beltane in their back field.

Jenny's visit to The Forest was, to my pleasant surprise, done without any need for me to be involved. She went with Myra, and she came back even more excited about the festival than she had been.

"What an amazing place to grow up!" was Jenny's impression. "Such a close community, and somehow they manage to keep that closeness without suffocating the individuals." She laughed. "I was almost ready to ask for asylum!"

The next couple of weeks were so full of planning, and meetings, and discussions, and brainstorming that I barely thought of Donald and Jonathan and their project at all. So it was a surprise when Donald called me the Wednesday before May Day to tell me they were traveling up again with plans to close on the farmhouse on Monday, May second.

Donald sounded excited. "Can you believe it's happening so fast? And Jonathan has already lined up a general contractor to head up the job of refurbishing."

"Moss does not grow on him, it seems."

I felt distracted; I had just finished going over a list of volunteers and what their assignments would be for preparations. That list wasn't just people from my congregation; it included people I hadn't met, as well as others I had, conscripted with the help of David Foster and Milton Bryant; after all, this was The Forest and Assisi, not just The Forest and the UU church.

Elaine had called this project ambitious. She'd been right. But for me, it was a good thing. If I'd had more than a few minutes between tasks, the feeling of inadequacy, of being too young and inexperienced to marshal this many people and manage this many moving parts—despite Jennie's capable support—would have made me shrink into a corner, a cowering mass of insecurity.

As I listened to Donald go over his plans in detail, I was looking under my desk for the pen I'd dropped so I could write myself a note to confirm with the company who would, at my personal expense, be setting up a large tent and several canvas shelters in case of rain. Rain was not predicted, but as I'd been told, the mountains make their own weather. And we were certainly surrounded by mountains. Besides, in full sun, shade was always welcome.

I stood. "Found it."

"What?"

"Nothing. Just dropped a pen."

"So we'll be staying at the same place, in Little Boundary."

That brought me up short. Had I missed hearing when they'd arrive? "Um, how long will you stay this time?"

"Just over a couple of weeks."

"So you'll be leaving…."

"The thirteenth."

I closed my eyes, calculating; arithmetic was not my strong suit.

"Spencer, you don't know when we're getting there, do you? Have you not been listening?" I heard the teasing humor in his voice.

"Busted. But it isn't that I'm not interested." I spent a few minutes talking about the May Day event, getting more and more worked up and frantic-sounding, even to my own ears. I couldn't stop myself.

"Whoa, Nellie!" Donald's laughter silenced my litany of fears and overextension. "You're not overwhelmed or anything. I can tell." He chuckled. "We're driving up tomorrow, you silly goose."

"Ah." My mind was a blank.

"Can I tell you something in confidence?"

My turn to chuckle. "Consider my vocation."

"Yes. Well. Here goes. Jonathan's out running around, so I can tell you that I'm feeling a little left out of the process. The project, I mean. On one hand, that's fine. I mean, what do I know about real estate, and closing costs, and lawyers' fees? But—shit, I don't know. Maybe I'm being petty."

"Is there a reason you feel you can say this only when he's not there to hear you? You haven't talked with him about it?"

"I've thought about that, sure. But in my mind, the conversation would not go well. I'd say, 'Listen, Jon Jon,'"

"Wait. You call him Jon Jon?"

He ignored me. "I'd say, 'Listen, Jon Jon, I realize you know all about this stuff, and I'm a total ignoramus, but why aren't you including me more?' And he says, 'How would you like to come up with a five-year plan that includes budgeting for food, and bedding, and heating and cooling, and lawn maintenance, and an amortized schedule for expenses like appliances and furniture? How would you like to write a grant for additional funding depending on projected occupancy and success? Oh, and how would you like to figure out exactly what success looks like?'"

I would have laughed, if he hadn't sounded genuinely unhappy. "Well, how about this. Someone should figure out how to get the word out to the kids who need to know you'll be there. I know you can write. And maybe you could come up with a plan to approach high school counselors and let them know about the project. Hell, Donald, you could even write a script about what it's like in one of those places and get the kids involved. They're sure to know about other kids who've been affected by the things your project wants to help with."

The line was silent for several seconds. Then, "Spencer Hill, you are a genius. Of course I can do that. I can do more than that. Just wait until Jonathan gets back!"

"Where is Jon Jon, anyway?"

He didn't miss a beat. "Oh, talking to people about financing, and legal stuff. I don't know."

"He seems to be taking a lot of time away from his job. Isn't he a guidance counselor?"

"Stuyvesant High School. Yes. Except that he resigned as soon as he made a firm decision to do this thing. It's not the same there without him."

I had no words. "I'm drawing a blank."

Now Donald's voice wasn't teasing. "You don't know how we met, do you."

"I—no."

"You never asked."

"You're right."

I heard his exasperated exhale. "Stuyvesant is one of the schools where I work with the theater department."

"Ah. Got it. I guess I didn't realize you were still doing that."

"Doing that again, you mean."

"Yes. Well, I never knew you were doing it before until you told me a few weeks ago."

"Mmmm hmmm. Out of sight, out of mind, am I?"

I felt my back stiffen. "That's hardly fair. You disappeared completely into that cult. For three years. And when you appeared again, you had an ill-tempered pit bull guarding you. So, okay, I'm sorry I never asked how you met Jonathan. But, Donald, you've never been out of mind."

"Never?" His tone told me I might be forgiven.

"Never."

"Cuz, you know, you are a little isolated up there."

"My thoughts travel freely."

"So, did I succeed?"

"What?"

"Are you less anxious about this festival, or whatever it is?"

I laughed hard enough that I had to sit down.

He said, "So while I'm up there, if I can't be useful to Jonathan for at least part of the time, can I help you with preparations?"

"You'd do that?"

"I'd love to do that. Do you have a skit?"

"A what?"

"You know, a little mini-play about the reason for the celebration."

"I know what a skit is, silly. And no, as far as I'm aware there's no skit."

"You should have one. Or something like it. What's this thing about?"

I was beginning to worry that our time on the phone was cutting into my work, but Donald's question intrigued me. So I gave him a quick rundown of Beltane and what it was all about. Donald asked a few questions, and then he had an idea that, despite as wonderful as it sounded, would—I knew—be very controversial.

"Sounds like you need something theatrical with a May Queen. What about that trans girl?"

My jaw dropped, my mouth closed, and then it opened and closed a few more times before I could speak. Donald spoke first.

"I think it would be really, really validating for her. Don't you?"

I shook myself, physically. "It would. It might also separate her completely from her family."

"And?"

"Donald, that's a pretty cavalier attitude."

"Isn't she already separated?"

"She still lives there."

"No. The boy lives there. The girl doesn't."

"Look, I can't argue with you about this. If you'd like to write a skit, it would need to be ready to work on it as soon as you get here. And I'd need to know as soon as possible what characters would be in it. The fewer the better, please. Are you really going to do this?"

"I'm going to hang up right now and march myself to the public library to look up Beltane. There might be something already written."

I shook my head in awe, and then realized I'd need to let Jenny know immediately in case she had something like this in mind.

Donald said, "Okay, so, ta ta for now. Expect us tomorrow. Well, expect a call from the inn, at least. And see about the girl."

I'd barely hung up from Donald, head still spinning, when my phone rang again. It was Jennie.

"Oh, Spencer! You've got to come see the maypole that Adam and a couple of his friends have just put up in the field! It must be more than fifteen feet tall, and all these gorgeous ribbons are attached at the top. Rainbow colors all around. It's unbelievable!"

"Wow. I thought that was going up tomorrow."

"Adam says it's going to rain tomorrow, so they wanted to get it in the ground today. That way when the wet ground loosens, they can shore it up afterward."

"Very sensible."

"Myra's here, too. So are you coming out?"

"Myra? She's not teaching today?"

"Substitute teacher. I don't know. Are you coming?"

"I have to make a couple of phone calls first." I told her briefly about Donald's idea, which she loved.

Then she said, "In a minute some folks are going to do a run-through of how to move around the pole and create a pattern."

I chuckled. "If I miss it today, I'll see it on Sunday."

I hung up, my hand resting on the phone. Clinging to the

phone, really. I needed to speak with David Foster, and I wasn't sure what I'd say.

He was in his office. "Spencer. How are things going with the Beltane preparations?"

"Really well, I think. They're putting up the maypole now. Jennie's supervising. Um, listen, there's been a suggestion I want to talk to you about."

He already knew about Jonathan's project, so I dived straight into Donald's idea about the Beltane skit, which would involve a May Queen from the town.

David loved the idea. "You're sure the Forest Dwellers don't already have one?"

"Myra hasn't mentioned anything. I'll ask, to be sure, but I suppose there's no harm in two of them, as long as they're compatible without being too much the same. But here's the thing."

I took a deep breath. David waited.

I repeated, "Here's the thing."

"You said that."

"The thing is that I want to see what you think about Kira being the May Queen."

"Oh, my."

"I confess I'm afraid of how her parents would react to this idea."

"Well, they've already informed me they aren't attending the festival."

"I see. Have they forbidden Kira and Molly to attend?"

"Molly's school class is attending, so they've allowed her to participate. I guess being surrounded by her classmates will keep her safe, in their opinion."

"And Kira?"

"I don't know that they've forbidden her. I've been meaning to suggest that 'Ralph' be allowed to go with Molly." He chuckled. "If I've learned anything about Miss Kira Blake, it's that she has a decidedly theatrical personality. But, Spencer, if Kira is given a big role and her parents didn't know...."

"They should not ever know. I mean, we'd need to keep her identity a secret in any case; as I understand it, she's not exactly proclaiming her identity to the world, so she'd need to be disguised."

"You're right that she's not, as they say, 'out.' So, yes, a disguise is essential. Her involvement would need to be kept from Molly as well, of course."

"How is Boyd getting along with the family?"

"Much better than I'd had any reason to hope."

"What if he escorted her? He could be in on the secret, safely enough."

There was a pause of several seconds. Then, "We're really going to do this, aren't we? I feel kind of slimy."

"It's for Kira."

"Yes. It is."

Jennie had been right about the maypole. By the time I got there, several people had just about finished their "dance" around it, and the pole itself was wrapped in a colorful, intricate pattern. The ribbons, twenty or more of them, were two inches wide each. They'd been tied to a green-painted metal piece that resembled the skeleton of a crown, and woven into its metal bones were bits of evergreen branches.

Adam and Myra were helping the dancers understand their moves, though because they were nearly done the two supervisors were mostly just watching, grinning broadly and nodding. Jennie was dancing, clearly enjoying herself immensely. She saw me just before the design was finished and laughed aloud.

Adam walked toward me. "You realize you'll be expected to do this on Sunday."

"Me? No. This is for the kids."

He grinned as though at a secret he was keeping from me.

Myra joined us, and we stood facing each other and grinning. Myra said, "This is really going to work."

"What if it rains after all?" I asked.

She laughed. "The ribbons will survive. And people aren't made of sugar. We dance, rain or shine."

"I have a question for you. Does the celebration typically involve any kind of skit, or play, anything like that?"

"We do a kind of procession, where the May Queen and Green Man see each other across an area strewn with flowers and meet in the middle. Why? What do you have in mind?"

Without revealing Kira's likely part, I told her and Adam about Donald's idea. "Donald was a professional actor for a number of years, and he's worked with school kids on various plays and skits before. He's intrigued by the idea of Beltane, and he's thinking it would be great to have a May Queen from the town. He's already doing research on the, um, Sabbat is what it's called, right?"

Adam scowled. "From the town...."

I readied myself for a skirmish. "Is that a problem?"

"Elaine has been the May Queen as long as I can remember. And Erik is the Green Man."

"Okay, but does it have to be that way?"

Myra laid a gentle hand on Adam's shoulder. "Elaine will be May Queen for *our* celebration, in The Forest. For the festival here, what a wonderful symbol it would be of what this year's Beltane is all about! That is, someone from each community."

Adam was only partly mollified. "So the Green Man here would be a Forest Dweller? Maybe. I think we should ask Erik."

Myra turned to me, and I got the sense that she saw asking Erik as a mere formality. "Why don't you tell Donald to write something up based on his Beltane research. Short, because it would be better, but also in case we don't do it."

Her hand was still on Adam's shoulder, and I was getting a better sense about who they were as a couple. My, um, activities with Adam aside, I'd never seen anything more than a solid friendship between them—nothing that pointed toward them being a couple who might marry at some point. But I was getting the sense that Adam needed someone who understood him well enough to smooth out some of his rough spots, and that Myra might just know a little something about how to do that.

To be honest, there were times I saw women as superior to men and wondered why I didn't want one as my life partner.

Myra asked, "Which girl did you have in mind?"

"It's, um, a bit of a secret. We're not planning to reveal her identity."

"How wonderful! How mysterious! So she'll be truly a Pagan symbol—almost a goddess—rather than a mere mortal."

"So you think it would be well received?"

She laughed. "I hope so! I think it shows Assisi is truly getting into the spirit of our Sabbat. Our tradition."

I phoned Boyd as soon as I got home. He told me he and David had already spoken, and not only was David fully on board, but also that Kira, who had promised to be silent about her excitement, was nonetheless thrilled at the role she would play. He said, "She wouldn't do it, I don't think, if she couldn't be anonymous. So the mystery will remain intact."

As independently as he'd been acting, Boyd seemed to be getting further and further away from being in line for a lay minister role. But time would tell.

CHAPTER 11

That evening I phoned Vanessa and Loraine to talk to them about May Day. I wasn't sure Vanessa would be up to it.

"She's already in bed," Loraine told me. "I think it's in Matthew where it says the spirit is willing but the flesh is weak. I don't think she'll be going. She really wants me to go, and take pictures. If Sheila can be here on Sunday, maybe I'll do that."

We chatted for a few minutes, and I mentioned that Donald and Jonathan were driving up again for closing on the farmhouse.

"I love what they're doing so much!" Loraine said. "How long will they be here this time?"

"Until the thirteenth, I think Donald said."

"They aren't still at the Pinewood, surely, for so long?"

"That's what he said, yes."

"Well…. You know I still own that little house I was living in before I moved in with Vanessa. My renter left last week, and I was trying to decide what to do with it. It's still furnished. Do you think your friends would like to stay there instead?"

"That's very generous."

"Not at all. They can pay me what they would have paid Pinewood."

I laughed. "It sounds perfect to me. I'll ask and let you know."

~

I was relieved when Myra called around nine that night to say that Elaine and Erik, though taken a little by surprise, were supportive of passing their roles on to younger actors for the combined celebration. A Forest Dweller boy named Seth would take the part of the Green Man.

"They did say," Myra added, "that the spirit of Beltane should not be toyed with." We agreed she should see what Donald was putting together as soon as possible.

~

Donald called as soon as he and Jonathan arrived at the Pinewood the next afternoon.

"I have the skit. Or, really, it's simpler than that; no speaking parts for the kids. I had to pare things down a little, given the time limitations. I think they'll love it! Short and sweet, just like you said. How soon can we get the actors together?"

"How many are there?"

"Not many. The queen and green fellow, of course, and a few non-speaking roles for kids who throw flowers and such."

"Costumes?"

"You know me so well. But not really. Cotton fabric to wrap the Queen and the Green Man in, toga-like. They'll wear crowns of flowers and leaves, and we'll paint their faces. Purple, I think, for the queen. The green goes without saying."

"Sounds great, Donald, but—well, I'm not sure how much of the raw material you'll find close by."

"No worries. I shopped in the city before we left."

I laughed. "Of course you did."

"So. Actors?"

"The boy will be someone from The Forest."

"Perfect! I love how this is coming together."

"On a different matter, I know you're ensconced there at the

Pinewood, but two weeks seems like a long time for a B&B. Would you prefer to stay in a small, furnished house here in Assisi? It's going wanting for renters, and the cost would be the same as the Pinewood."

It seemed as though Donald might have covered the phone with his hand before he lowered his voice. "I would *love* that. Just need to talk you-know-who into it."

"Why would he be reluctant?"

"Probably feels we owe this place, given that we reserved the room."

"I'll leave you to work that out. But it would make things a whole lot easier for your involvement in Beltane if you were closer. By the way," I added, "Myra Langtree, from The Forest, needs to see the script to ensure the integrity of the Beltane spirit."

"My. These folk do take this stuff rather seriously."

"Donald, it's their religion."

"Of course. Sorry."

Later that afternoon, I drove Myra to meet with Donald in the Pinewood restaurant and review his material. The weather was not pleasant, with spotty rain on and off. We drove in silence for a bit, the only sound being the swish of tires on wet pavement. For her part, Myra was so quiet I grew concerned. The only thing she'd said so far was in answer to my question of who was taking her class today at The Forest's grammar school.

I asked, "Everything okay?"

She let a few beats go by. "Feels weird. Going into Little Boundary. I mean, I'm fairly new to The Forest, so I don't have quite the same queasy feeling as others might. But this town? This is where the people who started that fire came from."

"Decades ago, but yes."

"You know, other than the few sculpting jobs Adam's had in Little Boundary, I don't think anyone from The Forest has gone there the whole time I've been here. Unless you count that day we rescued those horses."

"But—you all thought someone from Assisi had started the fire."

"Even so, the Burgos family legend burns bright. They were known to have been horrible to the community in their time."

"Do you think no one but you would have agreed to come with me today?"

She shrugged. "I don't know if I'd go that far, but they might have suggested Donald come to us instead."

For reasons I couldn't have articulated, I didn't say that Donald would have liked that. I didn't say he'd told me he wanted to visit The Forest.

Maggie Downing wore the same apron—or at any rate, an apron with the same pattern of raindrops on flowers—she'd had the last time I'd been here.

"Good day for hot cocoa," she assured us, "despite the season. But here in Vermont...." Her voice trailed off as if to say "expect anything." We ordered a plate full of her sugar cookies as well as the cocoa.

I wasn't surprised that Myra and Donald got along as though they had known each other all their lives. Donald opened with, "Sorry if I'm a little groggy. I napped the last several miles in the car. Kind of a snores d'oeuvre for this repast."

"Snores d'oeuvre!" Myra echoed, laughing. "I'll have to remember that."

I sat back and said little, amused by these two sprite-like people across the table from me. They leaned together over printed pages like children pouring over a list of chocolates.

"Donald, I love this description of the queen! It's almost heavenly."

"Mmmm. I want her to be nearly aliferous."

Myra sat up straight. "Not a word I know."

"It means winged. Like a bird, or an angel."

"I like that."

They went silent as Myra picked up a page and read to herself. When she set the page down, she looked at Donald. "This is marvelous. These phrasings, these descriptions—they're precisely what Beltane is all about."

"Thanks. I'm glad." He looked up at me. "We need someone for the speaking parts. The narration, if you will. Could that be you?"

I blinked, and Myra's expectant glance told me I had to take this suggestion seriously. "What does it say?"

Myra handed me a couple of pages. "We could of course ask Elaine to say something. Maybe she could say some of it, and you could. I like the idea of someone from each community having a part."

Donald turned to Myra. "D'you think it would be okay if Spencer added some of his own stuff? I mean, he is a preacher, after all."

It was true that what I was reading was essentially Pagan, but it was hardly antithetical to anything I might have said in church. "I wouldn't modify it very much," I said, flattered to think I'd have a part to play.

Donald emptied his mug and shuffled the papers in front of him. He handed them to me. "I made a few copies. I'll give you one, Myra, to take back, and you and Spencer can work things out with Elaine. Meanwhile, I need to meet with the kids. Costume fitting, and whatnot." He looked at me. "Any way I could have some time right away with the girl to go over her part?"

"It would need to be after school. Which is," I glanced at my watch, "any minute now, really. Maybe I can use the phone in your room?"

∼

By the time we left, we had arranged for Boyd to bring Kira to meet Donald in Loraine's empty house Friday. After she left, Seth would be brought from The Forest to learn about his part.

I've heard that when a dress rehearsal goes south, it bodes well for the real performance. So I began to worry about Sunday, because everything seemed to be going so well.

If there was a fly in the proverbial ointment, it was that Donald and Jonathan weren't seeing eye-to-eye about logistics. As Donald had suspected, Jonathan felt obligated to stay at the Pinewood for a least a few nights, whereas Donald—who knew Jonathan needed the car for tasks concerning the farmhouse—wanted to be in Assisi to be involved with finalizing the arrangements he was responsible for. In the end, Donald moved into Loraine's house, a ten-minute walk from mine, while Jonathan stayed at the Pinewood through Saturday night.

"He's not thrilled," Donald told me, waving a hand dismissively, "but too bad. His grumpiness is usually fugacious." He gave me a sideways glance and added, "Temporary. Fleeting."

It seemed to me that I was hearing Donald's unusual words far more frequently, the last couple of times I'd seen him, than when I'd known him before. Was this a bit of an overreaction, perhaps, to feeling restrained in Jonathan's hearing? I felt a bit of an unholy glee knowing that Donald felt free to express himself around me in a way Jonathan discouraged. Then I wondered whether Jonathan's reluctance to have Donald move without him to Assisi had a hint of jealousy in it. Jealousy about me, that is. But that was even less holy.

I met Jonathan and Donald at Loraine's old house late Friday morning to let them in and give them the key. Jonathan followed Donald into the house, carrying bundles of paraphernalia that would be needed for the production. When Jonathan left, even though he and Donald kissed in parting, it seemed to me as though there was some tension between them—nothing major, just enough to make me wonder what it was about.

As Donald moved his suitcases into one of the two bedrooms, I wandered into the kitchen. Loraine had stocked the place with the basics: eggs, cheese, milk, butter, bread, peanut butter, beer, ginger ale, store-bought chocolate chip cookies, and a pan of brownies. The freezer held ground beef and what looked like freshly frozen ice cubes, and in the cupboards I found boxes of pasta and a few jars of red sauce. I found plastic wrap, foil, even trash bags.

I lifted the handset from the wall phone beside the fridge to see if it was connected; a dial tone assured me it was. I had just turned toward the living room again when Donald reappeared.

"Spencer, do you have time to help me get set up for the kids this afternoon?"

"I have some time now, sure. What can I do?"

We worked for a while on the costumes. My efforts provided both of us with entertainment, as I proved to be less than useful.

"You really are hopeless at this," he said, wiping tears of laughter from his face. "I'll get Myra to help. She'll be here first thing tomorrow."

I had brought lunch, not knowing what I was going to find in the kitchen. Over tuna sandwiches and sliced cucumbers we chatted about how everything would work out.

I told him, "I need to let you in on arrangements for the May Queen." Of course he already knew a little something about "the trans girl," but I swore him to secrecy before telling him her name.

"Along with everyone else, her family in particular are to be kept in the dark," I told him. "As you know, they've been far from accepting."

"Intrigue. Fun."

By the time I had to leave, the kitchen table was ready for the actors. Costume materials were draped over chairs, and pads and pens sat on the table, ready to jot down ideas or for anyone to take notes if they wanted.

Donald walked me to the front door, smiling, clearly enjoying his involvement in this festival. We regarded each other for a moment, and then I asked, "Is Jonathan joining you for dinner?"

He shook his head. "He thinks he'll still be in Newport. Lots to work out in a couple of weeks."

I tried and failed to stop myself from asking, "Do you want to come to my place around six?"

He tilted his head slightly, looking very much the imp. "Love to."

CHAPTER 12

When Donald and I had been together in New York, I'd found him to be a courageous and creative cook. Most of the time our gustatorial adventures were successful, though there was the occasional failure when we'd give up and go out for our meal.

Since then, I had learned quite a bit about basic cooking, though (as I'd told Jonathan), my tool collection left something to be desired. Even so, I managed to put together a decent meal of homemade red sauce with Italian sausage over spaghetti, with a side salad, and I had some fresh ice cream to go with the last of that chocolate sauce Jonathan had made.

The first thing Donald did when he arrived was to wander over to the piano keyboard. He lifted the shiny black cover and toyed with a few keys while I watched.

When he lifted his face to look at me, his expression was unreadable. "Would you play for me?"

"If you like. Anything in particular?"

"That Chopin piece. The first thing you ever played for me."

"The Barcarolle. Opus 60. I haven't played it in a while."

"Why not?"

Why not, indeed? *Because it reminds me of you*. But I couldn't say that.

I shrugged. "There's so much other music. But if you can tolerate a few fumbles, I'll give it a go."

I propped up the lid of the black baby grand to release as much sound as possible. This room wasn't able to allow the piano's voice its fullness, its true resonance, but I wanted to give the instrument every opportunity to send its music as far as it could reach.

As I coaxed the opening notes from the keyboard, a rush of feelings nearly overwhelmed me. For years, this had been my favorite piece. The first time I'd played it for Donald, tears had come to his eyes.

My fingers knew the way. They seemed to work of their own accord, and the music flowed from the instrument. After the gentle, sunlit opening in a major key, the music fell into a minor mode. There were passages of hesitant longing, then liquid runs rising up and up to what surely ought to be a big cadence, only to fall back. The longing began again, and again the cadence was deceptive, dying back with a languid quality. Once more, and this third time, that cadence climbed to an intense, orgasmic peak that lasted just long enough to be gratifying. Then the intensity fell gradually, softly, into sweet, satisfying, melodic lines before a crescendo to the final cadence.

I let the final chord linger in the air for a few seconds before lifting my hands from the keyboard, and I looked up to where Donald stood. At some point, he had turned his back to the piano, and now as he stood there, arms crossed before him, I could see his shoulders rise and fall. I waited silently until he turned.

"You know," he said, his voice just a tiny bit hoarse, "it strikes me that lots of music pieces are like sex."

I stared at him, unsure what to say.

He added, "That false climax, then another, and then finally into release?" One side of his mouth lifted in a wry grin. "But it doesn't end until all those gentle, swaying phrases take you through a sweet afterglow. You don't hear that?"

I shrugged. "I've just never thought of it like that."

His arms dropped, and he rubbed his hands together. "So, what's for dinner?"

In the kitchen Donald picked up both the bottle of Chianti I had set aside for our dinner and the waiter-style, jackknife opener beside it. He examined the label and said, "Where do you get your wine up here? This looks like a very nice bottle. May I?" He held the opener up.

My memory of our time in New York was that the opener I used, which was not most people's choice as it required a little finesse, had been too much for Donald to bother with, and he had always waited for me to open wine bottles. I nodded, and while I told him about the trip I made to Newport periodically to replenish my wine supply, I watched as he handled the opener with apparent ease. He picked up the decanter I had set out and gently poured the wine into it.

I said, "It seems you've opened a few bottles of wine since the last time you and I shared one."

Eyes on the flow of garnet-colored liquid as it flowed into the decanter, he grinned. "Jonathan loves good wine, too. He insisted I learn how to open a bottle correctly. And by correctly, he means using just this style of opener." He set the bottle and the decanter down. "He says anything else is cheating."

"Cheating?"

"Well… his word was 'amateurish,' but I'm not sure I like that."

I didn't admit aloud that I felt the same way as Jonathan.

Dinner conversation was a little awkward at first. Donald praised the food and said it seemed I had learned something about cooking since the last time we'd shared a meal. I asked about progress on plans for the property. I wanted to ask whether Donald would be part-owner, but I wasn't sure how to phrase that without sounding nosy.

Then he brought up something I suspect he'd been holding onto with a certain amount of his own brand of unholy glee.

"I loved working with Kira. She's quite the drama queen. I'd thought maybe she'd be nervous about Sunday, but now I doubt it. And as for Seth...." He twirled spaghetti around his fork, eyes down, watching the process. "You'll never guess who brought him to Loraine's." He popped the laden fork into his mouth and watched my face as he chewed.

There he was. Puck. I was so busy enjoying this confirmation about Donald's recovery that I neglected to make a guess, or even to consider what the answer might be.

"Don't know?" he said after swallowing. "It was Adam."

I felt my jaw drop. "Adam? You met Adam?"

"I did indeed. If not for Jonathan, I'd might have done a lot more than meet him. Spencer, he's a god!"

I think I blushed. "He's not, really, though I know what you mean. He has his flaws."

"Name one."

"He can be a little prickly about certain things. Like, take offense where none is meant."

"That's all?"

"You said to name *one*."

"Name another."

Embarrassment sent a quirky grin sneaking across my face. To recover, I made a counter attack. "Name one of Jonathan's."

Donald made a face as though to say that wasn't fair, but he said, "He takes things awfully seriously. Sometimes he responds well when I try to lighten things up, and sometimes he doesn't."

I nodded. "I can see that. He seems very committed to things he feels are important. Like this project." I decided to take a risk. "And like you."

Donald, busying himself with his twirling fork, said nothing. I tried not to read anything into his silence.

He changed the subject. "So are you all ready with your part for Sunday? Have you changed very much of the script I wrote for you?"

"No big changes. Just a couple of minor things. I think you'll recognize it as your script. Don't be surprised if Elaine changes a few of her lines, though."

From there we talked more about the plans for Beltane, and Donald asked questions about The Forest.

"I wasn't kidding when I told you I'd love to see it. Is that allowed?"

"They're very particular about visitors. They don't like to be gawked at by curiosity-seekers. Like some kind of circus act, was how someone put it to me. But given your part in Beltane, I might be able to wrangle a visit for you."

"You get special dispensation because of Adam?"

I shook my head. "No; my relationship with Adam began after I got dispensation." I waved my fork, a piece of lettuce clinging to it. "It's complicated."

"I'll bet it has to do with that fire."

"In part, yes. I'll see what I can do to get an invitation for you."

After dessert, Donald and I took Klondike for a short walk. It was dark enough that I didn't think anyone would recognize us, but I was wrong. Or maybe Klondike—that large, white mass of a dog— gave us away.

We had walked as far as the high school, and I had told Donald a little about what Marshall had been like as a teacher, when a group of three teenage boys rolled past us on bicycles, headed for the school parking lot. One of them wheeled around and came back toward us.

"Hey, Rev! Hey, Klondike!"

Duncan Beale. I'd have known him anywhere. The black-dyed hair long enough to be teased into funky spikes, the glint of silver piercings in a few places, the black leather jacket. He half-stood, half-sat on his bike, watching us with interest.

"Hey, yourself."

"New boyfriend?"

"This is a friend from my New York City days. Donald Rainey. Donald, this is Duncan Beale, the son of one of my lay ministers."

Donald nodded, and they regarded each other for a moment. It the dull light it was hard to see the expression on Duncan's face. Then he turned to me. "Still on a piano break?"

"Yes, sorry. I meant to let you know we could start again next week, if you'd like."

"Sure thing. I got some new music to show you." He turned his bike toward where his friends had gone. "See ya!"

Donald and I walked for about five steps before he said, "Piano break?"

"I'm giving him piano lessons on Thursdays. With this Beltane project taking so much time, I'd given him a couple of weeks off."

"Sounds like he's ready to go back at it. Looks like quite a character."

"He's had a huge turnaround since I met him last fall." I started to give a description of the sullen, almost catatonic young man I'd met in September when I heard the sound of a bicycle approaching. I turned, and Duncan pulled up beside me.

"Meant to ask you, Rev. Whaddya know about how Ralph Blake is doing?"

I was on guard instantly, not sure how to respond. "Why do you ask?"

"Well, cuz he's not been in school lately, but I seen Molly around."

"Did you ask her?"

Duncan made a face. "She's, like, two grades below me."

I laughed. "Too young for you to talk to, then?"

He ignored that. "I was getting a group together. Ralph was gonna sing in it. But he's, like, fallen off the map."

"Did you call?"

"Yeah. His folks just said he couldn't come to the phone."

"What makes you think I know anything?"

He rolled his eyes. "Can't fool me, Rev. You know everything that goes on around here."

I chuckled, pleased; it was what I had told Vanessa, and now here it was coming to me. "Not sure I'll admit to that. But I do know the Blakes are in Reverend Foster's congregation. Next time I talk with him, I'll let him know you asked."

The look he gave me said he knew I was giving him the runaround, but he just nodded and headed back toward the parking lot. Donald and I watched for a moment, and then he said, "That's going to be a bit tricky."

"It was a challenge for me not to use the name 'Ralph.' And I will talk to David. Probably call him tonight."

"David?"

"Foster. The Protestant minister."

Klondike and I walked with Donald all the way back to Loraine's house, our conversation light and casual. At the door, though, we turned toward each other, and I could feel a current of something pass between us.

Donald held his right hand out. "Thanks for a lovely evening, Spencer."

I grinned and regarded his outstretched hand before I took it in mine. "It was a lovely evening."

He unlocked the door and turned to me just before opening it. "I told you once that Jonathan didn't play as well as you. Do you remember?"

"How could I forget?"

He nodded. "Good night."

CHAPTER 13

As Sunday approached, everyone involved grew predictably excited. Saturday was especially frenetic, if in a good way, with so many Assisi residents now able to throw themselves into their respective efforts and contributions now that it was the weekend. From setting up tables and chairs to preparing gallons of punch to baking brownies and cupcakes and cookies, it was thrilling to see what once seemed unlikely—a pipe dream—coming to life.

At the same time, there was a nagging doubt in the back of my mind. It concerned Kira. I had to admit to playing a part in rushing forward with the idea of Kira as May Queen. It had seemed like a wonderful, validating experience for her.

But now, I felt so unsure about its advisability that I sat down at my desk in a rare quiet moment early Saturday morning and drew a kind of flow chart that included the steps everyone involved had taken to make sure Kira would be as anonymous as she needed to be, given her parents' position. I wondered whether she had been unable to resist confiding in Molly. It wasn't that I doubted Molly, but she was young, and this was exciting, and she clearly supported Kira in her female identity.

Blocks and arrows, and straight lines and curly ones, filled the paper before me. I drew a small red triangle anywhere I thought there might be a vulnerability to Kira, and when I was done I saw too many of those to feel sanguine. Was it too late to replace her? And what would that do to her self-confidence? Would she feel destroyed at this point to be pulled out of a role that Boyd and David both said she was thrilled to have? Even Donald had said something that led me to believe she was really excited about it.

We could conceivably put Molly in Kira's place. The only thing Molly had to lose would be if her parents discovered her involvement. She had permission to be there with her class, even if not to be singled out in a critical role. So she might be in hot water. But Kira….

Kira stood to gain so much. Her female identity would be celebrated by everyone who saw her as the queen, even without knowing who she was outside that persona. As the queen, paired with a young man, the contrast would bolster her conviction and her certainty; it could give her strength she would need to carry forward as who she knew herself to be, whether she was attracted to boys or not.

But part of her identity was as a member of her family. Her parents were her parents; her sister was her sister. I could only imagine what the loss of that belonging would be. And it would be made worse if the Blakes sent her off to exactly one of those places Jonathan and Donald wanted to rescue teens from.

Marshall had been severely damaged by being subjected to conversion "therapy," so severely damaged, he had tried to kill himself while he was at that place. Kira had already made one attempt, in her own home.

Today, at nearly the eleventh hour, I was feeling more and more that it would be wise to replace her, with Molly or with some other girl from Assisi. With no speaking parts for the teens, it would not be logistically hard to do.

It seemed like a good idea at the time was no excuse.

I went to the MacPhersons' where I knew Myra, Jenny, Boyd, and probably David would be. I pulled Myra aside first.

"I'm having second thoughts about something."

Myra was smiling, excited anticipation nearly beaming from her face. "Oh?"

"It's about the May Queen."

"What about her?" Myra might not know who the queen was, but she knew of the need for secrecy.

I condensed my concerns into a few sentences, closing with "The best that could happen would be wonderful. The worst would be a horror beyond measure."

"Spencer, we've taken precautions. There should be no way for anyone to find out who she is. And even if they do—"

"Where's David?" I looked around but didn't see him,

"He told Boyd he'd be here around four."

I left her standing there, looking confused, and knocked on the MacPhersons' back door. Roberta answered. "Hello, Spencer."

"May I use your phone?"

She ushered me into the kitchen to a yellow wall phone and left, saying, "I'll give you some privacy."

I'd called David so many times recently that I knew the number. When he answered I launched into my concerns, trying not to sound panicky. I finished with, "Does Molly know?"

"She doesn't. I've been very clear with Kira that no one must know, even Molly. I'm convinced Kira understands the need for secrecy here, much as I wish it weren't necessary. But you sound genuinely worried."

"I am. I admit I've been as much behind this idea as anyone, and in principle I like it very much. But David, think what could happen if things go amiss. I made a list of vulnerabilities—places where Kira's cover could be blown—and there are too many of them for my liking."

There was silence on the line briefly. Then he said, "At this point, though, I'm worried about what she'd say, or do, if we pulled her out. Tell you what. I'll go and talk with her and see what she says. For all we know, she might be feeling afraid already. I'll do my best to assess the situation."

"Thank you. Please be sure she understands that it would be easy to find a replacement, even now."

Donald was waiting for me when I headed back into the field.

"Isn't this fabulous, Spencer? I'm so glad to be a part of it. The Forest Dwellers are delightful!"

I glanced around the field. "How many of them are here, do you think?"

"I've met three so far, but that includes Myra."

"Is Adam here?" Adam shouldn't know who Kira was, but I wanted to talk with someone who might understand my worries.

"Haven't seen him."

"You haven't told anyone who the queen is, have you?" I shook my head. "Stupid question. Of course you haven't."

"The words would have stuck in my throat." He watched my face as I continued to scour the scene with my eyes. "Spencer, what's going on?"

I took Donald's elbow and walked him off to the side of the activity where we couldn't be overheard. "I'm worried about Kira."

I told Donald about Marshall, about how his parents had sent him to be converted when he came out to them as gay, about how he had been treated when he was there. I described the scene Marshall had told me about. How he had tied heavy rocks into the legs of a pair of pants. How he had paddled in a canoe out onto the lake that was part of the camp. How he had capsized the boat. And how the two counselors who had rescued him had said that as bad as suicide was, maybe it wasn't as bad as being gay. And I told Donald how much that experience had continued to trouble Marshall, how vulnerable he had been when we'd been together, how easily emotional crises overcame him.

Donald listened until I stopped long enough to take a breath. He said, "You're worried this will happen to Kira?"

I hesitated, because it was really none of his business knowing what Kira had already done, but I really needed an ally. "Kira has already attempted suicide once."

Donald didn't seem shocked by this news. "What are you going to do?"

I let out a ragged breath. "I don't know. David's gone to talk with her, see if she might be feeling some trepidation, herself, and let her know we could find a replacement quickly if needed."

"So it's really up to her."

"I'm not sure it should be."

"Why not?"

"Do you remember what it was like to be her age? Because I do. I remember very well how little I understood truly dire consequences. Failing an exam, flubbing a piano piece during a recital, those things loomed large. But dying?" I shook my head. "I might as well have been immortal. Did you ever see the film *Little Big Man?*"

"Consider who you're talking to."

"I saw it a few years after it came out, when I was in my teens. There's a scene near the end when Dustin Hoffman's character walks up into the hills with the tribal chief. The chief says he's old and ready to die. He stands on a hilltop, looks at the sky, glances around, and says, 'It's a good day to die.' In the end, he doesn't. But, Donald, I thought I understood. At the time, I thought it would be possible for me to say that and mean it. But as a minister, I've been with several people who were in the process of dying. I know much better now what it is. Back then?" I shook my head. "Back then I didn't have a fucking idea what dying meant."

Donald gazed off into the distance for a moment. "I've never been to conversion therapy. Getting out of that cult wasn't exactly comparable. And I've never tried to kill myself." He looked back at me. "But what I do have, and you don't, is the experience of having your family find out something about you that they really, really, really—did I say 'really?'—*really* hate. The way I coped was to pretend. To lie. To hide, until I could get away. Marshall is braver than I was. And Kira is braver than I was."

"Or maybe yours was the more sensible way to handle it."

"Maybe. But I'll say this. After I came out to my folks, if something—*anything*—had appeared on the horizon that looked like affirmation? Man, I would have grabbed at it."

"So you think we should let Kira do this."

"I think she should understand, as well as she can, what could happen. And then she should decide."

I let out a long breath. "I think that's what David's doing. Helping her understand."

"And you got him to do that. You've done as much as you can. For now. If the shit does hit the fan, there might be more you can do. But let Kira be Kira. Don't yank this away from her now." He chuckled. "I'm a fine one to be giving advice. This was my bright idea, wasn't it?"

By six o'clock, the field was as ready as it could be for May Day. Festivities would begin at one tomorrow, after Assisi church services, and after a brief, private ceremony in The Forest. I tried to focus on my sermon for the following day, but my thoughts bounced around from worries about Kira to my feelings about my own culpability. That culpability was not limited to how easily I had gone along with the idea of Kira as the queen. It extended beyond that, or perhaps mixed in with that, to how much of my focus in the past weeks had been on Donald.

Each time I'd realized how comfortable Donald was using his odd vocabulary in my presence, I'd gloated silently, knowing Jonathan discouraged that whimsy.

When Donald had moved ahead of Jonathan into Loraine's house, I'd welcomed the time alone with Donald—working on the festival preparation, dinner, conversation, all of it filled with a sexual tension the likes of which I relished at the time and relived later. Never mind that we hadn't kissed, that we hadn't fucked, that we hadn't overtly rekindled the relationship that the Risen Christ cult had ended. There was something implicit between us, something not said aloud: *If it weren't for Jonathan….*

I couldn't be positive Donald heard that voice as clearly as I did, but I strongly suspected that he did. It was clear in the meeting of eyes. In the quick recall of a hand that had strayed too close to the other's. In the nervous laughter and the pulling away when one of us sensed we were physically too close for mere friendship. And it was in what he'd said to me on Loraine's doorstep: *Jonathan doesn't play as well as I do.* That word, play, referred overtly to the piano. But there was no doubt in my mind that both times he had said it, Donald was thinking of other things as well. Perhaps he was even thinking about how I'd made love to him.

The situation was untenable. And it had to end.

CHAPTER 14

Along with Jenny and a few other organizers, I was still on the field when David arrived a little after six. He approach me where I was struggling to understand the workings of the maypole. I handed my green ribbon off to whoever was next to me and followed David away from anyone who might overhear us.

"She's immovable," he told me. "I painted as full a picture as I could of what might happen, to no avail. I stopped short of actually telling her that I thought she should hand this off to someone else."

"What did she say?"

He glanced around, though no one was nearby. So it seemed less as though he was watching for an eavesdropper and more like he felt helpless.

"She said something like the worst has already happened, and she wasn't afraid of what her folks might say or do." He rubbed his face. "Spencer, I even tried to describe one of those conversion places. You know what she said?"

Of course I didn't; I shook my head.

"She said she'd already known about them. Said she wasn't afraid of them."

I scowled in confusion. But then something occurred to me that offered at least a little encouragement. "It sounds like she's found some source of courage, or determination, or something, and that it's unlikely she's thinking of suicide as an option. Does it strike you that way?"

"It does, but who knows whether she'd change her mind? Especially if she's sent away."

We stood silent for a moment, mostly staring down at the grass by our feet. If her courage was coming from her role as May Queen, no wonder she wouldn't give it up. And we'd just have to leave it at that.

I lifted my face to look at David. "On a related note, did you mention that Duncan Beale had asked about 'Ralph?'"

"Yes. I couldn't quite read Kira's reaction, but she didn't say anything about sending a response. Didn't suggest telling him anything."

I echoed what Donald had told me. "I guess it's up to her, then."

~

Sunday dawned bright and warm. It would be a glorious day for Beltane.

During church service, the air fairly sparkled with anticipation; it seemed the entire congregation was looking forward to the festivities. And that included Donald and Jonathan, who were seated in a pew close to the front.

My sermon, which was about communities sharing with each other and learning from each other, seemed to go over well enough; certainly it was appropriate to the day, if not one of my more brilliant oratories.

Few people hung around after the service; clearly, everyone wanted to get home and change before heading out to the MacPhersons'. I did speak with Jonathan, however, who had left the Pinewood and was now in residence with Donald at Loraine's.

"I didn't see Loraine Fuller here today," Jonathan said as he shook my hand. "I was hoping to thank her for her generosity."

"She's hoping to be at the festival. But if not, I'm sure you'll see her before you leave on the thirteenth. Meanwhile, I hope things are going well with your project."

He nodded. "I was just telling Donald about the house I've rented in Newport, starting in June. At some point, when the renovation is complete, we'll move into the farmhouse."

I glanced at Donald, wondering whether he would have liked to be involved in locating even a temporary domicile. His face held a smile, but it seemed perfunctory rather than pleased. Or was that just my bias showing?

As soon as I was changed and had walked Klondike briefly, I bundled dog and my contribution of a few cases of ginger ale into the Jeep and headed over to the festival. I caught myself in vanity, hoping no one would think these sodas were my sole contribution; renting those tents had cost a small fortune.

It was not quite one o'clock when I got there, but already the place was buzzing. Some of the activity was due to final set-up, but it was clear that folks were starting to arrive as participants.

I wished I could have had a birds-eye view of the field; there was so much to see. Areas had been roped off for where singing would take place, and Jennie had a cadre of people from all over Assisi around her for a final run-through of a couple of hymns. Lining most of the western outer rim of the field were tables, already laden with food and punch; placed in various clumps near these tables were smaller tables and folding chairs for anyone who wanted to sit while they ate. One large tent sheltering more tables and chairs was off to one side, and a few smaller shelters were scattered various places for anyone who wanted to get out of the sun. Almost out of sight beyond the food tables was a line of obligatory portable toilets.

I noticed that some people, including some of the children, wore necklaces made of colorfully-dyed leather thongs, threaded through single stones of various colors and sizes. These must be Forest Dwellers, I reasoned.

The maypole took center stage, and the space around it was clear, both for the dancers and for onlookers.

The corner at the far right, the northeastern corner, had nothing around it; this would be where the procession began. The plan was for that to take place at two, once the crowd was full and everyone had oriented themselves. From that corner, a path of dried hay had been strewn. In another venue it might have been a red carpet; here, the hay was perfect. It was bordered on either side by Y-sticks stuck into the ground, hemp roping set into the Y shapes.

I deposited my ginger ale and made my way toward that corner, Klondike in tow. As I stood, imagining the event, Elaine Gault approached me.

"Good afternoon, Spencer."

"And to you. I hope your own Beltane celebration was lovely."

She smiled. "We feel assured of a pleasant season for all."

Adam and a few other men approached, each carrying large burlap bags, which they deposited on either side of the hay path. They opened the tops of the bags but didn't take anything out. I was pretty sure I knew they contained greenery and flowers to be strewn in the path as the May Queen and Green Man made their appearances.

Elaine glanced at Klondike and smiled. "Is this the beast who helped you save that odd little man's horses last winter?"

I laughed. Odd little man was a perfect description for Alan Jermin. He was perhaps more malevolent than this term implied, but still somehow it fit.

On either side of where the hay path emerged from the woods were makeshift wooden platforms, about five feet above the ground, raw wood steps leading up to each. Leafy boughs had been draped on the edges like bunting. Elaine gestured toward them. "For us," she said. "Do you care which side you take?"

"I give you your choice." I had my notes with me, though I had memorized most of the text Donald had written for me, adding just enough to make it my own.

Elaine nodded toward the woods behind the platforms. "I believe our young actors have arrived."

Through the trees I could barely make out a group of people moving about. One of them was Donald, and I was sure he was helping to dress and prepare Kira and Seth, who—as far as I knew—had never met in their current identities. Both of them attended the Assisi high school, but Kira had always appeared there as Ralph. Would Seth know her? Would it matter?

I shook myself, mentally; there was not much I could do to protect her now. She had made her decision.

David Foster made his way out of the trees and approached me. "Our May Queen is nearly beside herself with excitement," he said. "Seth just seems nervous."

I asked, "Did they know each other?"

"I don't think Seth recognized Kira. I don't know how she managed it, but she looks very, very much like a girl."

I chuckled. "I suspect Boyd had something to do with that."

David laughed. "Very likely."

Elaine, listening intently, looked puzzled. I said to her, "Apologies if this seems cryptic. I'll explain it all later, if that's all right."

"As long as it isn't a problem for the event, that's fine."

Not wanting to call attention to what was going on behind the curtain of trees, Klondike and I wandered into the center of the grounds to admire the maypole. Long streamers of cloth in every bright color imaginable hung from the festooned crown at the top, awaiting dancers.

I fingered a bright red streamer. Behind me, I heard, "I like your Donald."

Adam.

As I turned to face him, standing this close, my breath caught. He was dressed as I had first seen him. Well, as I had first seen him dressed; my first sighting had been of his naked body at McGown Pond before he had dressed just as I saw him now. Bare-chested, he wore a long, dark brown, leather skirt. Ragged slits in the leather, at irregular intervals, started at the hem and went up to the middle of his thighs. There was a wide band of leather, fastened around his hips, far enough below his navel to reveal the beginnings of the inguinal ligament, that line that starts near the hip bones and leads diagonally down toward the genitals. A thin, leather thong was wrapped around the center of this band and fixed into a metal ring so that a single, long thread of leather dangled down the front of the skirt.

I wanted to fuck him right there on the grass. Instead, I raised an eyebrow. "Donald is not mine anymore."

"Isn't he?'

"What's that supposed to mean?"

Adam shrugged and glanced over to where Donald and Jonathan stood at a food table, their backs to us. "He suits you better than he suits Jonathan."

I gave him a half-smile that I hope communicated disbelief. "And you know this how?"

"I sense Jonathan's humor comes from underneath. Donald's is right on top. Like yours."

"I have no idea what you're talking about."

He nodded. "Give it time."

We stood side by side and glanced around as more and more people, both villagers and Forest Dwellers, made their way from the side road where cars were parked.

"You've done it, Spencer."

"We've all done it."

He turned to face me, hesitated just a few seconds, and embraced me.

Behind us I heard the first strains of a familiar hymn. The

singing had begun. Not everyone moved in that direction, but many did.

Over to the side was a long table with hymnals on it. Three people stood behind the table, asking anyone who wanted to use a hymnal to sign a log sheet; this was Jenny's plan to avoid losing any more than we could help. I knew some of those hymnals were from my church, some from David's, and some from Milton Bryant's. The people handing them out were all three Beales: Andrea, who was one of my lay ministers; her husband, Jacob; and their teenage son Duncan, my piano student, looking resplendent in his many silver piercings and with more silver jewelry than I would have thought he owned, sunlight glinting where his black clothing and hair set the white metal off to its greatest advantage.

Everywhere I looked, what I saw confirmed that we had, in fact, "done it." I had chosen very well in Jenny as my co-organizer. In fact, as much work as I had done—procuring the tents, recruiting David and his congregation, and Milton Bryant with his, and calling a special town hall to spread the word—it was Jenny who had done most of the grunt work. And she was still at it.

Then of course, there was Donald's contribution, working with the two teens, designing their looks, all the while keeping Kira's secret.

Although I would hardly say I knew everyone in Assisi, and far from everyone in The Forest, I didn't see anything that made me wonder if the two groups were keeping to themselves. The singing appeared to be especially useful in encouraging a mix of participants. At the food tables, it was clear that people were sharing tastings and even swapping recipes.

Klondike and I stood (well, he sat) where we could see almost everything that was going on. I was glad I'd worn my baseball cap; the visor shielded my eyes against the sun that was warming my shoulders and making Klondike's fur nearly sparkle. Every so often, white fluffs of cloud meandered vaguely across the blue sky, carefree and without purpose, causing shadows to wander the field just as many of us on the ground were doing. I didn't always see the clouds before I felt the cool of their shade on the back of my neck.

Several people stopped to chat, some I hadn't met before. It gave me a good opportunity to talk about the purpose of the day to people outside my congregation.

At one point, a voice behind me said, "So this is the famous Klondike."

I turned and saw Jeff Lawrence and his wife Linda, the couple who'd recently been through a third miscarriage. I smiled. "You never met him when he was Vanessa's dog?"

Linda lowered herself so she could fondle the dog's golden-tipped ears. "We heard about him occasionally." She stood. "Vanessa sometimes made him the central character in a story."

"A story? Do you mean as part of a sermon?"

Jeff laughed. "It made for some humor that helped her make important ethical points while keeping our attention."

"I'll have to try that," I said. "I'm sure my sermons could use some humor."

"You have your own style," Linda told me. "Though I won't discourage you from including Klondike whenever the spirit moves you."

I watched as they wandered toward the food tables, thinking what a shame it was that they hadn't managed to have a child yet. Maybe next time.

A few minutes later, Boyd approached with an older woman dressed mostly in spring green, which seemed very appropriate for the day. Though not tall, she stood straight and walked with purpose. Her short, white hair was carefully arranged, which seemed in conflict with the stark brown of her brows, two thin lines like arched caterpillars, neatly drawn.

"Mom," Boyd said to her, "this is Reverend Hill. Spencer, my mother, Mrs. Harper."

She extended a hand. I took it, but instead of a handshake I leaned over and planted a light kiss onto the mottled skin.

"Such a gentleman," she said. "But then it does often seem as though the best manners are exhibited by homosexuals."

As I glanced at Boyd, I heard his hoarse whisper: "Mother!"

She grinned at me, and in a flash I knew that she had meant her words to be a good-natured poke at her son rather than anything else.

I smiled back. "We are known for that. It's true. Are you enjoying the festival?"

"I had my doubts," she said, her voice tinged with humor, "what with all these non-Christians. But I can see it's all in good fun."

I was debating whether to expand her understanding of today's purpose or leave her with "good fun," when Boyd's eyes fell on something behind me. Boyd and his mother took their leave, and I turned to see David Foster, one arm gently resting against the back of a young girl.

"Reverend Hill, Molly Blake would like to make your acquaintance."

"I'm so happy to meet you, Molly." I held my hand out and she shook it, looking a little self-conscious.

"I wish Kira could be here," she said, "but thank you for being kind to her."

For the first time, I wondered how Kira had managed to leave the house without being caught. "And thank you, Molly, for being so supportive. I'm sure Kira is very grateful for you."

"Is this your dog?" Molly reached over to stroke the white fur.

"Yes. His name is Klondike."

"He's gorgeous."

David and Molly headed over to the drinks table. I watched them go, wishing I could tell Molly about Kira's secret role in today's pageant.

Kira's secret. Suddenly the warm-and-fuzzy feelings engendered by today's evident success changed as dramatically as if the puffs overhead had been chased away by towering columns of thunder. I expected Kira would have a wondrous moment today.

But what would follow it? Would it also be the end of her parents' patience? And if so, what would that mean?

If Kira wasn't terrified at the idea of conversion therapy, I was. Marshall's experience was as clear in my mind as it could be, given that I hadn't witnessed it myself.

Marshall. I'd had to accept at least some of the blame for his flight away from Assisi. Given my role in recruiting Kira as May Queen, would I also be culpable if her fate took a worse turn than it already had?

As if sensing my restlessness, Klondike looked up at me. I rubbed his ears. "Come on, boy. Let's walk for a bit. I need to be distracted."

CHAPTER 15

I think it was around one-thirty when I saw Loraine Fuller headed toward me. I looked for Vanessa, sorry and yet not surprised that she wasn't here. We exchanged a few words, and then she pointed out a problem I hadn't considered.

"What will you do with Klondike while you're speechifying?"

I glanced at the large white creature, sitting patiently beside me in the shade of one of the smaller tents. No words came to me.

Loraine laughed. "Figures. Tell you what. I'll take over until I'm ready to leave, or until you're ready to reclaim him."

We embraced as I handed her the lead.

It wasn't clear to me how so many people seemed to know that something was about to happen, but sometime around one forty-five folks began gathering at the far corner, standing on either side of the roping or at a respectful distance near the end of the hay path. I felt Elaine's hand on my shoulder, and we made our way to our platforms.

"I hope you brought your outdoor voice," she said, grinning.

I took the platform to the right after Elaine chose the left. On the platform was a music stand where I could set notes, or on which I could lean lightly, or perhaps it was there just to have something in front of me. A glance at Elaine told me she wasn't going to make any use of her stand at all. She stood straight but relaxed, giving off an almost palpable combination of self-possession, confidence, and benevolence. I did my best to follow her example.

Jenny and a few helpers led many children, some Forest Dwellers and some not, to where they could stand just outside the roping and close to the bags of leaves and flowers.

I glanced at my watch: one fifty-eight. Almost no one remained on the field; all but a few people were ready for this part of the festival.

I saw Elaine step forward, regal in what looked like a cloud of green silk shot through with threads of sunshine, her hair a silver and grey waterfall down her back. Self-consciously, I removed my cap.

The crowd hushed immediately. A slight smile on her face, Elaine graced the crowd with gentle glances. She spoke first, as we had arranged.

"For those who don't know me, I am Elaine Gault, Elder of the Forest Dweller community. And this is a momentous day." She glanced at me and then back at the crowd. "This young man, the Reverend Spencer Hill, has wrought a minor miracle. Because of his generous heart and perseverance, he led the way toward resolving decades of hatred and distrust between The Forest and the town of Assisi. But he didn't stop there."

It was everything I could do not to drop my jaw in surprise. I had expected her to say things about how we were both bringing town and forest together; I had not expected this calling-out.

Elaine looked at me. "Spencer Hill, you and Jenny Pratt have helped not only to bridge a long-standing rift, but also to strengthen the supports on either side of that bridge."

Relieved that someone else was being lauded, I looked toward the children for Jenny, extending an arm to where she stood. Elaine did the same. For her part, Jennie's face glowed nearly as red as the streamer I had fingered, and then she covered the lower half of her face with her hands, clearly as delighted as she was embarrassed.

Someone began clapping, and soon the entire crowd was applauding. A few people let out shrill whistles. After a moment, Elaine raised a hand, and a hush fell again.

"What non-Pagans call May Day, we in The Forest call Beltane.

Beltane is one of the four primary festivals, or sabbats, on the Wheel of the Year. Beltane is the time of year when we honor the union of Mother Earth, appearing here as the May Queen, with the forest god, the Green Man. Together, they bless us with good weather and fertile land. Beltane traditions revolve around fertility, and fire, and passion, and rebirth."

Elaine extended an arm toward me; my turn to speak. I used the correct pronunciation of the holiday Samhain, which is not pronounced how it looks.

"Last October, I learned about the veil that separates our world of the living from the world of those who have passed on. At Samhain, October thirty-first, that veil is very thin, making communication through it possible. I understand that the veil is just as thin now, at Beltane. The difference is that in the fall, we leave a time of plenty and prepare for the sleep of winter. Now all of us, in town and forest, celebrate Earth's awakening and the coming of new life."

Back to Elaine.

"New life." She paused and stood very still for a few seconds. "Long before the advent of Christianity, people celebrated sexuality because of its relationship to fertility and abundance. This is the season when animals give birth, bird eggs hatch, and flowers bloom. So Beltane is a celebration of life that cannot exist without sexuality. Those who don't know better might think that this means there will be wonton, unbridled pairings." She paused again to allow the crowd's chuckles to recede. "Not so. We celebrate with the flowers, but we do not cast or receive seed without regard for where it lands or what result it might have.

"Last night, we in The Forest prepared for Beltane. We performed rituals of protection over our livestock and crops. We created a purifying bonfire whose smoke carried protective energies with it, throughout our community, through the surrounding forest, and even extending to Assisi. Today, we ask the Beltane spirits to bless us."

I picked up the commentary. "In a little while, we will gather around the maypole. As you've heard, the focus on sexuality is not about wanton pairing. Rather, it celebrates life and the way life comes into being. The maypole can be considered a phallic symbol, penetrating the earth to ensure delivery of potent Beltane blessings from above. Dancers, holding the ribbons, will weave a pattern representing the intricacies and diversity of life. The resulting sheath is a symbol of Earth's womb, from which this life comes.

"Many of us here in Assisi worship a form of Christianity. We might be tempted to consider ancient traditions to be primitive. Perhaps even uncivilized. But I remind you of a ritual that is paramount, the most sacred part of the Christian year: Easter. It, too, celebrates life returning, ritualistically in the form of the Christ rising from the sleep of death." My turn to pause and look at the people gathered before me. "Anyone who enjoys the traditions of Easter eggs should keep in mind where those eggs come from, and what they represent in nature. And as for the rabbit...."

Elaine waited patiently for the crowd's laughter to diminish.

"Reverend Hill and I are not the main event here. We are merely the narrators, and our role is nearly done. Let us now prepare for the entrance you've come to see."

She turned slightly in the direction of the trees that served as a curtain through which Kira would come. "We welcome the May Queen."

People crowded a little forward and watched in silence as Adam appeared on foot, slowly leading a golden horse with a cream mane and tail. A few flowers had found their way into his hair. His garb, which had looked almost like a costume out on the open field, now spoke of deep woods and communion with mysterious spirits.

I had known horses would be involved at this point, but I was unprepared for the way the juxtaposition of animal energy and an almost ethereal beauty of this steed nearly made me lose my balance.

Seated on the horse was a young girl, her face painted purple. A large wreath of flowers hid her hair completely, and I credited Donald with hiding the vividly-colored hair which would likely have revealed Kira's identity. Wrapped around her body was a dark pink cloth, reminiscent of a Grecian robe. Adam halted as soon as the horse was fully out of the woods, and waited.

I knew this was Kira. And yet, it wasn't. This creature could easily have leapt from the pages of a book about faeries. She smiled, but it was not a smile of mirth. It radiated nobility, even magnanimity. She was truly the May Queen, blessing us all with beneficence and good will. I doubted any substitute could have projected what I felt from Kira.

I was so taken with this vision that I missed my queue. Elaine began the first words of the recitation we were to say together. I lifted my printed page and joined her on the second line.

"Leaves are budding across the land.
Magic rises around us in the forest.
The hedges are filled with laughter and love.
We have made for you a gift, a gathering of flowers picked
*   by our hands,*
woven into the circle of endless life
to encircle your head and to grace your beauty.
Queen of Spring, the bright colors of Nature herself
blend together to honor you this day.
Spring is here and the land is fertile, ready to offer up gifts
*   in your name.*

> *We pay you tribute, our lady, and ask your blessing this*
> *   Beltane."*

As we spoke, the children nearest Kira's horse tossed flowers and petals on the path before the animal.

In a somewhat theatrical tone, I said, "We welcome the Green Man."

Now it was Myra leading a horse, this one so dark brown as to appear nearly black. Myra had changed into clothing very similar to what Adam wore, though the color of her leather was lighter and had a drape to it his did not. Her long, reddish hair, too, was festooned with just enough flowers to avoid competing with the May Queen. She could have been one of the faeries over which the May Queen presided. She halted when she and her horse were beside Adam and his.

This dark steed carried young Seth, his face green. The cloth wrapping his body was brown. His head, too, was festooned with a wreath, all leaves. It seemed he was trying to imitate Kira's self-confidence, and he made a good attempt. It wasn't his fault that she outshone him.

Elaine joined me in another recitation.

> *"God of the Green, Lord of the Forest,*
> *We offer you our sacrifice.*
> *Green Man of the Woods,*
> *you bring life to the dawning spring.*
> *You are the deer in rut,*
> *mighty Horned One who roams the autumn woods*
> *until the hunter's arrow spills your lifeblood upon the*
> *   ground.*
> *God of the Green, Lord of the Forest,*
> *we offer you our sacrifice.*
> *We ask you for your blessing."*

A boy from my congregation, Oliver Teldale, ducked under the rope a little too fast and almost tripped, recovering just in time without dropping the clear glass jar full of honey. He held it toward Seth, but Seth was clearly too nervous to lean over enough to reach Oliver's hand and make the exchange. Myra stepped in and helped, and Seth accepted the sweet offering. Speaking together once more, Elaine and I gave our final speech.

"With thanks to the May Queen and the Green Man, and to God however you worship, we may now go forward with confidence, assured of the new life that will spring from the fertile ground. Amen, and blessed be."

I couldn't see where the applause began, but it exploded across the onlookers. Adam and Myra stood for several seconds before moving forward together, leading the horses along the hay path as children threw flowers and leaves before them. Elaine and I descended from our platforms and followed at a distance. The horses walked all the way over to the maypole, and I thought Kira and Seth might dismount, take a colored strip, and prepare for the dance. Instead, they stayed on their horses at a short distance where they could watch the action, royally beaming good will onto their happy subjects.

Off to the side, just far enough away to avoid tripping the dancers, were three people with instruments. They were dressed in a similar fashion to Adam and Myra, so I assumed they were Forest Dwellers. I saw a drum held by a man, his hand around a wooden piece behind the drum's skin, held more or less perpendicular to the ground. His other hand held what looked like a short, double-headed drumstick. One woman held a violin and a bow. And there was some kind of stringed instrument, a trapezoid shape, set flat on a wooden stand. The woman standing at the wide base held two small wooden sticks. I turned to Elaine, my face full of question.

Elaine pointed to each player starting with the man. "Bodhrán. Fiddle. Hammered dulcimer."

To my surprise, perhaps a hundred yards away was another pole, much shorter, with not quite as many colorful streamers on it.

Then, amidst the several youngsters gathered there, I saw Boyd Harper and Martha Foster, David's wife. They were doing their best to help the children, who all looked to be between the ages of four and maybe ten, get ready for a maypole dance of their own.

Adam, Myra, Jennie, and—to my surprise—Duncan Beale were the instructors at the large pole, making sure each of the Assisi folks who were participating had a streamer (Forest Dwellers already knew what to do) and then had them stand as far from the pole as the streamers would easily allow.

Adam held a blue streamer. "We have twenty-four ribbons. Three is an important number in so many traditions, and four is the number of the seasons. Three times four is twelve. We've doubled that for good measure."

Myra, beside Adam, held a yellow streamer. "The idea is that every other dancer moves clockwise, and the other dancers move counter-clockwise. Clockwise folks follow Adam. Start with ribbons up. Everyone else, follow me and hold your ribbons down. After you pass your first person coming in the opposite direction, you move your ribbon up or down, to be opposite the oncoming person's ribbon, for the next position. Next pass, change again. So you end up with 2 rings of people going opposite directions, going over and under the ribbons coming the other way."

The townsfolk looked a little perplexed. I was glad there were enough Forest Dwellers there who knew what do to.

Adam said, "If someone breaks the pattern, don't worry. It makes the dance fun, and the ribbons still look nice on the pole."

I hadn't noticed a group of teens standing off to the side of the instrumentalists. I heard a quiet tone from Jennie's pitch pipe, and then the singers altogether sang a song I'd heard them rehearsing: "Sumer is icumen in," the round they'd been singing the day I had stopped into the Teens for Truth meeting not long ago. Summer is a-coming in. Perfect.

They sang through the short song in unison, and then two girls began again. At the end of their first line, two boys started at the beginning, and then a boy and a girl picked up the third thread of the round. They sang it through a couple of times like that, and then one by one the different parts stopped, and the final line was carried by only one voice, a girl who'd been one of the first to join Teens for Truth: Darla Willis.

I smiled at her, remembering the crush she'd had on her English teacher, Marshall Savage. I wondered whether she knew the reason he'd had to leave in the middle of the year.

When the applause died down enough so she could be heard, Myra said, "Everyone ready?"

Clearly the Forest Dwellers were. They all shouted, "Let's dance!" And immediately the three instrumentalists began to play something that sounded to me like Irish Celtic music. Myra and Adam stepped to the walking-paced rhythm, moving in their respective directions and leading the way for those behind them.

As a watcher, I have to say the effect was a little dizzying. I had paid attention to the instructions; even so, trying to follow what everyone was doing wasn't nearly as much fun as just watching the overall effect and laughing with the dancers when something happened that wasn't perfect.

The music grew seamlessly faster as the ribbons got shorter, and toward the end it became truly frenetic.

Something nudged my thigh, and I looked down to see Klondike, Loraine on the other end of his leash.

"Ready to give him up?" I asked.

Loraine shook her head. "Nope. I think you're up next. Dancing, I mean."

"Oh, I don't think so." I nodded toward the pole. "They're all out of ribbon."

I don't know how the instrumentalists did it, but they managed to come to a rollicking cadence just as the dancers found themselves too close to the pole to go around any farther. Adam raised both arms, his blue streamer in one hand, and gave a triumphant, wordless howl. All the dancers shouted in response, and gradually —laughing and smiling—they moved away from the pole.

In less than a minute, two men—clearly Forest Dwellers—had

leaned extendable ladders against opposite sides of the pole while Adam and another man held the pole for stability. Using long-handled wooden hooks, the men on the ladders carefully untangled the ribbons, starting at the lowest point and working their way up, until all the streamers hung free again.

A voice behind me said, "Red for you, I think. I'll take a blue, and Jonathan wants green."

Donald took one of my arms and Jonathan took the other, and they marched me to the pole. Sensing the futility of any protest, I took the ribbon Donald handed me as other people came forward to claim a streamer of their own, and the music began again.

Round and round we went, and I think I did a respectable job of going over and under the other dancers at the right times. As before, the music grew louder and faster as the ribbons pulled us closer to the pole. I can't say now how it happened that I sent my ribbon in the wrong direction, or perhaps it was Donald who did that with his. In any event, with inches between us, our eyes met, and something from his eyes shot through me. I froze.

Behind me, and behind Donald, dancers bumped into us and into each other, until the entire ring of dancers came to a confused halt. Mortified, I expected the music would stop, calling further attention to my clumsiness, but it kept going until Adam, who had not been dancing this time, stepped forward and let out a sharp whistle.

Everyone turned to look at where he stood, hands on hips, eyes on me, an expression on his face like that of a parent about to correct a child who should have known better than to do what he'd just done. He heaved a dramatic sigh.

"I won't embarrass him further by telling you that it was Reverend Hill who bungled the dance so badly that—well, I don't have words for it. I've never seen a maypole dance bungled as badly as this. Not in my entire life."

He and Myra, laughing along with the dancers, wandered around the circle, disentangling where necessary, until everyone knew where they were and what they should do next. Adam signaled to the instrumentalists, and they picked up pretty much where they'd left off. The dance continued, though at a slower pace than before, until everyone met at the pole.

I accepted much ribbing as gracefully as I could, though I'm sure my face was nearly the color of the ribbon I'd held.

Loraine approached at one point, as the ladders were being carried off for the second time. She grinned at me. "We should have listened when you said you couldn't do this." She handed me the lead. "I've just given Klondike some water. And now, let me show you how this dance is supposed to be done."

She took her turn at the pole, a blue streamer in her hand. I leaned over and patted Klondike's side, hoping that the teasing was over. Ordinarily I'd suffer this kind of torment in good spirits; in my earlier life in Manhattan, I hadn't been aware of how weighed down I'd been by the carapace I'd formed to survive my austere upbringing. Since then, I had learned to laugh at myself as easily as anyone else can laugh at me. But in this case, the reason I'd fumbled was still too fresh in my mind.

Donald's eyes. I had sensed a message in them, carried on some kind of electric current that had shot into me. What had he wanted me to understand? What did I *want* to understand? And were those two things the same?

As though my thoughts had called to him, Donald appeared beside me. "I thought you acquitted yourself nicely, up there on the platform. It would seem the acting lessons I gave you a few years ago did some good."

His eyes now held nothing but bland friendliness. Whatever meaning had been in them was gone. I glanced around for Jonathan.

Donald interpreted my look. "He's recruiting."

"Recruiting?"

"Talking to the Catholic priest, last I checked. Spreading the word about the center."

Hoping to cover the intensity I still felt, I nodded. "Does it have a name yet? This center?"

"Jonathan is nothing if not a consensus builder. He's asking for ideas. I don't even know if he has anything in mind. He just wants to be sure that whatever it's called, the name communicates the goals well. And, of course, it needs to be memorable."

"Very wise approach. He's making sure people feel a part of the effort." My eyes found Milton Bryant and then Jonathan, apparently in earnest discussion. "And this is a great place for it."

"That's what he said."

We watched the dancers as they began to close in on the pole. Loraine was smiling broadly, clearly enjoying the dance, and I was certain she had made no mistakes whatever. They finished up at the pole, the music ended, and I wondered whether a fourth dance would begin. It looked as though Adam was about to ask if we had enough more interested dancers for the next round. But before he could speak, a commotion from the direction of the platforms drew everyone's attention.

I saw Seth, now in leather clothing like so many of the Forest Dwellers wore. Tall and proud and more confident than he'd seemed as the Green Man, he strode into the field, leading the cream-colored horse. And on that horse was Kira.

She was no longer the May Queen. Her bright pink hair was unadorned by a circlet of flowers, and her pink toga had been replaced by a flowing blue blouse over white jeans. On her feet were short boots, light brown, probably leather. She sat straight and proud, head held high, no smile on her face this time.

I don't think there was anyone whose eyes were not on her, some puzzled, some amused, and some—like mine—deeply concerned. I glanced around and caught the eye of David Foster, who made his way quickly over to me.

"What the hell...."

I said, "I take it you have no better idea than I have what's going on."

We stood silent, watching as Seth led Kira's horse to a spot near the maypole. I heard a small squeal, turned, and saw Molly, several feet away from me. Eyes wide, she appeared to be something between shocked and thrilled. I barely heard her say, "I knew it! I knew it was you!"

Kira's voice rang out.

"I am Kira Blake," she said. "I am Ralph Blake no longer. That name, and that person, are dead to me. I appear before you as a new person, released like a butterfly from the cocoon of the May Queen. This is who I am. Everyone here bears witness to my metamorphosis."

In the silence that followed Kira's announcement, I barely heard David say, "Now we know why she was so adamant about doing this."

CHAPTER 16

Boyd appeared beside me, snapping me out of my frozen state of shock. "Holy shit."

I asked, "You knew nothing of this?"

He shook his head. I handed him Klondike's leash and turned to David.

"Come on," I said. "Let's get her off the field."

From another direction, I saw Myra headed toward Kira as well. She took the reins from Seth, and David and I walked on either side of the horse as Myra led us all back to the space behind the platforms. No one said anything until Kira spoke.

"That was amazing." She turned briefly to look back at the crowd, where people were starting to converse. "I wanted to ride out on my own, but I've never been on a horse before today."

She chatted away about how she had made the blouse she wore, and how Seth had lent her his boots. It would seem that Kira and Seth had managed to get together outside of their sessions with Donald. I saw Myra give Seth a heavy look, but no one spoke except Kira until we were behind the trees and mostly out of sight of the field. I glanced back and saw that people were starting to mingle again, moving about almost as they had before, but I was pretty sure I sensed a change in the mood. Or maybe it was just that a few more clouds had appeared in the sky.

I heard someone behind us, and Molly came through the trees. Myra helped Kira off the horse, and the sisters embraced.

"You were magnificent!" Molly said.

Myra pulled Seth away from the group, no doubt to talk to him about his part in Kira's actions. David stepped between the girls.

"Molly, I need a minute or two with Kira. Can you stay with Reverend Hill?" He didn't wait for a response before walking with Kira in the opposite direction from Myra and Seth.

"What's going to happen now?" Molly wanted to know.

"I'm not sure," I admitted. "Molly, what can you tell me about how things are at home?"

She made a scoffing sound. "Better than they'll be after this."

I needed more. "So they aren't any closer to accepting Kira?"

Her head shook vigorously. "She barely comes out of her room. Even takes food up there rather than sit at the table. Mom and Dad keep calling her Ralph and making all kinds of comments about how they hope she's learning her lessons well from Boyd."

I couldn't tell whether Molly was in on Boyd's real mission.

She added, "They'll never let her out of the house after this."

That might be better, I thought, than sending her to the kind of place Jonathan wanted to save kids from.

Jonathan. Would he be able to help in some way?

David and Kira returned. He said, "I'm going to take Kira home. Molly, I believe you're here with friends, yes?" She nodded. "You should rejoin them now. Please don't say anything about Kira. Will you do that for me? And for her?"

Molly nodded again, gave Kira another hug, and headed back toward the field.

"Spencer, will you tell Martha where I've gone and let her know she'll need to get a ride home with someone?"

"I'll drive her home myself."

I watched as David and Kira skirted the outer edge of the field toward where the cars were parked. Then I went in search of

Martha Foster. I found her in a chair under one of the shade tents, talking to Jonathan. Perfect; I wanted to talk with him a well.

"May I join you?" I took a chair without waiting for an answer. "Martha, David has taken Kira home. I'd be happy to give you and your son a ride whenever you're ready to leave."

"Oh, thanks, but my neighbor is here as well. We'll go with her."

"You, um, I assume you're aware of what's been going on with Kira." She nodded, and I turned to Jonathan. "There's no secret to keep now, so I'd like to ask you about Kira. I don't know whether you have any suggestions at this point, but I'm thinking it's not out of the question for the Blakes to send Kira to some kind of conversion camp."

He sat up straight. "Have they said as much?"

"Not that I know of. But I do know they've been anything but accepting. And after today… who knows? It wouldn't surprise me if they turned her away, even if they don't send her anyplace."

He fondled his beard for a moment. "Do you know of anyone who might be able to take her in, even temporarily?"

"What a marvelous idea. Excuse me."

As I left the tent, I saw Boyd approaching. "What's going on?" he asked.

I told him what I knew, which wasn't much. "I have to find someone. Can you hang onto Klondike for a bit longer? I think he might like some water."

"No problem."

I wandered around the field, scouring faces for the people I was looking for. At the far end near the car parking area I saw them, no doubt headed for their car.

"Jeff!" I shouted. "Linda!" They turned, their faces expectant. I was a little out of breath when I caught up with them. "I need to run something by you. I'm sure you saw the girl on the horse."

"The May Queen," Jeff said. "Seems she's really a boy?"

I shook my head. Linda was about to speak, but I didn't wait. "She's transsexual. She was assigned male at birth, but she—how to put this—she has realized that she's actually a girl. It's a recognized disorder in the psychological and medical fields. At her age —sixteen—it's unlikely to change. But her biggest problem right now is her home life."

I gave them as thorough a description as I could in a couple of minutes, admitting my own culpability in facilitating her May Queen role. "Her minister, David Foster, and I felt it would be validating for her to do that. But her identity was not supposed to have been revealed, partly because of how very unaccepting her parents have been. She decided to do that on her own, and she orchestrated that—that exhibition, I guess I'd have to call it. Her parents didn't know she was even going to be here today."

Jeff wanted to know, "What do you think will happen?"

I shook my head. "I hesitate to think. But I must. Two possibilities are that they'll either send her away to a place that will promise to 'fix' her, which isn't possible, or they'll turn her out altogether."

I watched their faces for a moment, wondering if I should reveal the one secret I hadn't yet told them. But I was going to ask them to take her in, should that become necessary, so they deserved to know everything.

"There is a third possibility," I said. "She has already attempted suicide once. I don't know that she'd try again, especially now that she's so determined to be herself, but with a teenager you never know."

"How awful!" Linda turned to look at her husband.

He said, "And you're telling us this because…?"

Linda understood. She laid a gentle hand on Jeff's arm. "Kira might need a place to stay for a while." She turned to me. "Is that it?"

I nodded. "I know this is a huge thing to ask. And it might not be necessary. But if it is—"

Jeff interrupted me. "If it is, she can come to us. Though I would want to know more about this condition."

I let out a long breath of relief. "Thank you. Thank you so very much. Yes, I'll absolutely tell you everything I know. Reverend Foster's wife Martha is a doctor, and she has a copy of a document with extensive information."

Linda asked, "Would that be the DSM?"

"You know it?"

"I'm a psychologist."

I slapped the side of my head. "Of course! How could I forget? Then you know more about this condition than I do."

She added, "Kira should stay with her family if that's at all workable. But if it comes to the worst, our home is open."

I reclaimed Klondike and found an unoccupied table under one of the shade tents. I felt positively exhausted. I closed my eyes and sat very still for some amount of time, until I heard someone approach.

Donald set a cup of lemonade in front of me and sat in one of the other chairs. "You look strung out."

I regarded him for a moment. "Do you have any idea how Kira and Seth got together to arrange this exhibition?"

"Not really. I mean, they crossed paths once when Seth arrived a little early, before Kira had left one of our sessions. He took a good look at her, but I figured it was just a teenage boy ogling a teenage girl." He shrugged. "And maybe that was part of it. But, no."

I sipped my drink and closed my eyes again.

Donald asked, "What's going to happen now?"

"David took her home. He'll let me know whether steps need to be taken."

"Steps?"

"I've found a place for her to go if she needs to leave her home." Donald's silence made me open my eyes. I said, "What?"

"You are amazing."

He stood and walked away without another word. I followed

him with my eyes and saw him approach Jonathan, who was talking with Jenny. Donald slipped his arm around Jonathan's waist.

I closed my eyes again. And, as had happened a few times since I'd first seen the two of them together, a sense of incongruity fingered its way into my brain. This time, however, it had a clarity I hadn't noticed before. This time what I saw, as clearly as I'd seen Donald's arm on Jonathan, was that Donald seemed different when he was with Jonathan. Different from when he was with me.

The Donald I had known in New York had been full of fun, silly at times, but he'd also displayed a confidence that had seemed to come from deep within him. There had been times I hadn't taken that depth seriously and had pushed back on one thing or another, and each time I had failed. By that, I mean Donald's depth had held him in place.

In the time I'd spent alone with him this spring, I'd seen some of that depth. But in the time I'd spent with him and Jonathan together, Donald had seemed superficial, even flighty. The silly part of him seemed to have taken over. And, it appeared, that was fine as long as it didn't extend into Donald's whimsical vocabulary.

What was this about? What was going on? Was Donald some kind of chameleon changing color depending on the environment? The context? Was there something about Jonathan, about how he saw Donald, that sent a message of what he wanted from Donald? And did Donald change his behavior to accommodate what Jonathan wanted?

And what about Bruce Cobb? Donald had allowed himself to be cowed by that bully in a way I would never have expected of him. Of course, he had just come out of something that would challenge the self-confidence of most people; deprogramming can go only so far to reconstruct a personality that had been subsumed by a religious cult.

Still....

And then of course, there was me. If Donald was submissive to

Bruce's bullying, and whimsical to Jonathan's pragmatism, did that say anything about how Donald was with me? Had his confidence been a contrast to some lack of it in me? It was true, I believed, that I had gained quite a bit of confidence in the last few years. Was there something else about me that brought out a contrast in him, and if so, what would it be? Not that it mattered. He was not "with" me any longer. But Adam's words—*He suits you better than he suits Jonathan*—haunted me.

I sat, deep in contemplation, for a few minutes, Klondike lying peacefully at my feet, until I felt him stir. A glance told me he was on alert, and an instant later he was on his feet. Ears stiff and forward, the fur between his shoulders raised, he uttered a long, low growl. As I stood, but before I could turn and look in the direction of the dog's glare, I heard it: voices, many of them, in a sing-song pattern. A large group of people, perhaps thirty of them marching as one, approached from the direction of the parked cars.

And then I was aware of a change in the crowd around me, the festival-goers. I turned away from the newcomers to see many of the original crowd—not all, though probably most who were still at the festival—form a group of their own, each holding a sheet of paper. They moved as though they were not surprised at what was happening, just forming a group for some common reason, facing the newcomers. The next thing I heard was Erik Stillman's confident voice, raised in song, the same tune as that of the newcomers, though not in unison with them. Immediately other voices joined his.

Holding Klondike's lead securely, I turned in place from one group to the other, trying to understand what was happening. The newcomers moved slowly but steadily onto the field, singing as they went. I knew the hymn: "Onward, Christian Soldiers." Opposite them, Erik and his group—which included both Forest Dwellers and Assisi residents, and even Father Bryant—stood still, facing the oncoming group, singing… singing what? It was the same tune, but different words. The singers consulted their sheets of paper as they sang.

One more look back at the oncoming crowd was all it took for me to recognize Alan Jermin, the closed-minded, self-righteous pastor of Little Boundary's Assembly of God church—the "odd little man," as Elaine Gault had labeled him. Of course, he was easy to spot, as he marched in front and held up a large, wooden cross.

These were the people who had invaded Assisi last winter, knocking on doors, ostensibly proselytizing but in reality—or in addition—looking for me and for Marshall. In an instant, I felt exonerated: It was *their* fault! Their fault, *not* mine! *They* had forced Marshall to flee.

Anger welled up in me so profound that Klondike's leash shook in my hand. As though he picked up on my feelings, the dog barked several times.

Only once before had I heard Klondike bark in any way that wasn't playful, when he'd come close to attacking someone who'd threatened me physically. The sound surprised me enough to shake me out of my fury, and I strained my ears to listen.

> Onward, Christian soldiers, marching as to war,
> With the cross of Jesus going on before!
> Christ, the royal Master, leads against the foe;
> Forward into battle, see his banner go!

These war-like lines came, of course, from the new group. The other group, my group, had evidently rewritten the words. I couldn't quite make them out, given the cacophony of the conflicting groups, so I gave Klondike's leash one quick jerk, as Vanessa had taught me, to distract him from the new group, and we walked quickly to where Erik stood. He clearly didn't need his sheet of paper, so he handed it to me, and I sang with my group.

> Onward, Pagan people, circling round the wood,
> Sharing all the goodness, and, of course, the food!
> Love, the royal Master, leads against the hate;

Let hate not come near us. Keep it at the gate!

We didn't march forward. We stood where we were, immovable. After maybe the second time through the lines, I noticed that some singers were using the word "loving" instead of "Pagan" in the first line, and I grinned. I changed my word as well; it felt more inclusive, and even more powerful against the hatred of Jermin's group.

Then I heard the instrumentalists pick up the melody and play with my group. Because we were not singing in unison with Jermin's crowd, this accompaniment made our group louder. Shivers ran through me several times as we repeated these lines, facing the new crowd. Even as Alan Jermin came nearly toe-to-toe with Erik, acknowledging me not at all, Erik didn't budge. He kept his gaze just above Jermin's head and kept singing.

At a gesture from Jermin, the "Christian" crowd, still singing, began to encircle my group, though there weren't quite enough of them to go all the way around. I worried that violence hovered. Then I saw that those who had not been singing with my group, others at the festival who had been observing this confrontation, began to encircle Jermin's crowd. Their silence was perhaps more ominous than any singing.

Despite the apparent calm of my group, I became even more concerned about the possibility of violence. Then, in my peripheral vision, I saw the figure of Ben Marks, Assisi's police chief, moving onto the field from behind the Jermin crowd. He was dressed in his uniform. Behind him were several other policemen and policewomen, some with Assisi insignia and some I didn't recognize. They followed Ben and then fanned out around the field, not close to the singers, but in full view of everyone.

Suddenly children appeared, clearly Forest Dwellers because of the leather necklaces, carrying burlap bags. They skipped and frolicked through Jermin's crowd, throwing flowers and leaves into the air, and Erik raised his arms. The crowd and the instruments finished that repetition, and then something wonderful happened.

The instruments began a lively, cheerful tune, and the children returned to stand somewhere behind Erik. I thought perhaps this was another song for the crowd, but—no. A few at a time, people began laughing. It was quiet at first, but it spread throughout our group, and soon I was guffawing with the best of them. We laughed, and laughed, and the music grew more and more lively.

I glanced at Ben where he stood just behind Alan Jermin and saw that he was struggling not to laugh; he must have felt his job was to be stern and, above all, not to side with anyone. But before long, the contagion had spread, and most of the police officers were at least chuckling.

We laughed until the singing of Jermin's crowd petered out, at which point he raised his cross higher. The laughter quieted, and in the relative silence Jermin shouted, "This is not over!"

Erik gave him what could only be seen as a mock salute, and he began laughing again, joined quickly by the crowd behind him.

Jermin, clearly infuriated and (I hoped) maybe even embarrassed, turned and walked back in the direction he had come, and members of his group fell into step behind him. I watched to see whether I knew anyone, hoping vehemently that I would not. I didn't want (or expect) to see Maggie Downing there, for example. I was sure I would recognize Jermin's wife, or the maid who had been at their house the day of the horse rescue, and I didn't see either of them.

The laughter followed Jermin's group all the way off the field, and then Erik raised his arms again and began to clap, and everyone on the field except the police officers followed suit.

A memory from my childhood appeared suddenly in my mind. With parents who—despite leaving their religious vocations behind—were God-focused, and with my own stern demeanor and evident carapace, I was often ridiculed. My father had been fond of saying, "Be a fool for God, Spencer. Be a fool for Jesus." I wondered whether Alan Jermin would view today's rout of his group with the spiritual intentions Father had hoped to instill in me.

When the clapping faded, Erik shouted, "Thank you, all of you! Now, I'm famished. Laughter makes me hungry!" And he turned toward the food tables.

I hooked a hand around one of his arms, slowing his progress.

"Very well played," I said quietly. "Now, I'd love to hear how you organized all of this without my finding out about any of it."

He chuckled. "It was important that you didn't know."

"Why?"

"Plausible deniability."

I shook my head in wonder. "Fine, but how did *you* know? I mean, how did you know this would even happen?"

"Ah. For that information, you'll need to speak with Myra."

"I'll do that. Meanwhile, I sure as hell don't know how you managed it. I doubt there were more than twenty people here today I didn't speak with directly at one point or another. And no one gave anything away." I clapped him on the back once, stood still, and said, "Well done."

He grinned. "There is no greater power than the one others do not believe you possess. Now, I really am famished."

Aware of movement behind me, I turned and saw Donald nearly skipping toward me.

"Were you surprised?"

His eyes sparkled with a light that made my heart ache with longing. This was my Puck, the Puck I had fallen in love with, the Puck whose love was now given to the deserving Jonathan. I reached deep into my heart to look for a place that was glad for them. Failing, I vowed to look harder, later.

I did my best to smile. "I was. Very."

"Jonathan wrote the better words."

Behind Donald, at a more respectable pace, Jonathan approached. I reached out my right hand as he drew near.

"Well done," I said. "Thank you both, so much, for helping to make today wonderful."

We chatted for a few minutes, and although I asked, they couldn't tell me any more about how this encounter had come about beyond their individual contributions. I led Klondike away and went to find Myra. This mystery was nagging sorely at me.

~

"Imagine, if you will," Myra began when I had found her, "a cloak-shrouded figure, a woman, moving quietly along the path leading from Little Boundary toward The Forest. Imagine her knocking tentatively on the door of the large common house where you've met with Erik before. Imagine her—"

"All right, enough." I chuckled. "Just tell me."

"Fine. Remember when you and Adam and I followed Klondike to the burning barn last winter? And after the rescue, the good pastor," she raised a hand to her mouth and cleared her throat meaningfully, "and his wife appeared, and he was beyond rude to us?"

"An unforgettable afternoon, for so many reasons."

"That cloaked figure was Joan Jermin, Alan's wife."

I felt my eyes widen. "What? What did you say?"

Myra nodded. "She turned traitor, you might say, or at least enough to warn Erik of what her husband was planning. She said it was because of how we'd saved her children's lives, and of how rude her husband had been to us. Pretty wild, huh?"

"That's one word for it."

"Elaine says it shows love can win over hatred, and that good deeds send out ripples. I think that's what gave Erik the idea of laughing."

I shook my head, amazed. "And Jonathan Ehrlich wrote the improved text?"

"He did. I really like that guy. Kind of a waste that he's gay." She laughed at my surprised face. "I'm allowed to say that! By the way, mum's the word on the identity of the spy. She'd be in deep shit if her husband found out."

I nodded. "Weren't you concerned that something unpleasant might happen to the children who went into that crowd?"

She shook her head. "Not at all. They had very, very clear instructions. And they didn't stay long at all, just long enough to make a point."

I felt a hand on my shoulder and turned to see Ben Marks. "Reverend," he said.

I reached for his hand and shook it firmly. "Thank you. I'm so glad your presence alone was all that was needed today."

He nodded. "I confess I was more than a little concerned when Shane told me what was going to happen."

"Wait. Shane MacPherson knew about this as well?"

He laughed. "Reverend, I think everyone but you knew it was going to happen. And you'll be even more surprised to hear now much Vanessa Doyle had to do with it."

I squinted at him, my entire face a question mark.

"Yes, indeed. She and I talked about the best way for my crew to be present without being confrontational. She even suggested I recruit the officers who came from Little Boundary."

For the umpteenth time, I felt my head shaking slowly in astonishment. For here was more evidence that this day signaled the beginning of an end to the enmity among these three communities. If only we could somehow lose the Assembly of God.

CHAPTER 17

By late afternoon, the Beltane crowd had thinned significantly. My work was not over, however; I was in charge of the volunteer clean-up crew. I gave the care of Klondike to Duncan Beale who, I felt, had done enough today and could reasonably be relieved from the work, though I heard him decline a ride home with his parents; it was clear to me that he had enjoyed himself fully and had relished the various responsibilities he'd fulfilled. He was clearly not ready to go home.

As I handed the leash to Duncan, I said, "He should have more water."

"No prob."

Adam found me just before five where I stood with a large trash bag in my left hand and a trash stabber in the other. "We're all heading home," he told me. "There are a few more rituals for us back in The Forest. Sorry to leave you to this mess."

I gave him a tired grin. "I have a feeling most of it came from Assisi residents."

"Yeah, well. I wasn't gonna say that, but…." He tilted his head. "You look exhausted."

I inhaled deeply and nodded. "It's been a rather full day. And I still have to find out how things are going with Kira."

"Oh? Why is that on your plate?"

"Shit," I said, scrunching my face. "I have to call David. I hope the MacPherson's haven't gone out; I need their phone."

"Again, why is this your problem?"

"If Kira's parents turn her out after her public display of—I don't know, transformation, I've identified a place she can go. But David had already left before I made those arrangements."

Adam glanced around the field where roughly thirty people were busy picking up litter and putting chairs away. "I think they can spare you for a few minutes. Come with me."

We walked toward the house together. At the back door Adam took my bag and stabber, set them on the ground, and knocked on the door. Roberta answered.

"We have an exhausted minister here, Gramma. He needs to use the phone, if that's okay, and then he needs a cup of your herb tea. What do you say?"

Roberta smiled and reached for my hand. "Come in, Reverend. I think you've earned a few minutes' rest."

Adam gave me a quick hug and headed out, on his way home.

After a phone call letting David know about the offer from the Lawrences, I sank gratefully onto a chair at the kitchen table and closed my eyes. A few minutes later, Roberta set a dark blue ceramic mug in front of me, full of steaming liquid that smelled wonderful.

"Mint and ginseng," she said. "And here are some ginger cookies for a sugar boost."

I thanked her and lifted the mug, feeling a little energy returning just by inhaling the steam.

She sat in the chair next to me and regarded me for a moment, her grey eyes soft with something like tenderness. "Shane wasn't convinced this would work." She chuckled. "Neither was I, to be truthful. But you've pulled it off."

"With much, much help."

"More than you know."

I glanced at her. "That sounds cryptic."

"That young man, Jonathan, took it upon himself to spread the word in Little Boundary. About Beltane, I mean. About this festival."

I pulled back slightly in surprise.

She added, "Quite a few of the folks here today are not from Assisi or The Forest. They're from Little Boundary."

"Really? That's wonderful. I didn't know." So I wasn't the only one removing barriers. If I had to see Donald with someone else, I was glad it was with Jonathan. And that's when I found that place in my heart I'd sought earlier.

Roberta said, "He's got quite the marketing savvy. He was also all over the field today, talking up his place in Newport."

"I did know that."

"I gather he found quite a few contributors. Very clever of him to set it up as a charity."

I nodded and swallowed a mouthful of cookie. "He's a clever fellow, no question. With a very worthy cause. I wonder if he came up with a name for the place yet."

"I think he has. Prospect House."

"Prospect House," I echoed, allowing the words to feel their way around the inside of my mouth and in my brain. "I like it."

"So do I. I wish Shane and I had more disposable money. We'd contribute if we could."

"You've contributed so much already. Your field was the best possible place for this to happen. I only hope the grass recovers."

"A little grass is nothing compared to what happened here today."

I glanced out of the window toward the field. "Where's Shane?"

She laughed. "He's out there. I'm sure he's telling people how to do everything the way he thinks it should be done."

Brushing crumbs off my hands, I said, "And I'm someone he should be instructing." I drained my mug. "Thanks for this. I feel refreshed enough to tackle more trash."

~

At home later, I barely had energy to pick over a selection of food I'd brought from the festival. Even Klondike, usually inexhaustible, ate slowly.

With some gentle music on the stereo, I reclined on the couch, Klondike snoring softly from where he lay on the floor under the piano. I didn't realize I'd fallen asleep until the phone woke me. A glance at my watch told me it was nearly eleven o'clock.

"Spencer, it's David."

Uncharitably, I thought, *Christ. Now what?*

"I'm calling from the hospital in Newport."

I jerked awake. "Kira?"

"Her father beat her rather badly. Molly called me in a panic about an hour ago and said Kira had run away. But she didn't go far. I found her nearly collapsed on the road, about half a mile from her house. Her face was bloody, and she had trouble walking because of the pain."

"My god in heaven. How bad is it? What did the doctor say?"

"Martha rode with us. She didn't think anything was broken, and the ER doctor agreed. But—my god, Spencer, you should see the welts on her back and legs."

My heart hurt. My eyes stung. "What can I do?"

"You said the Lawrences would take her in. Can you let them know we need to take them up on their offer?"

"Tonight? Will Kira be released tonight?"

I heard him exhale. "No. Sorry; I'm just feeling a little frantic. They're keeping her overnight, and maybe one more day, for observation and to fill her full of antibiotics in case of infection. Tomorrow morning, though, can you tell them?"

"I will. Um, so did you speak to the Blakes?"

"Not yet. But tomorrow Martha and I will both go there to pack up as many of Kira's things as we can manage, provided the Blakes will let us."

"Provided…." I echoed. "Christ. Do they even know Kira will not be coming home?"

"I don't know, and I don't care. I mean, I did tell them I had a family willing to let her stay with them, but I didn't tell them who." He paused, and then, "Shit, Spencer, I'm gonna have to tell Ben Marks about this, aren't I?"

"I suspect the ER doctor will report the incident there, in Newport. They won't have a choice; this is child abuse. They're required to report it."

After a few seconds of silence, I heard, "You're right. I guess I knew that. This just gets worse and worse. If Kira's father goes to prison, I don't know whether her mother would want her back or want her dead."

"Let's take one step at a time. For now, we know Kira will be safe at the Lawrences. And when police call in at the Blakes, at the very least her father will know better than to risk something worse for himself by trying to find her. I hope."

"So I should stop worrying. Right."

"It's like a rocking chair. It gives you something to do, but doesn't get you anywhere." His laugh was tinged with anxiety, but it was a laugh. "If you want to worry about something, consider where Molly falls in all this. She wasn't complicit in Kira's involvement today, but will that protect her?"

"She sounded all right when she called me. If she's home tomorrow when Martha and I go there… hold on. Martha's gesturing at me."

He must have covered the phone with a hand, because for a few minutes all I heard was muffled sounds. Then, "That was a resident psych consultant, checking in on Kira. Seems the doctor had already called the police here in Newport, and they've arrested Howard. Kira's father."

I was fully awake by this point. "I don't know whether this is appropriate, but do you think I should go and check on Molly and her mother?"

"I'd be so grateful. Just wait long enough for me to call her and make sure she's willing to see you, someone she doesn't know."

"Wait. Is Boyd's cover blown? Do you think Mrs. Blake knows what his role really was?"

"Could be. Not worth the risk. I'd rather you went, if she'll agree."

He called back quickly and gave me the address.

Mrs. Blake and Molly were both in tears when I arrived. Molly threw herself at me and wrapped her arms around my chest.

She sobbed, "Kira's in the hospital. They've arrested Daddy."

I hugged her gently. "I know, sweetheart." I wanted to tell her what a good thing it was she had phoned David, but I didn't yet know where Mrs. Blake stood, or whether she knew Molly had called him. I led her to a couch upholstered in a brown and red plaid and turned to her mother, a plump woman wrapped in a threadbare blue terrycloth robe, her short auburn hair crying out for a comb. One side of her face was conspicuously tending toward purple.

"Mrs. Blake, I—"

"Vera, please." Instead of reaching a hand toward me, she made use of a facial tissue she was holding.

"And I'm Spencer. Spencer Hill."

"David said you'd stop by."

"Can I get something for you? Water? Tea?"

She let out an odd chuckle. "Something stronger. And for Molly."

"I can fetch you something, but I can't give spirits to Molly."

"I can."

True. I looked around and found a bottle of brandy and brought it and a couple of small glasses to Vera, who had sat next to Molly. She poured a splash into each glass and handed one to Molly, who sipped it and grimaced.

"Do you good," Vera said, and she downed hers.

I sat in what was probably Howard's usual chair and said, "I assume Reverend Foster is keeping you updated on Kira's condition." I saw her wince at the name, which I had used without thinking, but she said nothing. Molly glanced at me, eyes wide, and then she took another sip of brandy. I asked, "Did anyone give you an idea of what will happen next, regarding the arrest?"

"Depends on whether I want to bail him out."

The air around me was thick with questions. I struggled with which to ask first, especially given that Molly was present. Vera spoke before I could decide.

"And I don't think I will." She set the glass down and sat back, arms crossed in front of her. "I tried to stop him. I want you to know that. I want everyone to know that."

Molly defended her mother. "She did. He hit her, too."

I wanted to ask Molly to let me talk to her mother alone, but she was already in the thick of things. "Vera, may I ask, has he struck you before?"

"Threatened. Never did it."

I nodded. It seemed unlikely he would have struck Molly at all, but the police might well ask that question at some point. I'd just wanted to get a sense of the man. And I liked him less by the minute.

I had more questions. *Tread lightly, Spencer.* "I believe Reverend Foster has told you we've found a place for Kira to stay for a while, so things can get sorted out."

Vera's eyes shot to mine at my second mention of the name Kira. I waited.

Finally she said, "You do that so easily."

"What's that?" As if I didn't know.

"That name. And 'her,' not 'him.' I don't know if I'll be able to get used to that."

I recalled the point Boyd had made to Kira. "This might seem very sudden to you."

"Damn right." She glanced quickly at Molly, evidently regretting her language. "I mean, yeah, it did."

"I believe Kira is trying to understand that it would come as a shock to you, but she's having to balance that with being true to herself."

"As he—she sees it."

At Vera's change in pronouns, I felt my shoulders release some of the tension they'd been holding. "And as unsettling as that might be for you, it does seem to be how she sees it."

I wanted to say that Kira was the only one who *could* say, that she would know who she is better than anyone else. But I wasn't about to have Vera think I was telling her she didn't know her own child.

Molly's eyes had followed these comments, shooting from Vera to me and back again. I suspected she wanted to say something but wasn't sure how it would be received.

Vera heaved a deep sigh, and into the silence that followed, Molly said, "I think she knows. She knows who she is."

Vera glanced at her younger daughter and turned a tortured face to me. "How could this happen?"

"I've read a little about transsexualism, emphasis on 'a little.' I can't say that I understand it. But even if we have trouble accepting it, and even if we suspect that she'll change her mind and be Ralph again, that change would be easier if everyone in her life believed what she's telling us now. If we say, 'Thanks for telling us about yourself, Kira. That's important for us to know,' then if she feels pulled within herself to go back to Ralph it will be easier to tell you that, too. The stronger the resistance, the more she'll dig her heels in, and the harder it would be for her to tell you anything, one way or another."

Vera nodded. "Believe it or not, I told Howie that. He wouldn't hear it." I saw her eyes fill with tears again. "Will I ever get him—her—back?"

Even more tension left me as I heard her words. She wanted her child back. That was step one.

"It won't be up to me, or Reverend Foster. As I understand it, social services will be involved, and I don't know what might happen after that."

I wanted to ask if she'd divorce Howard, or at least keep him out of the house and out of Kira's life, if he didn't go to prison. But someone else, someone whose job it was to make that suggestion, would talk to Vera about her options.

She said, "You and David, though, won't you be asked about it?"

That hadn't occurred to me. "He might, as your pastor. I doubt they'd come to me."

She gave me a glance I couldn't interpret. Then, "You're gay, aren't you." Not a question.

"I am."

She shook her head. "I don't understand that, either. But they aren't likely to ask for your opinion, so it doesn't matter."

That stung. I wasn't sure that was true, but there was no point in arguing with her about it.

I folded my hands in my lap. "There are often things we don't understand about each other. That makes it even more important that we listen to each other, that we truly hear what others are trying to tell us about themselves."

"My child is still a *child*."

"In many ways, yes. But she's sixteen. She's past puberty, past the time in her life when sexual maturity begins. In my opinion, we have no choice but to take her at her word."

"But—" Vera halted, as though not quite sure what she was going to say.

"I think what's important right now is to recognize that this is about Kira. While you and Molly and your husband are important, this particular issue isn't about you. Your husband, in beating Kira, tried to make it all about him. And without overlooking Molly and your own needs, I believe you understand that Kira is the priority right now."

"She's made sure of *that*." No *he*. It was *she* this time. I took heart. Then she added, "You're a minister, though. Isn't there something in the Bible that you can say? Something that might help?"

There was no point in explaining that UU philosophy doesn't rely particularly on Biblical scripture, or that I was unaccustomed to looking to it for support as much as David probably did. But there was something I believed would be appropriate.

"In Paul's first letter to the Corinthians, he reminds us about what Jesus said at the last supper, about eating and drinking in memory of him. Paul wrote in Greek, and the word he used for remembering had a specific meaning in Greek philosophy."

I saw Vera's eyes start to glaze over. I chuckled. "Don't worry. This isn't heavy-going. The word referred to the belief that we know who we are before we're born, and as we're born we forget what we knew. Part of our life's work is to recover who our soul has always been. That is, the truth about who we are is buried deep within us, waiting for us to figure it out." This philosophy, which both Jesus and Paul as Jews would have known about, was central to Judaism. I was not about to tell Vera that.

"So," I let out a breath and sat back, "perhaps for Kira, her realization about herself is something that was true for her soul before she was born. Who can say? I can't, and I don't think anyone can, other than Kira. It's certainly true that each of us understands ourself better as we grow older. This could well be part of her journey of discovery."

The look on Vera's face told me she wasn't entirely convinced I'd provided her with something scripturally useful. I tried again.

"In the Gospel According to Matthew, Jesus tells us that the two most important commandments are to love God with everything we are, and to love others as we love ourselves. The more we know about ourselves, the more we have to love God with. And that second commandment would make no sense unless we love ourselves. So underlying these two commandments are instructions to know ourselves and love ourselves. Putting these two thoughts together, we need to let Kira come to love God as the person she discovers herself to be."

There was a little light in Vera's eyes, but I wanted more.

"I wouldn't let anyone tell me who I am. I don't think you would, either. Nor should Kira."

It was clear to me that I wasn't likely to be able to offer more comfort to Vera or Molly right now, and I was sure I was beginning to repeat myself. I left a card with my contact information on it and took my leave.

"Call me anytime, if you think I can help."

CHAPTER 18

As I drove up to my house I saw a figure sitting on the doorstep. Boyd again? But no. It looked like Duncan Beale. And then I saw the bicycle off to the side, leaning against a tree.

Duncan waited for me to park the Jeep and approach before he stood.

"Duncan? It's past midnight. What are you doing here? Don't you have school tomorrow?"

He answered only one of my questions. "I need to talk to you. It's important."

"All right." I opened the door to find an anxious Klondike awaiting my return. "Just let me put him in the back yard in case— you know." I thought Duncan would offer some rejoinder about what Klondike might need to do, but he was silent. So this was indeed important.

When I returned, Duncan was on the couch, leaning a little forward, elbows on knees and hands clasped. I sat in the easy chair.

"So, Duncan, what's going on?"

"It's about what happened. At the field."

He looked at me as though hoping I would understand him without his having to specify.

"You mean Kira Blake's revelation?" He shook his head, not in negation, but as though trying to clear his thoughts. I added, "I take it this came as a surprise to you."

"No shit, Sherlock." I merely watched his face until he said, "Sorry."

"How well did you know her as Ralph?"

He sat back, arms limp at his sides. "Hell—heck, man, we were gonna start a band. Some friends, I mean. And Ralph, or whoever the f… whoever that is, was gonna be our main singer."

I waited, but he just stared at me. So I asked, "Is there any reason Kira can't be your singer? It's still the same voice, the same musical talent. The same person, inside. No?"

"Everybody's gonna know!"

"What will they know, Duncan? Because I'll tell you what I see. I see a teenager with more guts than I can imagine needing, a teenager who made a very public announcement that she knew was not going to meet with a lot of approval. She shed all her protection, all the lies she'd been wrapping around herself for what must have seemed to her like a very long time. Do I think that was the best way to do it? Not really, no. But I admire her profoundly for doing it."

He gripped his black-dyed hair with both hands, the silver rings on his fingers shining through that darkness. "So you believe this shit?" No apology, no taking back the obscenity this time. "You believe Ralph is really a girl?"

I leaned forward and rested my eyes on my clasped hands, trying to formulate the gentlest response. "I know this, Duncan. If someone told me I was really straight, I would not only not believe them. I would protest. Now, I don't know whether you're straight or not; none of my business. But if you are—"

"I'm straight, okay? Let's get that out of the way right now."

"No, you're not. You're gay."

"No fucking way."

"You are. I can tell. I know who you are better than you do."

It looked as though he was about to protest again, but instead, he said, "I see what you're doing."

"Good. Then you can see what some people are doing to Kira. Don't be one of them."

He stood and paced for a moment. "How can I help it?"

I held my arm toward the couch and he sat down again. "Let me give you an image. Let's say for a moment that you see yourself as a table, and on that table are all the things other people think they know about you. Your favorite color, the brand of potato chips or the flavor of ice cream you like best, how you look with the piercings and the hair style and the leather jacket. There's lots more; everything others see. What kind of table are you?"

"Whaddya mean?"

"Are you an oak dining table? A steel workbench? A kidney-shaped table of brushed nickel?"

"The workbench."

"Great. So you and the person who was Ralph happened to meet, and you saw you had a lot in common, including that you were both boys. Or, that's how you saw Ralph. So in a way, you might easily have assumed that everything you knew about Ralph was on top of a workbench a lot like yours. Then, suddenly, that workbench changes to a table made from a large, irregularly-shaped slice of a tree trunk. It's highly polished, and you can see the grain variations and the age rings. It's a pretty cool table, but it's not shaped like the workbench anymore, so everything you thought you knew about Ralph falls off onto the ground. What do you do now?"

I could almost smell the wood burning, he was thinking so hard. Then, "Is there a right answer?"

"The answer depends on whether you want to leave this person behind or keep them in your life. In the former case, the answer is obvious. In the latter, though, you have a job to do. I could tell you that all the stuff on the ground is still the person you know, that the only thing that changed was the workbench. But that's not likely to help you. Your job, then, is to take a good look at that tree-trunk table, and when you're ready, you pick up the things that fell off, maybe one at a time, and you put them back. When you've finished, you'll be able to see that although the change was very important, most of the things you knew about that person are pretty much the same."

He watched me intently, but I couldn't read his expression.

"If Kira agrees, your band still has a singer if you want one. The same singer you thought you had before. In fact, now that Kira has made herself a person of public interest, that could be good for your band. Everyone will want to come to your performances. At first, it will be to see Kira. But if you're good, they'll be back to hear you. All of you." Of course, things could go the other way, but everything was hypothetical at this point.

He watched my face for a moment and then dropped his eyes. In a sudden motion, he stood. "I gotta think this over."

"Excellent idea. And now, let's put your bike into the back of my car, and I'll drive you home."

When I finally went to bed that night, or that very early morning as it was by then, I left Klondike outside in the fenced back yard, turned the ringer off on my phone, and gave myself permission to sleep late.

Rain pelting against my bedroom window woke me up, but not until ten o'clock. The degree to which my body felt stiff surprised me until I remembered all the clean-up work I'd done, bending over and standing up and walking and bending over and standing up and walking and bending over....

I stayed in the shower longer than was reasonable, but the warm rivulets of water running through my hair, across my shoulders, down my back and legs tempted me in two ways. One was to luxuriate in the sensual pleasure of the water's caresses. The other was to embrace my semi-hard cock with my soapy hands and give it a good cleaning, letting it add its own warm contribution to the swirling foam at my feet.

A lot of men name their penises. Mine had earned his name in my late teens, and the name had been confirmed by the time I had failed—as I'd seen it at the time—to become the Episcopal priest my parents and I had always thought I would be. The failure was because I was gay. So in a way, I felt betrayed. The name Judas had become unavoidably attached to that member.

I had never told anyone his name. I don't recall knowing whether any of the men I'd been with had named theirs. It didn't matter. But as I gazed at the sated, flaccid fellow, relaxed and happily resting on my palm, I chuckled.

"Would you like a new name?" I asked him, and waited.

After a moment, he seemed to smile and say, "I kind of like the name Judas."

A puff of breath escaped me and revealed my surprise. "But why? Will you betray me?"

"Judas did his best to keep Jesus real. To make him remember that he was human. I think sometimes you need to be reminded of that, yourself."

As that remonstrance landed, I laughed. "Aren't you worried that I'll resent you and stop pleasuring you?"

If his laughter had been audible, it would have reverberated off the tiled walls around me.

Klondike was not happy with me, having spent so much time in the cold rain. He'd taken refuge in the massive structure Vanessa had called his dog house, so he wasn't wet, and that thick fur was designed for temperatures far below anything May in Vermont had to offer. Nevertheless, he gave me a sulky look when I brought him inside and fed him breakfast.

My answering machine was full of messages from people

thanking me for organizing the Beltane celebrations, so perhaps it was a good thing that Judas was on the job.

There were a couple of messages that required a return call. I was jotting down reminders when the phone began blinking, and I realized the ringer was still off. I turned it on, and the phone responded with a shrill ring.

"Spencer Hill, here."

"It's done." Donald. But what was "done?" Oh! The closing was today, on the farmhouse near Derby.

"Congratulations. So you're a property owner, now, eh?"

"Well… sort of."

"Explain?"

"My name's not on the documents. Just Jonathan's."

I let a beat go by. "And you're okay with that? Aren't you going to live there with him?"

"Well, yeah, but this is his baby. All the charity rigamarole is in his name. And of course I have no money to speak of, so I can't contribute."

"Aren't you still going to do a lot of outreach? Won't you be helping with all kinds of things once it gets going?"

Silence. A good five seconds of it.

"Spencer, don't harp on this, okay? It's not a big deal."

Something told me it was a bigger deal than Donald wanted me to know, but I let it drop. "When do I get to see it?"

"Um, well, anytime, I suppose. I was kind of hoping you'd have time today. Jonathan is there now."

"Where are *you?*"

"At Loraine's."

"You—you weren't at the closing?"

"No. We decided it was better that way. So, you wanna drive over?"

My brain struggled to understand what "better" would mean, but I knew he didn't want me to question it. "Maybe after lunch? I have some things to do here first."

Before I made myself a late breakfast, I called the Lawrences and let them know where things stood.

"I don't know what's going to happen next," I told Linda. "I'm not even sure when Kira will be released from the hospital. And, under these circumstances, are you and Jeff still willing to take her in?"

"Of course. But what circumstances are you referring to?"

"I don't have any idea what will happen with Howard Blake. That is, whether he'll be released any time soon. But we know now that he can be violent. It's not inconceivable that he'd show up on your doorstep, despite keeping Kira's whereabouts as secret as possible."

Linda laughed softly. "Our next-door neighbor is Police Chief Ben Marks."

I left to get Donald around one thirty. The rain had stopped, and the air felt clean and moist. Warm sunshine glanced off of wet leaves, which seemed to have unfurled and broadened overnight, delighted to receive the nourishing rays. As though the Beltane appeals to the gods and goddesses of Nature had met with approval, the very earth seemed renewed, ready for prolific fecundity.

I had always loved springtime in Manhattan. Even there, although concrete and tarmac covered almost all surfaces, the freshness of the air itself had drawn me into Gramercy Park, to which my family had a key. I had always thought that was the perfect celebration for the season. And I suppose it was, for a city boy. But I was a city boy no longer, and everywhere I looked, everything I saw, confirmed the renewal of life. Maybe, one day, I would be fortunate enough to experience the renewal of love, as well.

I felt rather than heard the sigh that rose from somewhere deep inside my body.

Donald was waiting outside when I pulled up to Loraine's house. To my eyes, he looked as fresh as the season, in khaki trousers and a soft yellow cotton shirt, sleeves rolled half-way up his forearms, a pale blue cotton sweater draped over his shoulders.

"Isn't this weather glorious?" He climbed into the Jeep and promptly rolled down his window.

I grinned. "Glorious? Is that the best you can do, with your dictionary brain?"

He seemed to ignore me as he faced his open window and inhaled deeply. "Ah, petrichor. That smell that comes from the earth after a soaking rain."

"That's more like it," I said as I steered the car onto the road.

Donald's sigh was heavy with satisfaction. "Spring is the best time for komorebi."

I waited perhaps thirty seconds. Then, "I give up."

"It's a Japanese word for sunlight filtered through the leaves of trees."

"Go ahead. Get it all over with now so you can restrict yourself to a normal vocabulary once we get to the farmhouse." I wanted to say *once Jonathan can hear you.*

"I know, I know. He does get testy. But, really, there's nothing so gratifying as redamancy. Loving someone who loves you back."

So many responses bounced around my brain that I ended up not saying anything for several minutes. Like, *Yes; I remember what that felt like.* Or, *Are you sure that describes your situation?* Or, *I envy you; I love someone who isn't in a position to do that.*

Instead, what I did say could reasonably be said to undermine Donald's feeling of being loved by his partner. "Can you tell me why it was better that you didn't attend the closing?"

"Sure. We're not ready to publicize our relationship. It's a small community, so the attorneys and the realtor probably know absolutely everybody. Also, Jonathan feels working with the contractor overseeing renovations will go more smoothly if there's no suggestion that he might be gay. Jonathan, I mean."

Silently chastising myself for ill will, I admitted, "He's probably right."

~

The approach to Prospect House, as it was to be called henceforth, was a fairly long dirt driveway off of a road that seemed to go nowhere else. There were trees along the road, but the farmhouse was set somewhat uphill from the road in an open field. The building was rambling and large, brick walls on the two-story main portion and white-painted clapboards, badly in need of attention, covering the sides of extensions that must have been added on over the years. The roof seemed sound, at least from the outside, but I felt sure Jonathan would make no assumptions about it.

Grass that hadn't been mowed in who knew how long, brown and dried with green shoots poking up from beneath, surrounded the building and guarded the front entry as though daring anyone to pass. Off to the right was an area surrounded by a somewhat dilapidated fence, probably a long-neglected garden. On the other side of the house was a large barn that appeared to be in better shape than the house, its clapboards painted the traditional red.

Jonathan's rented car was parked off to the side next to a dirty white van, "Stafford & Son, Contractors" painted in red on the side. I pulled in beside the van. Donald was out almost before I cut the engine.

"Come see the view!"

I followed as he led the way between the house and the garden, through grasses bent after spending months beneath snow, the occasional pricker bush catching at the legs of my jeans. Donald came to a halt at the top of a slope, hands on his hips and a beatific smile on his face.

Before us, the slope led down to the banks of a small river. Trees and bushes lined the edges, nearly obscuring the rushing blue water. On the other side were a few houses, very far apart, and in the distance beyond them were mountains and more mountains.

Donald pointed more or less north. "Canada. Right there. Well, several miles, but you can actually see into it in clear weather like this."

As we stood gazing into the distance, I felt my hair lift with the light breeze. With no trees nearby, the May sunshine warmed my shoulders and back, as if beginning to fulfill the promise of Beltane.

"This is a gorgeous setting," I said, and then turned to face the house. "Am I allowed inside?"

Donald continued to face Canada. "You may, if you like."

I turned back. "You won't come?"

Still he faced away from me. "Not while the contractor is there. You go ahead."

"Donald…."

His face when he looked at me seemed almost artificial, or perhaps composed, as though to conceal the genuine version beneath. "Like I told you, Jonathan and I both feel it would be better if the crew doing the renovation don't know the goal of Prospect House. And if they see Jonathan as gay, there could be problems that wouldn't crop up otherwise." He shrugged. "Maybe Jonathan can pass. You can. Me? Not so much."

He gave me a smile that, for his sake, I wanted to believe.

I would like to have before and after images of the property, but not if it meant ostracism of Donald. Not if it meant he had to remain out of sight as though somehow not quite acceptable.

I told him, "Well, really, what I want to see is the finished product." It wasn't exactly a lie. "Shall we go back to the car?"

I thought he might protest and say that I should see inside the house, but he didn't. It felt to me as though he was grateful not to be left standing alone outside, or waiting alone in the car—grateful not to be in danger of feeling unworthy, or as though he wore a sign that read UNCLEAN or was required to carry a bell to warn the godly of his approach.

A little histrionic, Spencer, don't you think? I responded to that voice in my head with, *Fitting, though.*

~

On the way back to Assisi, a drive of about forty minutes, neither of us spoke for a while. Donald held his arm out of the open car window, occasionally leaning far enough toward it to allow the wind to have its way with his hair.

I broke the silence. "When do I get to see the house you've rented while work is going on at the farm?"

Donald sat back and turned his face toward me. "Once we're moved in, I think. No point before that." He was quiet for a moment. Then, "Do you know how Kira is doing after her announcement yesterday?"

"I do." I glanced quickly at him and back to the road. "She's in the hospital. It seems her father beat her quite badly."

"What?" His tone carried appropriate horror.

"He's been arrested."

"Oh. My. God." Silence, for several seconds. "So will she go stay with those people you talked to yesterday?"

"Most likely. Her mother is struggling to find a way to accept her, but whether that's the best environment for Kira right now isn't clear."

"And if her father gets out on bail, or whatever…."

"There is that, yes." A few miles went by, images of Kira no doubt occupying each of our minds. I said, "I need to check in with David Foster when I get back, to see how she's doing."

"Is there anything I can do to help?"

I shook my head. "I don't even know if there's anything *I* can do at this point."

"Okay. I have stuff to do, anyway. I'm working on your idea of skits for school kids."

It took me a moment to remember what that idea had been about, and when I did, I chuckled. "I can just see you in high school drama class, directing heart-warming scenes about how much better life can be, with Prospect House helping to make that possible."

"Yup. That's me."

CHAPTER 19

D avid called me Wednesday afternoon to let me know he and Boyd had successfully packed up a significant representation of Kira's belongings and then moved them, and her, into the Lawrences'.

"She seems indomitable," he told me. "No more hint of the suicidal thoughts that put her in the hospital last time."

"What a relief!"

"And I'm talking with her teachers to work out how to catch her up on schoolwork. I'm hoping she'll be up to going back in person soon."

"As Kira?"

He chuckled. "Who else? And how could we stop her, anyway?"

I expected Duncan tomorrow afternoon for his piano lesson, and I felt that would be a good time to get a clearer sense of his reaction to seeing Kira, and no more of Ralph, in classes. Maybe our conversation had helped him come to terms with the change.

I spoke to Donald several times over the next week, though I saw little of him. I was relieved, for his sake, to learn that Jonathan discussed with him the details of work at Prospect House, including him in the project as much as possible given the visitation constraints.

The following Wednesday, May eleventh, I had dinner with Jonathan and Donald, who were still in Loraine's house. Jonathan cooked a small pork roast, stabbed all over with slivers of garlic and small twigs of rosemary. I brought a devil's food cake that I'd made from a mix; I had yet to learn how to bake one from scratch. But it was appreciated, nonetheless; in putting it together I'd done my best to slice horizontally through the two layers I'd cooked, so that there were four thin layers with frosting in between.

"What fun!" Donald clapped his hands when a slice appeared before him. "Chocolate lasagna!"

Dinner conversation was largely about progress at the house in Derby.

"We've decided how much to expand the kitchen," Jonathan told me. "It'll be big enough for groups of kids to learn to cook for themselves."

I heard the "we" introducing that statement and rejoiced for Donald's sake.

"The barn looked to be in good shape," I offered.

"Goats!" I heard glee in Donald's voice. "We're going to have goats. They'll live in the barn, and they can eat the poison ivy that's growing all over the back field."

"The kids will learn to take care of them," Jonathan said. "It's remarkably healing of oneself to take care of others. We might even get set up for cheese-making."

By the time I got home, I felt a sense of delight for all the wonderful things that were planned for Prospect House. And I did my best to feel equally glad picturing Donald, with Jonathan, working with the teens and with each other.

As planned, Jonathan and Donald drove back to New York on

Thursday. They would pack up their apartment in the city and move into the house in Newport on Wednesday, June first.

That afternoon I packed Klondike into the Jeep and headed toward Little Boundary. I felt the need for a bit of an escape, and there was a hike—more of a walk, really—that Marshall and I had taken once, one that I had particularly enjoyed. It hadn't involved the kind of steep hike that he had loved, but part of the trail skirted a sheep meadow, and the lowing of those fluffy animals seemed to call to me. I needed something gentle, something easy, something refreshing and nourishing. And it was a beautiful day.

Plus I needed to counteract the sense of emptiness I was pretty sure had to do with Donald leaving the area.

As usual, Klondike charged ahead on the trail, and then back to me, and then into the woods, and then back. I had the whistle if needed, but the dog seemed to know that I preferred not to be called on to be the disciplinarian today. My pace was slow and easy, and I breathed deeply of the sweet air, scented lightly by blossoms on the occasional apple tree that had survived as the forest had overtaken a long-neglected orchard. These trees were gnarled and twisted, the blossoms were few and might or might not grow into fruit, but the occasional whiff of perfume renewed me.

Soon the meadow came into view. The trail followed along a wire fence with wooden posts that delineated the edge of that property, keeping the forest and any hikers outside. At a place where the elevation offered a sweeping view of the meadow, I stopped and leaned gently on my walking stick. In the distance were sheep, though they weren't the fluffy things I'd seen in the past.

"Of course," I said quietly. "They've been sheared. Tis the season."

Suddenly Klondike was beside me, ears pricked forward, at full attention. I followed his gaze and noticed two dogs, apparently border collies based on the distinctive black-and-white patterns of their fairly long fur, working to corral some of the sheep. I looked down at Klondike and noticed his ears twitching every so often before I realized that I could barely hear the sharp whistles made by a man to communicate with the dogs.

Klondike and I watched in fascination as the collies worked, lowering their heads as they moved toward the sheep, in the manner of predators chasing prey. From this distance, it was almost like watching a ballet, with troupes of white dancers flowing gracefully over green, undulating swells of land. I laughed aloud in delight a few times at the precision that felt like a performance.

It was Klondike who sensed another presence. His low growl and a sudden turn of his head away from the herding spectacle alerted me, and I turned to see a man approaching on the other side of the fence. Perhaps in his forties, he was short with a powerful-looking physique. His leathery skin had already collected enough of the spring sun's rays to begin darkening.

The brim on his canvas hat barely revealed his eyes, which were trained on me with a look that said he was trying to decide how threatening to be.

"Good afternoon," I said, and nodded.

The man stopped about four feet from me, and Klondike moved to be as close to him as possible. He wasn't growling any longer, but he was definitely watchful.

The man squinted at me through the wires of the fence as though trying to figure something out. Then, "Ain't you that gay minister from Assisi?"

It was not a question I cared to answer directly. "I'm Spencer Hill. My church is the Unitarian Universalist of Assisi. And you are—?"

"I saw you. You and those heathens."

With a start, I realized he must have been one of Alan Jermin's congregation, the ones who'd marched onto the MacPhersons' field at Beltane.

"They're actually very nice people. I don't think the word 'heathen' applies very well."

"They ain't Christian. And neither are you."

He had me there.

The man spat on the ground. "You just stay on that side of the fence." He turned and walked away in the direction he'd come, Klondike and I watching him stride off.

I turned back to the sheep-herding performance, struggling to regain my sense of peace.

No use.

"Come on, boy," I said to Klondike. "We'll come back another day. Maybe he won't bother us next time."

The drive home took us past the Assembly of God church. There were two men adding letters to the marquee in front, a recent addition that was so large it was probably meant to be imposing. In reality, it was ugly and offensive. As I drew near, the men completed their job. The letters read:

REASON IS FAITH'S GREATEST ENEMY

"Klondike, my boy," I said to my dog, "one's faith must be pretty damn puny for reason to be its enemy."

Bucolic. Pastoral. Peaceful. All these words applied to the next couple of weeks. The frantic Beltane preparations, the turmoil around the changes in Kira's life, the visit by Jonathan and Donald —hell, just the presence of Donald—had left me feeling depleted and in need of some down-time. I didn't even see much of Adam, what with how much there was for everyone to do in The Forest: caring for newborn animals, completing the last of the ground preparations for planting, transplanting the hardier crops from indoor starter seed beds to their outdoor locations, and so many other seasonal tasks I couldn't keep track of, tasks I had little understanding of.

But there was a cloud bank gathering, in the distance but

threatening, with a darkness that deepened slowly but perceptibly. I knew I would need to address it, and my heart and my brain wrestled with each other to arrive at agreement for how to do that.

As gratifying as the response had been to the invasion of the Assembly of God at Beltane, the aftermath was disturbing. No one said anything to me directly, probably because—as a minister—I'm expected to be nice to everyone.

Had Jermin and his crew done something reprehensible? Yes; I thought so. But the negativity I sensed in Assisi, the birth and progression of something akin to malevolence toward those invaders, troubled me deeply. Should we push back against their ignorance, their prejudice, their narrow-mindedness? Yes, but not with malevolence.

What was most disturbing about the storm clouds I felt gathering around me was that although on the surface it represented something I'd worked for for months—a genuine connection between Assisi and The Forest—what lay beneath was dark and ugly. I wasn't so much of a Pollyanna that I expected all would be sweetness and light. But this? No; hostility toward a common object was decidedly not the connection I wanted.

The time also contained a few surprises. One surprise was that Boyd Harper asked me to meet him in the church office.

"I realize that I haven't done very much to recommend myself as a lay minister here," he opened. "I'm sorry for that, because it's what I had intended, and it's what I had hoped you were thinking about. So I'm sorry if I've wasted your time, but I've decided against pursuing that option."

I hoped my relief did not show on my face or in my voice. "I see. And is there anything in particular that brought you to this decision?"

"Yes. There is. In fact, I'm very much hoping to get involved with Prospect House. I spoke with Jonathan Ehrlich at length about it, in general terms at least, at the Beltane celebration. But I didn't get his contact information. I'm hoping you'd be willing to share that with me."

I paused for a few seconds as several thoughts ran through my mind, including the fact that I couldn't recall seeing Boyd look so happy before today. His focus on helping Kira, his direct approach to problems, and his determination all seemed in line with the kind of work Jonathan was hoping to accomplish.

I wrote on a slip of paper and handed it to Boyd. "Your idea surprised me at first, but after a moment's reflection it makes sense to me. But isn't it rather far from your mother?"

"Yes. About that." He looked down at the paper in his hands and then up at me. "Mom started another fire. I'd told her I was food shopping and would make dinner when I got home. But when I got back, she'd started making something herself, turned the stove on, and then went to read her book."

I pictured the woman I'd met at Beltane, with her makeup carefully applied, her clothing deliberately chosen for the event, and her teasing wit. It was hard to take in that she wasn't always like that. My heart ached for both her and her son.

Boyd added, "It was much less damaging this time, but it convinced her—and me—that she can't really be left alone, and neither of us wants me to be there every minute. I've found a retirement home in Newport that she likes, so we'll be selling her house, and I'll find an apartment or something like that there."

"Will you need any help getting yourself and your mother packed up and moved?"

"Thanks, but her church will help with that."

I stood and held my hand out. We shook hands, and I told him, "I hope everything works out for you. I have a feeling you'd be a boon to the work Jonathan plans."

"Thank you."

Another surprise concerned Myra Langtree.

As my congregation gathered for service on Sunday, May twenty-ninth, I noticed that Myra was in one of the pews toward the back, sitting alone. Of course I would have to wait until after the service to speak to her, but I found myself looking in her direction several times.

My sermon for that day had been inspired by two things. Well, three. One was the man who had told me to stay on my side of the fence the day Klondike and I had watched the shorn sheep on the hillsides. Another was that sign, newly installed at the Assembly of God, with its ridiculously ignorant message. But the real impetus was the negativity I'd felt encroaching on our community after that ungodly invasion by Alan Jermin and his closed-minded crowd.

As I stood, ready to speak, it occurred to me that my message today would apply at least as well to The Forest as it would to me, and as it would to Alan Jermin and his ilk.

"Consider the dandelion. Tooth of the lion, as it could be translated from the original French, so called because of the spiky shape of its leaves. And it's about as tough as a lion. Maybe tougher. With its long taproot, it survives in all climates, hot and dusty to cold and snowy. Those toothy leaves can be added to salad greens or boiled like spinach. We can use the taproot to benefit the health of our liver and our kidneys, as a diuretic and blood cleanser. The sap soothes bee stings. It's self-pollinating, and its seeds don't need a period of dormancy. And if all that isn't enough, we can even use the blossoms for two things: making wine, and keeping young children entertained as they huff and puff and send the white fluff spiders off for new adventures. The dandelion is a wonder of nature.

"But if we see those spiky leaves, those brilliant yellow blossoms, or—horrors!—those fluffy-headed seeds appear in the middle of a field of peas, or beans, or cucumbers, or if they show their faces in the middle of a swath of otherwise impeccable lawn grass, it's an invader to be treated like some kind of terrorist. Out come the trowels, or the hoes, or even the chemical weed killers.

"For that's what we call the dandelion. That's the category we assign to it. A weed.

"As Unitarian Universalists, Ralph Waldo Emerson is perhaps the closest thing we have to a saint. He once described weeds as plants whose virtues we haven't yet discovered. But the dandelion has many virtues. Many benefits. So in what way is it a weed?

"A man ironically named Michael Pollan—though he spells it differently from that stuff that's the bane of allergy sufferers—wrote a book entitled *Second Nature,* in which he categorizes plants according to how cultured they are, how hard they are to grow, and the color of their flowers. At the top are the civilized, aristocratic plants such as roses and orchids. The lowliest plants, then, are the proletariat. The peasants. The great unwashed. That is, the weeds. The unwanted. The pariahs."

I paused, giving everyone a chance to consider whether they might be seen by someone as a weed, or whether they saw others that way.

"But what if we don't know the benefits of something we call a weed? What if we didn't know about the dandelion's many benefits to our health and well-being? What if we just saw it appear where we didn't think it belonged?

"And conversely, what if, instead of eradicating it on sight, we took the time to understand what lies beneath its appearance, or beyond the context in which we see it?"

I paused again, this time for effect. When I spoke next, I pitched my voice to be deep and loud.

"Are people weeds? Or is it just that we sometimes treat them that way? And what would tempt us to do that? Do they look different from us? Do they believe in things we don't agree with?"

I lowered my voice to a harsh whisper.

"Do they frighten us?"

I took a deep breath and closed my eyes briefly, and then gazed with softened eyes around the congregation.

"The inherent worth and dignity of every person. Justice, equity, and compassion in human relations. Acceptance of one another, and encouragement to spiritual growth in our congregations. A free and responsible search for truth and meaning. The right of conscience and the use of the democratic process within our congregations and in society at large. The goal of world community with peace, liberty, and justice for all. And respect for the interdependent web of all existence, of which we are a part. These are our principles as Unitarian Universalists.

"We can respond to weeds with poison. But poison is something we give to others that damages us. So, instead, let's do our best to *understand* the plants—or people—that look like weeds." I chuckled. "Mind you, they might still be weeds. But if they truly deserve that description, perhaps they are to be pitied rather than vilified. Being Unitarian Universalists does not make us better. But let's do our best to mean it makes us more loving."

I'm sure that ministers everywhere find themselves in relative darkness when it comes to knowing whether the messages in our sermons landed the way we hoped. My "weeds" sermon, containing as it did a fist-in-velvet reprimand, probably meant that people who saw themselves in it avoided me as they left the church that day. Or perhaps a few of them were among those who chuckled and told me, "Excellent sermon for spring, Pastor Hill. Dandelions, indeed!"

I managed to keep track of Myra, though it didn't seem as though she was in any hurry to leave. When the crowd had mostly wandered outside, I found my way to where she sat, off to the end of a back pew. I sat beside her.

"I'm delighted to see you here," I told her. "You came alone?"

She eyed me briefly, as though contemplating a response. Then she smiled. "Yes. As far as I know, I'm the only one from The Forest who wants to join your congregation."

I blinked stupidly, my mind grasping at random words that held no meaning and had no function here.

Myra laughed. "Yes, I imagine you're having a hard time parsing that. Is there somewhere we could talk privately?"

I led her to the parish office and closed the door. We sat on a bench in the front hall, and I waited for her to speak.

"I'm leaving The Forest."

As flummoxed as I was, I managed, "Can you tell me why?"

She sighed and stared before her, seemingly at nothing in the office. "I thought leaving Sedona and coming here would bring me closer to the way of life in the Pagan community. Instead, it's clarified things for me in a different way."

She turned back toward me. "I still love and respect that way of life. But I don't see myself living it, still, as I grow older. I don't see myself as a wife and mother, raising children in that life." She gave a humorless chuckle. "I'm not sure I see myself as a wife or a mother at all. And I've come to realize that I'm not a good fit as a companion for Adam."

In my ministry, I've learned how not to reveal being stunned by information that takes me unawares. So I was able to say, "I see. And have you told anyone there?"

"I have. Erik and Elaine both know. Adam and I have had several conversations about it. He hasn't mentioned it to you?"

I shook my head.

She nodded. "That's to his credit. I did ask that he say nothing until I'd reached a decision and told others, myself."

"Have you... have you moved out of The Forest?"

"I'm in the process of moving into the house Loraine Fuller is renting out, now that she's with Vanessa."

"Really? Donald and Jonathan were just there."

"Yes. That's how I knew about it."

"And you'd like to join us? As a Unitarian Universalist?"

"I've been doing some reading, and some research, and somewhere—can't remember where—I saw something. Let me see if I can recall it."

She closed her eyes as if reading from the insides of her eyelids, and I saw her fingers move, counting while she spoke.

"You might be a Unitarian Universalist and not know it if you believe there is no conflict between religion and science, if you believe all the world's religions contain some wisdom, if you believe religion should be a search for truth and meaning in life, if you believe we are a part of the interdependent web of nature and not the master of it, if you yearn to be part of a community of seekers after truth, and if you believe working for social justice is a spiritual act."

She opened her eyes, and they seemed to bore into mine. "Is that accurate?"

I nearly laughed with the delight that started in my heart and spread throughout all of my being. "I couldn't have said it better."

"So. What do I need to do?"

"I can provide you with some literature about UU, which you might not have encountered in your research. But as you've probably learned, there is no formal process for coming into the church. We have no dogma, no doctrine to which anyone must swear allegiance. You don't even have to leave other belief systems behind. You could remain Pagan and still be a UU. As you'll see in the material, we encourage everyone to discover their own spiritual path, to ask questions, and to look deeply for answers. We find those answers everywhere—from other religions, from science, from everyday interactions with each other. And sometimes we learn to get comfortable with the questions when answers seem elusive."

"So I just attend services?"

I laughed. "If only all the UUs in Assisi did that every week!"

I shifted my position to face her more directly. "In essence, you join the community. I already know quite a bit about you that fits smoothly into the UU tradition. But I wonder if you can tell me a little more about how you made this decision."

She gave me a wry smile. "Don't tell anyone I said this, but I was beginning to find living as a committed Pagan to be a little confining."

I'm sure I revealed my surprise at that point. My experiences with Forest Dwellers had been anything but confining. "In what ways?"

"I get a little tired of all the sabbats and festivals and ceremonies. They all seem to run into each other for me. I don't mean to disparage them, or criticize in any way. I can see the meaning in them, and I don't doubt the sincerity of the practitioners." She sighed and shrugged. "I guess I just want to live a day-to-day kind of life. Who knows? Maybe I'll return to a more ritualized life at some point. But right now, I want to find out more about who I am outside of that lifestyle."

I shook my head, puzzled. "I have to say, Myra, the picture you draw has very little in common with my perception of what life is like in The Forest. But you are the one who lived it. And I don't know how to tell you how very welcome you will be in the Assisi congregation."

We smiled at each other for a moment, and then I asked, "What can I do to make your move into town as smooth as possible? Do you need anything in the way of furniture that isn't already there?"

She shook her head. "As you know, the house has Loraine's furniture in it. Adam has been driving me back and forth as I pack a few things to bring with me. The only thing I don't have is a car. I do have some money, so if there's someone who can help me find a good used car, that would be very helpful."

"As it happens, I do know of someone. Johnny Caldwell. May I have him call you at Loraine's? I mean, at home?"

She laughed. "You can give him that number. But I might be more reachable in The Forest until school is out. I'll continue teaching at the grammar school there, but until I have a car, it's best if I don't live outside the community."

"And will you teach there again in the fall?"

"That's the plan. Yes."

Again, that warm feeling spread through me. Last fall, after I'd learned of the reason for the rift between The Forest and Assis, and even after the truth had come out, I'd told myself to settle for a slow and halting progression of good will between the communities. I'd given up my first idea, that there would be a real interchange between us. Elaine Gault had deemed me Assis's ambassador to The Forest, but the job description had felt amorphous. Then, Myra had suggested a Beltane collaboration. And now she would live in Assisi and teach school in The Forest.

I did my best to appear calm, but internally I was nearly beside myself with joy.

Myra and I chatted for a few more minutes, and then she left to walk "home" and work on getting settled in. After I called Johnny, who was a mechanic in my congregation, I sat at my office desk and allowed Myra's news to sink in. She was so well-suited to the UU tradition that I was almost surprised I hadn't thought already that this might happen.

Sure, she and Adam had been considering marriage in a vague kind of way, and sure, she had come from a Pagan community in Sedona not terribly unlike The Forest, but she fit so well into my congregation. She had slid seamlessly into the position Marshall had left, to work with Jenny on Teens for Truth, and she'd seemed completely at home working with people outside The Forest in Beltane preparations. I wondered whether this would be the first time she had lived alone, and whether it would make her feel lonely. But she was still part of a community. Mine.

CHAPTER 20

I was just finishing my lunch of leftover tuna casserole Monday when Jenny Pratt called me.

"Myra's just given me her news!" Apparently Jenny saw no reason to contain her own excitement. "This is beyond wonderful!"

I chuckled. "I agree. She's already part of our community in so many ways."

"Which brings me to my reason for calling. What do you think of asking her to be a lay minister? I mean," she spoke hurriedly as though to stave off interruption, "she's already familiar with so many of our congregation, and her spirituality couldn't be a better fit. She's been so, so helpful with the teens, and—"

I laughed. "Jenny, Jenny. Slow down! Or, actually, there's no need to make your case any stronger. That thought occurred to me last night, just as I was about to fall asleep." I smiled at the phone. Then, "I trust you've said nothing to her about it yet."

"Oh, no. Of course not. I just wanted to make sure you're considering it. And, as you know, Andrea and I are spread kind of thin these days."

She was right about that. It had been a challenge for the two of them since Marshall had left, months ago, and Loraine's exit from that role had followed. I'd done what I could to fill the gap, but the roles are different enough, and my own job was busy enough, that there was only so much I could do.

"Yes, and I'm sorry that's true. As you know I was considering Boyd, but he's—"

"I haven't told you this, but Andrea and I both don't think he'd be a great choice for us. Nothing against him, but…." Her voice trailed off.

"I agree. Though there was no reason for you to avoid telling me what you thought. And did you know that he's decided to move to Newport?"

"Oh! No. I didn't know."

"Well, unless you tell me something to change my mind, I'm thinking that once Myra has moved into Loraine's, I'll give her another week or so and then talk to her about the lay minister role, see if she's interested. How does that sound?"

"That's good. Andrea and I can certainly hold out until then. And, Spencer?"

"Yes?"

"I don't know whether Andrea has said anything to you, but I want you to know how very happy we are that if we had to lose Vanessa as our minister, it was you who came to us."

The room suddenly became blurry from the tears that arose. I wasn't sure I trusted my voice, but I said, "Thank you. Thank you so much."

The good news about Myra helped distract me from spending too much time thinking about Donald and Jonathan moving into their Newport rental house on Wednesday. I couldn't even call to wish them welcome to the area, because if they had a phone installed I didn't know the number.

Saturday afternoon I was just getting ready to walk Klondike down to McGowan Pond when an unfamiliar car parked in front of my house. It was a Jeep, a lot like mine, only dark red where mine was dark green. And at the wheel was Myra Langtree.

From my front steps, I watched as she climbed out, a big smile on her pretty face. She waved an arm as she approached.

"Isn't this perfect?" she said. "I can't thank you enough for getting Johnny to help me."

"Come in, come in! Tell me all about it."

She saw that Klondike was on his lead. "Are you heading out?"

"We were going to McGowan's. But I want to hear about your car first."

She laughed, a delightful, musical sound. "Pile in! I'll drive us there and walk with you."

As she drove, Myra told me she and Johnny had met late Monday afternoon and again later that week.

"He seems to have scouted everywhere in the world. He even had a friend drive him down to St. Johnsbury Thursday so he could see this car. And then," she gave me a look as if to test the credibility of what she was about to say, "he bought the car himself and drove it back. He knew how much I could spend, and he was determined to find a car that would be able to get me in and out of The Forest in bad weather. Of course, I paid him back. And isn't this a beauty?"

"It is. I love mine. What year is this?"

"Nineteen eighty. Yours?"

"Nineteen eighty-four."

She parked, and we walked the trail in companionable silence for a time. As we approached the pond, I asked whether Adam had ever told her I'd seen him here, sky clad.

Again, that musical laugh. "He did. Only at the time, he didn't think very much of you."

I chuckled. "Nor did his opinion improve for quite some time."

She smiled at me. "He's changed his tune since then. Sings your praises, even."

"That's nice to hear. I'm quite fond of him."

On the far side of the pond, we found moderately comfortable rocks to sit on, and I let Klondike roam for a bit.

Myra glanced at me. "May I tell you something in confidence? Something that—well, something I'm not quite sure you want to hear?"

"Whoa. With that preamble, how can I refuse?"

"It's something Adam said about you. And Donald."

She bent over to pick up a couple of pebbles as though to deflect from the possible significance of what she was going to say. I said nothing.

"He doesn't think Donald will stay with Johnathan. He thinks Donald will want to be with you again."

My chest felt suddenly tight, and part of that stress moved up into my throat. As calmly as possible, I said, "What makes him think that?"

"He likes Jonathan, for the most part, though he sees him as limited."

"Limited?"

"He says you and Donald are both multi-faceted, and that although Jonathan has depth, his personality is—I think Adam used the word singular."

"I see. Well, that's interesting. Though I can't say it seems very likely to happen."

We gave that some space, in which I allowed myself to wonder if Adam had seen what I'd seen—that Donald seemed more or less limited to the role of comic to Jonathan's straight man. Could Adam be so perceptive that he'd picked up on my own impressions? In a moment of weakness, I wanted Adam to be right. I wanted him to have seen that, with me, Donald felt he could express all of himself, not just the submissive, and not just the clown.

But—be with me again? Why? How? Was it even remotely possible that Donald would want to be a minister's partner? It was absurd.

I stood so suddenly that Myra seemed startled.

"Klondike! Here, boy!" The dog came running, and I made a show of ruffling his ears and butting my forehead against his. It was affection, but it was also a distraction. I didn't want Myra to see how her words had affected me. I didn't want to admit it to myself.

Myra and I walked in silence for maybe five minutes, Klondike trotting beside us, unleashed. Then Myra asked, "How well do you know Johnny?"

Glad of the change in subject matter, I didn't pick up immediately why she might be asking. "Not well, exactly. I do know that he's often among the first to offer help to someone in the congregation, if it's something he can do."

"He doesn't wear a ring. Do you know if he's partnered?"

That question woke me up, and suddenly I knew why she was asking. Johnny was only a few years older than she was. I wouldn't have called him handsome; he had the sort of face that was so homely it was lovable. If he was going to develop a belly, it wasn't evident yet. He was soft-spoken, and when he spoke it was because he had something to say.

And he had driven to St. Johnsbury to get Myra's car.

"As far as I know, he's single. He was seeing a young woman last fall, I believe. At least, they often came to church together. But they don't even sit together any longer."

I was dying—dying!—to ask why she wanted to know, to comment on her observation about his ringless hand.

She said nothing else for a couple of minutes. Then, "He offered to help me move the last of my things into Loraine's after school lets out on the tenth."

Feigning lack of curiosity, I asked, "What did you tell him?"

"Nothing, yet. But I'm inclined to accept."

I turned to face her and smiled. "I would, if I were you."

She stepped closer to me and slipped her arm through mine.

During service the next day, Myra sat with Jenny. I could see where Johnny Caldwell sat, but I couldn't tell whether he was with anyone in particular. However, I could tell that several times he glanced to where Myra sat. I kept having to suppress my smiles.

And the next Saturday, while I was out walking Klondike, I happened to see the red Jeep driving nearby, in the direction of Loraine's house, which I needed to start thinking of as Myra's. Through the Jeep's open windows, I saw that Myra was at the wheel, and Johnny Caldwell was in the passenger seat.

I did nothing to hide my smile that time.

For the next several days, I spent a lot of energy trying in vain to put out of my mind what Adam had told Myra about Donald. I also spent energy trying not to focus on the lack of a phone call from Newport. Surely, Donald being Donald would want to tell me about the move, no? And about progress at Prospect House?

I wanted to hear from him. And I didn't want to hear from him.

Friday was my birthday, not a day I was accustomed to celebrating beyond merely noticing. My parents had always done just enough: my favorite meal, a cake, and a few gifts. I hadn't told anyone here in Assisi about the date. Partly it was that I didn't want them to feel obliged to make a fuss. Partly it was just that given my history, I wasn't expecting one.

Klondike and I had finished our dinners Friday evening when the phone rang. It was Andrea Beale.

She sounded quite distressed. "Spencer! Something terrible has happened!"

"What? What's wrong?"

"Someone has vandalized the piano at the church."

At first I had no words. Then, "How bad is it?"

"I think you should come and see for yourself. I'm here now."

Not knowing how long I'd be gone, I tied Klondike behind the house, all the while wondering how someone could have done that. My house was right next door; wouldn't I have heard something? Had someone waited until I'd gone out?

I used my long legs to hasten toward the church. The lights were on inside, and I expected to see the business manager, John Thompson, inside, because he had a key. Andrea waited, apparently anxious, at the open double doors. Without a word, she stepped aside, and I strode in, my eyes on the piano, which from this distance didn't seem harmed. I'd made it about half-way down the center aisle before I stopped suddenly.

"Surprise!"

My heart jumped into my throat as crowds of people leapt up from hiding places between pews near the front of the church, and colorful streamers shot into the air.

My jaw was nearly on my chest as the next shouts nearly knocked me over. "Happy birthday!"

All around me, people were laughing, no doubt congratulating themselves at the success of their ploy. I stood, hands on my head, tears in my eyes, and looked from face to smiling face. Never in my life had anyone thrown a birthday party for me, let alone a surprise party.

I closed my eyes and felt a couple of tears squeeze from under my eyelids, and I let feelings wash over me. Amazement. Wonder. Joy. And, above all, love.

People began to crowd close to me with hugs and handshakes and smiles. I was enraptured. Couldn't get enough.

Eventually the hugs and handshakes thinned out, and as I looked around again I saw Vanessa in her wheelchair, grinning broadly. I moved toward her and knelt, taking her hands in mine.

"Did you tell them?" I asked. She would have known, having had access to my personal records.

"I did."

I glanced up at Loraine, behind Vanessa. She, too, had a smile like Vanessa's, and like my smiling face hers showed signs of happy tears.

I stood and turned to look around again, and my eyes met Donald's.

"I don't think I ever knew when your birthday was," he said. "By the time June came around, the year we were together, I was already in thrall to that… you know."

I took a deep breath, and as I let it out Donald stepped forward and wrapped his arms around me. I let my head fall against his and hugged him back. I don't know how long I would have stood there if Jenny hadn't clapped her hands for attention.

"Okay, everyone!" she called. "Cake and goodies in the function hall!"

Donald took my arm and we moved with the crowd. Someone else took my other arm, and before I looked I expected it to be Jonathan. But it wasn't.

Adam.

"Quite the production," he said. "And I still haven't figured out how mad I am at you for stealing Myra away from us."

His smile belied his assertion of anger, and the three of us walked arm-in-arm toward the hall.

There were perhaps five multi-tiered cakes waiting for us, each one with the initials "S H" scrawled on top in bold, colorful icing. Only one had candles, and I obliged everyone by making a silent wish—that the Universe would help me act in the best way possible for my congregation and for myself in the coming year—and blowing them out.

As is often the case, giving people something to eat quieted the crowd a little, and I had time to ask Donald about his move.

The first thing I said, though, was, "Jonathan's not here?"

He shook his head, his mouth full of cake.

Myra, beside him, said, "Donald's been at mine since last night. He's been helping get this whole event ready."

I looked at Donald. "But how did you even know about this?"

Donald gave Myra a significant look I couldn't interpret, and then he said, "Myra and, um, a friend, drove out to Prospect

House Sunday afternoon, and invited us. Jonathan was pretty busy, so Myra and I hatched a plan."

A friend.... I glanced at Myra, who blushed. A glance over her shoulder confirmed my suspicion; Johnny was not far away.

I glanced around for Vanessa to thank her for getting everything in motion, but I didn't see her. I couldn't see Loraine, either, so I knew they must have gone home. Vanessa's energy would not have lasted very long here. It was something of a miracle that she was still with us, considering that her doctors had expected the cancer to overtake her completely a month ago. I sent a quick message of thanks to the Universe.

At one point I managed to slip off alone to a corner of the room where I could look around at all these wonderful people. They were all here for me. For me! There had been planning and scheming and secrecy, time and energy spent for my party. So many of these people had worked their way into my time, into my life, into my heart. And, it seems, I'd managed to mean something to them as well.

Just before I stepped back into the friendly fray I caught sight of David and Martha Foster. Very near them was Boyd Harper, standing protectively near Kira. And then I saw Linda and Jeff Lawrence. I'd been able to support them in the process of becoming Kira's foster parents, a huge win for everyone.

Food disappeared gradually, as did the punch and soft drinks. Andrea and Jenny shooed me out before quite everyone had left, insisting that I mustn't lift a finger by way of clean-up. It was at that point that it struck me that no one had brought a wrapped gift. None needed; I felt I'd been given the best gift I could possibly have received.

Adam walked me home, and then into the house, and then into my bedroom.

"Happy birthday, Spencer," he said as he began to undress me. His mouth covered mine and our tongues played with each other as my dick filled with excitement and my clothes dropped. Adam nearly ripped his own clothes off before pushing me onto the bed. He took me into his mouth with a force that made me gasp.

I was barely aware of my hands clenching bedclothes, of my jaw straining toward the ceiling, of my harsh, rasping cries as he sucked and slid, his teeth barely touching me in all the right ways, his fingers digging into my ass as though to puncture the very muscle.

I came with a scream that sounded foreign to my ears and lay on my back, panting, until Adam flipped me over. I heard a condom wrapper tear and felt the slippery coolness of lube, and then he entered me with a tenderness I couldn't recall him ever displaying in the past. He moved in and out of me with a sweetness that nearly made me weep. Even in orgasm, he was gentle in a way that carried a deep sadness.

We lay together, silent, for several minutes. And then I looked at his face. I saw unshed tears.

"What?" I asked. "Is something wrong?"

His mouth formed a soft smile, and he stroked my face and then my hair. "I wanted our last time to be special."

"What do you mean?"

He kissed me and said, "I'm pretty sure we won't be doing this again."

I felt tears form in my own eyes. "Why do you say that?"

He kissed me again and rose from the bed.

"Adam?"

As he dressed he watched me, and I half-sat, half-reclined, not knowing what to say, what to do, feeling a profound sadness that Adam wouldn't account for.

Then he kissed me deeply. "I will miss you, Spencer Hill."

And he left.

CHAPTER 21

I lay on the bed in a confounding profusion of emotions, a mix of the elation from my surprise party and the confusion from Adam's words and his departure. What was he telling me? That we'd be together like this never again? But why?

Through my open bedroom window I was barely aware of a light breeze that carried with it the scent of soft rain as it strikes the dry earth. Petrichor, Donald had called it.

Donald. Was Adam leaving this part of our relationship behind because of what he believed would happen?

I'll have to talk to him, I decided. *I'll have to tell him he's mistaken.*

Klondike's soft bark roused me from my thoughts. No doubt he wanted to come in from the rain, doghouse notwithstanding. I threw on my bathrobe, went downstairs and let him in, gave him a treat, and took a glass and a bottle of Scotch into the living room. I sat in a large upholstered chair, in the dark, musing about how much darker the black piano was than the room around it, pouring more Scotch a few times as my glass became repeatedly empty.

I couldn't recall ever feeling as confused as I felt that night. These Forest Dwellers, these special people, had shown me that they have powers and sensitivities I'd never witnessed in anyone before.

I'd seen wonders. And yet I'd never seen Adam exhibit anything that could remotely be called paranormal, or even mystical. Had I just missed it? Was he, in fact, able to see or feel what was going to happen? Did he have a perception that allowed him to know what would happen between Donald and me? Perhaps I could ask Myra whether she'd witnessed anything like this about Adam.

∾

I awoke just after dawn, slumped on my side in the chair, still in my robe. Klondike lay on the rug near me, head on his paws, his eyes on my face. When he saw I was awake, he did that thing I've heard domesticated dogs have learned how to do to ingratiate themselves to humans, or vice versa. His eyes looked up at me as first one eyebrow and then the other lifted and dropped. Wolves, I had been told, and other wild canids, didn't do this. Probably they didn't care much about people, anyway.

Klondike lifted his head and then his large body as I sat up.

"Breakfast, boy?"

He seemed to smile, his black-lined mouth opening to reveal the pink tongue. For just a moment I allowed myself to admire him, with his thick white fur, merry black eyes, moist black nose, and his floppy, golden-tipped ears.

I smiled back and stood, a little unsteady after the prodigious amount of Scotch I had consumed last night.

∾

Around five thirty I had just come home from a few parish visits, including a couple of stops to thank people who, I was sure, had been the main organizers for my party. High on that list was Vanessa. Each time I saw her, I wondered how many more times I would have that pleasure.

As my car drew close to home, I saw Donald sitting on my

doorstep. He looked up as I drew near. I would have expected him to smile. He didn't, and I grew concerned.

He waited until I had parked the car and was approaching him before he stood. "Did you enjoy your party?" Now he smiled, but it wasn't his usual, light-hearted grin.

"I certainly did. And I thank you for your part in it."

He was silent for several seconds. Then, "Do you have a few minutes for me?"

"Only a few?" I smiled. "As many as you'd like. Do you want to come inside?"

He glanced toward the door and then at me. "Could we walk somewhere?"

"Of course. I know a nice walk up near a sheep farm. Is it okay if I bring Klondike?"

~

We walked in silence for a while along a part of the trail I hadn't followed before, one that was wide enough for us to be side by side. Around us, and along the sides of the trail, all kinds of grasses and other plants had shot up from the ground, many with tiny white flowers, others boasting slightly larger purple or blue blossoms.

Donald broke the silence. "Why do you think we don't often see red wildflowers?"

"Hmmm. I've never thought about it."

"I remember that tree with pink fur we saw earlier this spring."

"The redbud. No more fur on it now, I'm afraid." He said nothing else, so I decided to prod. "I get the impression there's something on your mind."

Donald stopped walking. I stopped and turned toward him. He stood almost like a statue, eyes gazing forward at nothing that would have caught my attention. I waited while he let out a couple of long breaths.

Still facing forward, eyes almost glazed, he said, "I'm leaving Jonathan."

Stunned. I was stunned. At first no words of my own came to mind, just Myra's: *He doesn't think Donald will stay with Jonathan.* In truth, I spent several seconds wondering if I could speak at all. It was a massive effort to block out Myra's other words: *He thinks Donald will want to be with you again.*

Finally I said, "May I ask why?"

He moved forward again, and I fell into step with him as Klondike emerged from the woods off to the side and took a position beside me.

"So many reasons." I waited, and he added, "Mostly, it's that I don't much like myself when I'm with him. It's taken me months to realize this. I'm tired of always being the cheerful one. So lately I've been letting that role fall away if I didn't feel like playing it. When I do that, we don't get along."

Playing a role.... Of course! This was the actor in Donald. Suddenly it made sense; it was clear why I'd seen him submissive to Bruce, and then whimsical with Jonathan. I asked, "You were reading your audience?"

He stopped again and turned toward me, his eyes intense. "Exactly! That's exactly what it's like. I knew you'd understand."

"Have you told him?"

"Yeah."

"What did he say?"

By some silent agreement we moved forward again. He said, "I'd rather not go into that."

"What are you going to do now?"

"I have a bit of a plan. But only a bit. Myra's going to drive me to Montpelier tomorrow. I'll catch a train there to New York and stay with Ruth and Nelson for a while. Not sure how long. I want to be sure that the city isn't still calling to me."

I swallowed and cleared my throat. Pitching my tone to be as even as possible, I said, "Do you think it might be?"

He released an exasperated sigh. His tone petulant, he nearly whined, "I don't know."

I let several seconds go by. "It sounds like you're trying to choose between a life supporting Jonathan's dream and a life in which you could resume your own. Or at least, a dream that used to be yours."

"You're proving my point, you know."

"Which point would that be?"

"When I try to talk to Jonathan about this, it's obvious he's not taking me seriously. And if I keep going, he says things that imply —he'd never say this directly—that my acting career was frivolous. That it contributed nothing to the betterment of mankind."

I laughed. "Sorry. Really. It's just that I could almost hear Jonathan's voice for a minute."

"You can laugh if you want. But he actually held you up as an example."

"Of what? Mankind's betterment?"

"Yes! Your ministry. Helping people. Forging a spiritual path."

My turn to stop dead in my tracks. "What utter bullshit." I'd lost track of the number of times I'd wondered about how much room Jonathan was making for Donald in their relationship. Now I was angry. And in my defense of Donald I neglected to realize that I was pointing him south, away from me. "When you do what you love, you connect with people. You help them connect with each other."

"Will you tell me how you see acting doing that?"

Flustered, I raised my arms and let them fall back to my sides. "Acting… acting gives the audience a safe way to see inside the minds and hearts of someone else, but safely, because it's fiction. It also holds up a mirror. Let's people see themselves in a way nothing else can." I heard rather than intended for my voice to rise. "It's almost like calling Shakespeare frivolous!"

"Or Anthony Shaffer. Or Peter Shaffer."

We stared into each other's eyes, and I had no doubt that both our minds were traveling back in time, back to nineteen eighty-three, to the classroom where our eyes had met for the first time. To the acting class where I'd hoped to improve my elocution skills, to be better able to deliver a sermon that would move members of future congregations. Donald had offered to work one-on-one with me for reasons that had to do only loosely with the fact that his father had been a minister. We had started with *Sleuth* by Anthony Shaffer. I had gone on to read his brother Peter's work, *Equus*, which had given me insights into my own life I don't think I would have seen in any other way.

As I pictured that classroom, I remembered asking Donald why he, clearly an accomplished actor, was taking the class. What had he said? I couldn't recall. So I asked again, now, here, on this dirt trail, many miles away from that classroom in New York City.

"Why did you sign up for that class?"

His face took on a teasing look, tongue-in-cheek, and he tilted his head slightly. "What did I tell you at the time?"

"Nothing that made any sense."

He laughed, head thrown back, mouth wide open to release an astounding mirth. "Oh, Spencer! You innocent." He gasped a few breaths as his laughter subsided. The mirth remained. "I followed you in."

"You *what?*"

"Oh, I did sign up for the class after that, so I could keep coming. But I'd seen you on the street, on your way to class that first day. At first all I noticed was that you were drop-dead gorgeous. But there was something else, something that seemed like a darkness that had been placed on you. Into you. Not something that came *from* you. And I wanted to see if I could lift it."

We stood, motionless, wordless. And then Donald said, "Crepuscular."

My laugh came from something akin to relief. "Now, that one, I know. It refers to twilight, to the gloaming. It's what's happening around us right now."

"What a wonderful word. Gloaming."

As though shot from a gun, Klondike darted away from us and

up the trail. It was not a normal burst of energy. He was after something. I reached for my whistle as I trotted after him, Donald on my heels. I kept my eyes on the dog's white fur, starkly visible in the dusky light, even as he kept increasing the distance between us. Before I saw that we were approaching the fence that bounded the sheep pasture, Klondike had found an opening near the ground and had dived under it and out onto the grass on the other side.

"Klondike!" I called. "Here, boy!" I blew the whistle, again and again as Donald examined the place the dog had breached.

"How did he get through here?" Donald said, almost to himself. "We'd have to strip naked or all our clothes would catch."

At a distance of about three hundred yards I could see the two border collies I'd watched in the past. They seemed frantic to get the sheep herded into a tight bunch. For their part, the sheep seemed unwilling or unable to do anything they were told, clearly terrified of something. I scoured the area for another human and saw no one. I heard none of the sharp whistles that had guided the collies before.

"Look!" Donald raised an arm and pointed just off to the side of where the sheep were milling about.

Three shapes, then four, then five, just dark enough to be difficult to see in this light and at this distance, approached from the direction of the woods. They had the appearance of dogs, but I knew they were something else.

"Wolves?" Donald's voice was hushed, intense.

"Coyotes."

Suddenly there were three more of them, circling around to either side of the sheep, heads up and looking around, in a near-trot that made it look as though they had springs in their feet. Klondike, meanwhile, had reached the collies, and he worked with them to corral the sheep. My initial thought was, *How did he know to do that?*

Then all hell, as they say, broke loose. Coyotes were closing in from three sides, ignoring the sheep for the moment, and focusing on the dogs. None of them barked. And I knew what that meant. An attack was imminent.

I couldn't say now how I managed it, for that fence was not made for climbing. Somehow I was on the other side, legs pumping, feet slamming the ground. Some part of my mind heard Donald call to me.

"Spencer! No! You can't do anything!"

In broad daylight, I'm sure I would have seen fur flying in all directions. Four of the coyotes had charged the dogs, and I heard growling and yapping and snarling. I watched the white of Klondike's fur, expecting any second to see red spreading through it.

As I got close enough to see the flash of white teeth, one of the coyotes that had been circling around the perimeter of the fray moved toward me. I'm not a sheep, but the sight of that wild predator, head down, teeth bared, gave me pause, and I stopped running. The animal stood still, a barrier between me and the fight, as my panting breath rasped in and out of my chest.

Desperate, frustrated, I watched as the battle raged. And then I heard a sharp yelp, and one of the coyotes was down, Klondike's teeth in its throat. Then a border collie yelped, and Klondike turned on the coyote that had its teeth sunk into one of the collies' front legs. He grabbed the neck of the attacker and shook it, hard, several times. Another coyote down. The other collie was in the thick of it with yet another coyote, and I think the collie would have won.

Suddenly the sharp crack of a gun sounded, and then another, as two men carrying rifles came racing onto the field, white T-shirts blazing through the dusk like white hats on the good guys. They had fired into the air, but the coyotes seemed to recognize a threat they didn't want to face. All but the two downed animals turned and ran toward the woods.

With my canine guard no longer facing me down, I ran toward the dogs where they stood, panting, tongues hanging out. They stared in the direction the coyotes had gone, but somehow they knew better than to chase after them. One collie tried to move and nearly fell, no doubt the one with a damaged leg.

Klondike had moved to stand over one of the downed coyotes, and I could see that it was badly injured but still alive. One of the men moved toward it and aimed his gun at the animal's head, dispatching it completely with a loud crack that sent Klondike jumping sideways.

By this time I was at my dog's side, my eyes seeking everywhere for injury. There was blood on his snout and across is forehead, but I couldn't tell whether any of it was his. More blood soaked the fur on his left flank, and when I touched it he yelped. So; he was not unscathed, and my heart twisted. *How was I going to get him to a vet? What could I do?*

The men busied themselves with their own concerns, and I heard one of them shout. "Why aren't those sheep penned? Should have been in there an hour ago!"

The only answer from the second man was, "I'll get the truck."

The first man looked in my direction. "Who are you, and what kind of dog is that?"

My breath was still coming in deep gasps from running and from panic over Klondike's condition. "Spencer Hill. And he's a Great Pyrenees."

"I think he got both of them." I knew he meant the coyotes.

"How is the collie?" I asked.

"Not good. Might have to put her down. Russell's getting the truck. Where's your vehicle?"

"Quite a way from here." I pointed in the general direction of the trail head.

"Bring him along. He needs attention, too."

From over his shoulder a pickup truck approached. At the same moment, behind me I heard Donald's voice. Somehow he'd got through the fence. "Give me your keys."

"What?"

"I'll drive the Jeep back and wait for you at the house. You go with Klondike."

CHAPTER 22

I sat in the back of the truck with the three dogs, the poor collie with the hurt leg whimpering, yelping quietly with each hard bump the truck encountered. Klondike lay with his undamaged side pressed against my leg, head resting on his front paws. If I didn't know better, I'd have said he knew we were on our way to help him.

The sign at the clinic, Little Boundary Veterinary, was not lit, but there were lights inside. The place had clearly already closed for the night, and yet somehow they were expecting us. I didn't know how, and I didn't care.

There were two veterinarians in separate examination rooms. One of the men carried the worst collie into one, the other dog following. The second man motioned to me to take Klondike into the other room. The dog was able to walk, but he was obviously favoring his left side.

As it turned out, most of the visible blood was not from Klondike, but his side wound was bad enough that the vet administered a sedative so she could clean the wound thoroughly and stitch it up. As she shaved the fur around the wound, she said to me, "Has he received all his shots?"

"Yes."

"You're sure? Because anything that coyote was carrying has been introduced to your dog."

"I'm positive." And I was; Vanessa had referred me to her vet, and Klondike's shots were current as of March.

"I'm giving him a heavy dose of antibiotics. You should bring him back here for another shot in a week. Or you can see your own vet. But it's extremely important. We'll also want to be sure there's no evidence of rabies."

"I understand." For some reason, my hands chose this moment to begin shaking. I pushed them into my pockets, both to get them to stop and to hide them from the vet.

As she stitched the wound, I said, "I don't know whether you'll be able to tell me anything, but it surprised me how Klondike knew to work together with the two border collies. They were all three trying to herd the sheep into a corner."

"Makes sense. The sheep would be easier to protect that way. Border collies are possibly the most intelligent dog breed, though poodles give them a run for their money."

"Poodles? Really?"

"Yup."

"Okay, but Klondike has never been taught to herd."

She finished stitching and reached for some bandaging gauze. "Great Pyrenees dogs were bred specifically to keep wolves and other predators away from herd animals. The thick coat allows them to work on snowy mountains, and the white fur blends in with the snow and with sheep, if that's what they're guarding. So Klondike here might have been doing more guarding than actual herding. I wouldn't use a GP instead of a border collie for herding. But it can handle itself against coyotes. I understand he killed two of them, and this is all the damage they did." She gave the bandaged would a gentle tap.

I declined to correct her; Klondike hadn't actually killed the second one. But if the gun hadn't finished off the injured coyote, I felt sure Klondike would have dispatched it.

She told me Klondike would be groggy for a few hours, and

she fastened a cone around his neck. "Keep this on him until your vet says he doesn't need it. Don't put him outside alone until the collar comes off, and don't feed him until after ten tonight, and then only if he seems fully alert. Otherwise he could choke." She stepped back. "Can you carry him?"

"I'm sure I can."

"Because one of the brothers, Russell or Tim, could help you."

I slipped my arms under Klondike's partially limp body. He was not light, but I was tall and strong enough. "I can manage. Thank you very much."

I was about to leave the examination room to see about the bill, Klondike's head lolling against my shoulder, when the vet said, "That dog is a hero."

I carried my hero into the waiting room. One of the men was there, watching for me.

"I'll help you get him into the truck bed," he said, and followed me out.

When Klondike was settled as well as we could manage, the man held his right hand out. "Russell Williamson."

"Spencer Hill."

"That's some dog you have. What's his name?"

"Klondike."

Russell laughed. "Great name. I need to go back in. He'll be fine where he is for a bit. You can come, or you can wait here."

"I need to pay the bill."

Russell shook his head. "Oh, no. That's ours. No telling how many sheep Klondike saved, and maybe our dogs as well."

I thought he'd go back in at that point, but he didn't. "You from around here?" he asked.

I looked at his face, actually seeing it for the first time. He wasn't the man who had spat on the ground and told me to stay on my side of the fence. I didn't think his brother was, either, so it must have been a hired assistant. Uncharitably, I hoped that man had been the one who hadn't penned the sheep when he was supposed to.

"I live in Assisi. I was walking the trail on the other side of the pasture fence when Klondike bolted. I had no idea why until I followed him."

"How'd he get past the fence?"

"He found a weakness under the wire."

"Huh. I wonder if that's how the coyotes got in. Have to look for that. How big is it? Did you crawl under?"

I shook my head. "Climbed it."

"No shit. Well, I guess you're tall enough. Assis, you say? I hear they got a faggot pastor there."

"Yeah. That would be me."

I couldn't read his expression, but after a pause he said, "Stepped in that one, eh? Sorry about that."

An awkward moment, to say the least. I thought he'd leave at that point for sure and go inside. I intended to wait here with Klondike. But Russell stood there, gazing around, perhaps trying to appear casual and like he hadn't just insulted me.

"You involved in that Pagan festival a while back?" His tone was odd; I couldn't tell what was behind it, but something was.

Tread carefully, Spencer. "I was one of the organizers, yes." I let a couple of beats go by before adding, "Were you one of the group who came onto the field late in the afternoon?"

He shook his head. "Nope. Tim was, though." He turned to look at me. "I don't take to all that negative preaching."

"So you're in the Assembly of God?"

He nodded. "Ain't real happy with it, though." He fell silent.

I wanted to know more. "Anything in particular bother you?"

He shrugged, a casual movement that belied his next words. "Seems to me if you get that excited about what folks are doing wrong, you gotta be messing in stuff that ain't your business."

I laughed. I laughed longer and louder than I would have if not already on the edge of fear for Klondike, fear that was behind me but still making itself known.

Russell and I glanced at each other. I said, "May I quote you?"

"You heard my words. That's enough." He turned as though

about to go back into the clinic, but turned back and held out his hand. "Thanks to you and Klondike here for coming to the rescue."

We shook hands, a firm manly grasp, and he headed inside.

By the time Russell and Tim dropped Klondike and me home, I felt almost as limp and useless as my groggy dog. It was harder now to carry him inside, but Donald was there and opened the door.

Donald waited until I had stumbled into the kitchen to lay Klondike onto his soft bed before he spoke. We stood side by side and regarded the pile of drugged white fur, his left side shaved and bandaged, his head poking out absurdly from the large plastic collar that would keep him from biting at the wound.

Donald's voice was quiet. "Will he be okay?"

I nodded. "I'll call his vet Monday and see how soon I can bring him in for a follow-up. He'll need an antibiotic booster soon."

After another minute or so, Donald told me, "I've thrown some sandwiches together for dinner. Figured that might be about all you'd want."

I consumed two sandwiches and a large helping of potato chips in the time it took Donald to finish half that. It was as though one of those wild animals had torn a hole in *my* side, and everything I ate fell through it as soon as I swallowed.

I downed the last drops of my ginger ale, unsure whether I'd be able to stay awake long enough for Donald and me to continue our trail conversation.

He sat back in his chair. "How are the other dogs?"

"I think one of them wasn't badly hurt. The other?" I shook my head. "One of the men thought she might not make it. She's still at the clinic, overnight."

"Lots of dogs do just fine on three legs."

"Not working dogs."

"But—surely, they wouldn't put it down just because it couldn't herd sheep anymore."

I let out a long, exhausted breath. "I'm sure I can't say."

He watched me for a minute. "Will you check in with them to find out?"

I rubbed my face. "Hadn't thought of that. I guess I could."

"Cuz if they don't want a damaged dog, someone else might. Maybe someone here."

That got my attention. Woke me up. "You know, that's a great idea."

He bit his lip. "It's good to hear someone say that."

"Oh, sweet man." I wasn't angry with Jonathan any longer, just sad for Donald.

His gaze fell to the table, and before I could say anything else, a tear landed on his empty dinner plate. He leaned his elbows on the table, dropped his head into his hands, and wept.

It's funny how a whole train of thoughts can pass through one's mind in a matter of nanoseconds. In the time it took me to push my chair back from the table, move over to Donald, lift him up by his shoulders, and wrap my arms around him, a memory had come flooding back in great detail.

It had been last fall—I couldn't recall the date—that Marshall Savage had sat at this table and described the horrors of the conversion camp he'd been sent to, the one where he'd tried to drown himself. I had been sitting in the same chair I'd used tonight, and Donald had sat where Marshall had been. Marshall, like Donald, had begun weeping, and I had moved around the table to hold him and let him cry.

Marshall had needed to leave Assisi, in the process leaving me. Donald needed to leave Jonathan, and in the process, leave me.

After a few minutes, Donald pulled away and went in search of facial tissues. I started after-dinner clean-up, and he came behind me, his arms wrapping around my waist, his head resting on the back of my shoulder.

I closed my eyes, which were burning with my own unshed

tears. I was sure now that I still loved this man. And I wanted so much to turn to him, take his face in my hands, kiss him several times, and ask him to please, please stay with me, live with me, be my life partner. But I couldn't do that.

Donald was leaving Jonathan because he felt as though he wasn't seen as a whole person with dreams and goals of his own. If I said what I wanted—wanted so much!—to say, I would be acting in no better faith than Jonathan.

We stood there like that for perhaps two minutes. Then he pulled slowly away.

"I should get back to Myra's. I haven't finished packing."

I nodded and followed him to the front door. Just before opening it, he turned to me suddenly.

"Spencer? I have to do this. I know you see that. But I'm not sure which way things will go."

I nodded. "Sure. I understand."

"But—I guess—shit. What I want to say is what if I don't fit there anymore? In New York?"

"I—don't know how to answer that. What are you asking?"

His eyes locked onto mine, sending a message I didn't dare interpret. I know what I wanted that message to be, but he needed to be the one to say it. My breath was shaky, making its way in and out of me in small, static bursts.

Ask it! I wanted to shout. *Please! I cannot!*

He stepped back, away from me, shook his head. "Never mind." He opened the door.

The voice in my head was shouting at me. *Tell him how you feel!*

"Donald?" He turned, and on his face I saw hope. Or maybe that's just what I wanted to see. "I want you to feel completely free to do what you need to do. For you."

"See, now, it's this kind of thing that makes me love you. Well, must be off. Though I confess to a certain degree of resfeber." He grinned. "Anxiety mixed with anticipation when beginning a journey."

I watched him walk away. I thought he might look back, wave, blow a kiss, anything. He didn't.

This parting, this new separation was not just for Donald's sake. Ruth had once said that I needed to ask myself if I was romantically attracted to men who needed help. *My* help. Not long after he'd gone into the cult, she'd described Donald—"Donnie," to her—as someone who might have appeared to me to have it all together, that as an actor he would know how to come across that way. But she'd said it wasn't real. She'd said I'd been a stabilizing influence on him.

Thinking about that now made me laugh. At that point in my life, I'd been anything but stable. I'd despaired of a life's work—a calling to God—that I'd thought would be mine. My mother had just died a sudden, horrible death. I wasn't exactly suicidal, but I wasn't far away from thoughts of it.

I believed now that what Ruth had seen was that together Donald and I had stabilized each other. It was beyond fortunate for me that when he disappeared into that cult, I had a terrific therapist to help me pick up the pieces. And, in fact, I'd leaned on Ruth herself to some extent. And she'd led me to UU.

So this parting was for both Donald and me. He needed to know what most fulfilled him. And I needed to know two things. One was that if he chose me, it was because he knew that what we were, what we could be, our life together, would be what fulfilled him. The other was that I would know the same thing about him.

That night, his words—*the kind of thing that makes me love you*—echoed in all my dreams.

CHAPTER 23

Myra wasn't in church Sunday. She was driving Donald to Montpelier, I was sure. Following some silent agreement, Donald and I hadn't spoken since the night before. There was nothing more to say. Not yet.

Klondike had recovered well enough that I'd fed him dinner at midnight, and today I'd taken him on a short walk and then left him sleeping on his bed. So far he hadn't pawed at the collar, but that activity might begin at any time.

Loraine was in church, without Vanessa. I wasn't inclined to inform anyone about what had happened with Klondike until he was well out of danger. I knew the story of his heroism would upset Vanessa, and she didn't need that.

At home after the service, I called the Little Boundary clinic. I was surprised when someone answered on Sunday, a young-sounding male voice, probably a vet assistant, or technician, or something. I introduced myself and asked about the border collie.

"Yeah, she's here. So's Russell Williamson, trying to decide what to do."

"Is there any way I could speak to him? I might be able to help."

A minute went by before I heard Russell's voice. "Yeah?"

"Listen, I understand you're debating what to do about the collie. Do you have a plan?"

I heard him let out a long breath. "Not really much choice."

"But she's still alive?"

"Not for long." I could have sworn I heard his voice crack.

"Would it be all right if I take her?"

There was silence, and then, "She needs a passel of work. Surgery. They'd have to take the leg. Stay here for several days. Lots of follow-up."

"And I can see why she'd lose her job as a herder. But—"

"No, what I mean is, it's expensive. You wanna pay for that?"

"Yes. Yes, I would."

More silence. Then, "Her name is Nellie." I think we both let out a sigh of relief. I heard him call to someone and say, "The preacher's gonna take care of her. Do everything you can, yeah?"

Back on the phone, he said, "She's a great dog."

"I watched her work one day, with the other collie. All of you were amazing. It was like watching a ballet."

He chuckled. "Never heard it called *that* before."

"Are you going to replace her?"

"The dogs are insured. They're critical to the farm. So, yeah. We hope to find one that's already been at least partly trained, so it can come up to speed with our other dog quickly."

"The insurance wouldn't cover an injury that takes her out of the job, I guess?"

"That's right. You gonna keep her yourself?"

"I'm not sure. I certainly will, if I don't find someone I'm sure can be a good owner, especially given her handicap. I'd be happy to let you know."

"Yeah. Good."

I smiled; the guy had a heart, but he didn't want to show me too much of it at once. "Do I need to talk to someone about billing and such?"

"Hang on." He left the phone, then came back and told me to come to the clinic Monday to settle things and agree on a plan. The last thing he said before we hung up was, "Just so you know, there's still a chance she won't make it."

"I understand. I'll support whatever they need to do."

I'd just finished breakfast Monday when Myra called.

"How's the collie?"

It took me a few seconds to realize that, of course, Donald would have told Myra all about the attack on the drive yesterday.

"Nellie. The sheep farmers were about to put her down. She's going to lose at least part of the leg the coyote mangled. And even if she survives, they can't use her for herding anymore. I think they might have kept her as a pet, but the surgery and all that was going to be too expensive."

"But—she's still alive?"

"Sorry; yes. I said I'd pay the vet bill, and if she survives I'll take her. She'll need some rehab, I think. I wouldn't mind taking her, but I'm kind of hoping to find her a good home."

She laughed. "You've already found one."

"What's that, now?"

"Me! I'd love to have a border collie. Nellie, you say?"

"Nellie. And that's wonderful news. I'm headed to the clinic in a few minutes. Do you want to come with me? I'm going to talk to the vet about what happens next, and to pay the bill."

"Yes! I really would. But I have classes."

Right; school wasn't quite out yet for the summer. "What time could you go?"

We agreed on a time, and then I said, "Um… Donald got off on the train all right, I take it?"

"He did. He told me all about what he's going to do, back in the city. Re-establish old contacts, see if he can land a role or however you say that. Maybe even look into earning some money teaching acting. Not in a school, though; he doesn't want to go back to school and get a degree. I gather he used to do some volunteer teaching."

"Yes. Where Jonathan used to work. That's how they met."

"Poor Jonathan."

"Wait. Poor *Jonathan?*"

"Yes. He's losing a fantastic partner, not only a life partner, but also a partner in his efforts. Though Donald did tell me it wasn't out of the question that he'd support the effort in some way."

My mind tried and failed to draw that picture. And anyway, it was still focused on all the plans Donald had for testing his return to his old life, which would keep him away from me.

The veterinarian, whose name I hadn't picked up on Saturday but who was in fact Dr. Wanda Devlin, seemed relieved to see me. It made me wonder if she'd had doubts about getting paid for Nellie's work.

"How's Klondike?" she asked after I had introduced Myra.

"He seems to be fine. He's in the car, actually, parked in the shade with all the windows cracked."

"Would you bring him in? I'd like to check the wound. No charge."

Myra said, "I'll get him," and I handed her the key.

Dr. Devlin and I talked about finances, and Russell had been right; this was going to be very expensive. But I had the money, thanks to my parents, and Nellie was certainly worth it, even if the effort failed.

After examining Klondike and changing his bandage, Dr. Devlin wanted to speak with both Myra and me to go over next steps.

"It's going to be touch-and-go at first," she said. "The Williamsons had kept up with her care to now, shots, check-ups, things like that. If Klondike suffers from after-effects, he's got a great chance for survival. He's strong, and his wound is not very deep. But Nellie's front right leg was in very bad shape. Her health was good, but there's a better-than-nothing chance of infection. She'll be here for at least a week, maybe longer. I realize you have your own vet, but I'd advise against moving Nellie at this point."

Myra and I agreed that Nellie should stay where she was, with a doctor who already knew her. Dr. Devlin and Myra talked for several minutes, with the vet no doubt wanting to be sure Nellie would be cared for. And then we went in to see the dog.

We weren't allowed too close, and we weren't allowed to touch her. She lay on her left side, woozy from pain-killers. Where her right front leg had been there was a gap that tore at my heart. She wore a softer cone collar than Klondike's.

I glanced at Myra and saw that her eyes were filled with tears.

The vet noticed this, too. "I'm sure you feel very sorry for her right now," she told Myra, "but once she's with you, the best thing for her will be if you treat her like any other dog. The border collie is an incredibly smart animal, and she will take advantage of any weakness you show, which will make it harder for you to work with her as she heals."

Myra brushed at her eyes. "I understand."

Dr. Devlin hadn't smiled in my presence until that moment. "I hope Nellie and Klondike will be good friends."

On the drive home I broached the topic I had promised Jenny I would.

"There's something I want to ask you about," I opened. "You should understand that any response is acceptable."

"I'm intrigued."

"It's based on a combination of things, including how well you know several members of our congregation, what I know about your own spirituality, your work with Teens for Truth, and finally your recent adoption of UU."

"I see. Do I have permission to anticipate you?"

"Anticipate me?"

"Your question. I think I know what it is."

"Do you, now. Well, you might, but I have another question I'd wager you haven't anticipated. Go ahead; what do you think I'll ask?"

She gave me an assessing glance. "It's true there's only one question I think I know. And if I'm right, the answer is that I'd be absolutely delighted to be a lay minister in my new church."

I laughed. "Very good. And I might be even more delighted than you. I know Jenny and Andrea will be thrilled. I'll set up a meeting with all four of us to get things started."

"Wonderful! And the other question?"

"The other question has more to do with your life in The Forest. I know you have the ability to read people's energy, at least to some extent. Erik sees and interprets auras. Elaine is no doubt capable of things I can't even image." I paused to see if she confirmed what I'd said.

She told me, "I wouldn't dare guess at Elaine's powers or capabilities. In fact, the Forest Dwellers don't see these characteristics as anything special. They mostly don't discuss them unless someone needs help that a certain person can give. What's the question?"

"What about Adam?"

She hesitated. "Why do you ask?"

"He's said a couple of things in the past weeks that added up to what you told me during our recent walk to McGowan Pond. Things that all pointed to exactly what happened with Donald, how he left Jonathan, and how he feels about me. Adam seems to think Donald is open to what might happen with us if he doesn't find a place for himself in New York again."

She took a minute, looking out of the window in silence. I let her think.

Finally she said, "I want to avoid being overly specific here. Adam has said many things in the past that make it sound as though he has some window into the future. I admit that much of what he thinks will happen, does come to pass. But *those* predictions tend to center on personalities."

"I'm not sure I understand."

"If he were to say, for example, that lightning from a thunderstorm next week would strike a tree and block the road into The Forest, his record tells me that there's maybe a ten percent chance of that happening. But when he has a strong feeling about what people will do in their relationships with each other, he's usually spot on. Otherwise I would never have repeated what he said."

"Interesting. And did he predict that you would leave The Forest?"

She chuckled. "He said that at the end of my very first week, after I'd moved from Sedona almost four years ago now. So I'm not sure how much credibility to give that one."

"He said nothing about it more recently?"

"Well…. He started acting differently toward me a couple of months ago. Nothing definitive, nothing negative or unfriendly. But I got the sense he was gradually creating space between us. And to be honest, when I noticed that, I had already been wondering what it would be like to leave. So it's possible he picked up on that. But no. He said nothing."

"I suppose he might not have wanted to influence you." I had a keen appreciation for what that reluctance felt like; it had hung like a cloud over my time with Donald ever since he'd told me he was leaving Jonathan. Maybe longer. It had prevented me from saying more as Donald was leaving me to return to New York.

Myra said, "That would be very like him. Adam is a man of unquestionable integrity."

"Yeah. I think I sensed that with some certainty when I found out that although the two of you were considering a life of partnership, he had told you that he and I had a kind of relationship of our own."

"Yes. That was very like him. And I get the sense that the physically intimate aspect of your friendship with him is over."

"He told you that?"

"In his way. Not in so many words."

We drove in silence for a couple of minutes while a thought bounced around my brain and I struggled to form words to express it.

"Perhaps you can't answer this, but given that he's pretty sure about that, I'm wondering how likely it is—how strongly he feels, and how truly likely it is—that Donald would want to be with me. Here."

"And how much hope you should pin on it?"

"Yes." No point in beating about the proverbial bush.

"If I were in your shoes…." I heard her exhale, a long breath that seemed to carry away any inhibition to tell me her honest opinion. "I think Adam's image is of Donald having some success in what he's there to do, but that he will find it unfulfilling, and that his feelings for you will sully any accomplishment that doesn't include you."

It was better than I could have hoped. And yet the exhilaration I felt was tinged with an undertow of fear that a life here, with me, would leave him unfulfilled in other ways. But that was a discussion he and I would have only if Adam was right.

I resolved to put it out of my mind. I almost succeeded.

CHAPTER 24

Tuesday afternoon when I returned from a few pastoral visits and a tedious but necessary meeting about church finances, a car I didn't recognize was parked in front of my house, and Jonathan Ehrlich sat on my front steps. It was perhaps indicative of how fragmented my mind was lately that the first thing that went through my mind was, *Why are people always sitting on my front steps?*

He waited until I was a few feet from him before standing.

"I need to talk to you."

I almost said, *I'm not surprised.* Instead: "Please. Come in."

He didn't sit anywhere despite my invitation; he stood with his back to the piano as though to deny its presence.

"Can I offer you something? Coffee? Tea?"

"It's about Donald."

No tea, then. Fine. I waited for Jonathan to speak again.

"He says his leaving had nothing to do with you. Is that true?"

I opened my mouth, shut it again, and finally said, "I don't know how to answer that. Certainly I did nothing, said nothing, to encourage him to make *any* changes. As I understand it, he needs to test himself, to see if he left something years ago that he needs to go back to."

Jonathan's fists clenched and unclenched. It was frustration, I was sure. Nothing more.

"He didn't say anything about coming back to you? To a relationship with you?"

He nearly had. He had come exquisitely, agonizingly close. "No. And neither did I." A barking, humorless laugh escaped me. "Can you seriously see him as the partner of a minister in a rural community like Assisi? Running bring-and-buy events? Organizing bake sales? Leading a knitting group?" I threw my head back and laughed, a horrible sound that sent a knife into my heart because of the truth I was about to admit. "Can you see him partnered with a minister *at all?*"

"You're saying that's kind of what he would have been with me?"

I shook my head. "I'm saying that each of us must do what fulfills us. Prospect House, and the hope and help it will bring, fulfills you. And I completely understand that fulfillment, because mine isn't wildly different. But was it a dream the two of you shared? Or was it yours, and Donald tried to share it because he loved you? I can't say. But I think he has answered the question."

Jonathan's eyes welled with tears.

"Jonathan, I truly believe he loved you. Maybe loves you still. I don't know what he said to you. But if he can love you and leave you, it's because something calls to him too powerfully for him to ignore it. You're not wrong, if you think I still love him. I do. But would I ever ask him to share this life?"

"So now you're saying I was wrong to ask him to share mine?"

I ran a hand through my hair. "I'm saying this isn't about you. It isn't about me. It's about Donald, and he needed to make it about him when he realized that he wasn't fully in the dream you have."

"So I should just let him go?"

"Do you have a choice?"

We stared at each other across a space that should have been filled with connection; after all, we both loved this man who had left each of us for something he might not achieve. But instead, the space felt more like a chasm across which I was trying to throw a line of communication to someone who didn't even see it, or who let it land unheeded at his feet.

Even as I felt my heart twist with the belief that events would prove Adam wrong, the juxtaposition of what this connection with Jonathan should have been and what it was dropped a seed into my brain, a seed that would become a message for my congregation. Even in this painful moment, I was working on a sermon.

My laugh then was more like an ironic chuckle. "Jonathan, it seems to me that both you and I are where we need to be. Donald left to figure out where he needs to be. I pray he finds it, wherever and whatever that turns out to be."

Jonathan's car left black marks on the road.

After Jonathan left, Klondike made it clear he needed a walk. Rather than go someplace where I'd meet people, I headed for the trail behind the high school.

There were about five kids, mostly boys but with one girl clearly holding her own, doing fancy maneuvers with their bicycles in the parking lot. I was pretty sure one of the boys was Duncan Beale, but I didn't want to stop. Choosing a path as far from the kids as possible, I kept my eyes straight ahead and got onto the trail without being noticed. Or, at least, without anyone calling to me.

At first my mind was a jumble. Thoughts twisted around each other, a tangled knot of multi-colored yarn that felt like it would never be useful again. But then I passed a spot that held a challenging memory.

It looked very different now, compared to when Klondike and I had come out in a December snowstorm to look for Marshall. It wasn't long after he'd been fired from his teaching job for "conduct unbecoming" or some such ridiculousness. He'd been fired because, thanks to the Assembly of God bigots and a homophobic vice principle, it had been discovered that he was gay. And one awful night he'd disappeared into a snowstorm.

Klondike and I had gone out looking for him. It was the dog who'd found him, huddled in a mass of crisscrossed branches on the side of this trail, curled into a ball and nearly hypothermic.

Now, months later, I stared nearly sightlessly at the green leaves on vines that covered the tangle, wondering where Marshall was and what he was doing, what his life was like now. I understood why he had left, though that didn't mean I wanted to lose him from my life. But, clearly, he'd needed to lose me.

Klondike let me know he was ready to move on.

Ready to move on. And yet, here I was, having been left again by yet another man I cared for.

I tried to outpace the cloud of self-pity that followed just behind my head, ready to engulf me. I reminded myself of how things had changed in good ways all around me, some of it due to my own actions, my own intentions. The strife between The Forest and Assisi was all but over. My lay minister problem was resolved, as was the question about Boyd Harper's suitability for the role. I'd made an acquaintance—if not quite a friend—in a member of the Assembly of God congregation, someone who might not be an advocate for open-mindedness, but someone who saw my business as my business, and who wasn't entirely on board with Alan Jermin's rantings. And Klondike, bless his snowy-white head and huge canine heart, had been a true hero, saving the lives of sheep and dogs, though it was sad that he'd had to take out couple of coyotes in the process. And our congregation had gained a marvelous new member in Myra Langtree.

I noticed that Klondike was still favoring his left side a little, which he'd been doing since his encounter with coyotes. But he'd let me change his bandage, and the wound seemed to be healing. We had an appointment for Thursday afternoon with his own vet.

"Klondike, old boy," he looked at me expectantly, and I patted his back between his shoulder blades, avoiding the cone, "that's twice now you've rescued some animals in Little Boundary, horses and now border collies. And both times, it was for members of that insane church. You'd think they might appreciate you. Us. Don't see it happening, though."

We encountered no one on our walk, and on the way back my mind went onto quite a different topic of meditation.

It was my parents' love letters.

It seems likely that most children don't really come to know their parents as people; that's the natural order of things. And maybe the parents don't ever stop thinking of their offspring as children, no matter how old they are. But had I been especially blind? Had my eyes been so effectively hooded against seeing other people, caring about their lives, that all I had seen was my own life, blind to who my parents had been? Had I seen only my own troubles?

And if that were true, then was I somehow making up for that obliviousness by dedicating my life to a career focused on others? It didn't feel like compensation. It felt right. It felt good. I truly believed I had found my calling, my vocation.

A voice in my head told me, *You're doing it again, Spencer, making this about you. Where's Judas when you need him? Didn't this monologue start with your parents?*

I laughed aloud, and Klondike gave me another quizzical look.

Ah, yes. Parents. And those letters. Those letters!

I hadn't read any more since that day in the storage unit. The box containing them was tucked away in a bureau drawer in my bedroom. Maybe if I read through a few more I'd get a better sense of my parents as people.

They had given up so much. So very much. For my father, the Catholic priesthood. For my mother, a nun's life dedicated to God and doing his work. Why?

Again, that voice. This time it said: *For love.*

For love.

At some point, Father must have thrown off his inhibitions, deserted his calling, and proposed to Mother. I couldn't imagine her being the instigator. And how sure was he, I wondered, that he was doing the right thing? That he wasn't pulling her away from the life she should have had?

Back to me, which seemed all right as long as I was aware of it. Back to Donald. What would have happened if I'd thrown off my own inhibitions, the ones that held me back so Donald could make his own choice? What if I'd said, "Don't go. Stay here. Be with me. Be my husband." What would he have done?

What would he give up for love? What would I?

I wasn't about to foreswear my calling, follow him to New York, and talk him into a life with me there. Does that mean I wouldn't give up my calling for him? Well.... No, actually. It wasn't out of the question for me to be given a post in or near Manhattan, though those posts were probably in high demand by ministers with longer careers, illustrious ones, which I knew better than to think described mine at present. So, I supposed, maybe I would have to take a hiatus if I followed Donald to New York.

As for him, all right, so I didn't try to stop him from leaving. But if I had, would he have given up the possibility of restarting his acting career? For love? He was the one who'd said he loved me. I hadn't responded, even though I loved him.

And then there was the question of love, itself. Did I love Donald? Yes. Did he love me? He'd said so. But if I were to give up my calling, would it be for love? Because Love, capital L, *is* my calling. I can't give up on Love. But would giving up my calling for love necessarily be giving up on Love?

Enough! These were not puzzles I was going to solve. Not today, at least.

I distracted myself by singing hymns aloud, Klondike showing the good sense to ignore me.

It did not take Donald long to get back into the acting scene. He called one evening in the last week of June.

"Congratulate me. And then tell me to break a leg." He sounded beyond elated.

"In that order?"

"Yes, please." I obliged and then waited. "Aren't you going to ask me what for?"

I laughed. "As though you could stop yourself telling me."

"Fine. I'm the official understudy in an off-Broadway production for a part that should sound very familiar to you. The character's name is Milo Tindle."

Milo…. Milo…. Why does that sound so familiar?

And then it came to me. "*Sleuth?* You're in the cast for *Sleuth?*"

Sleuth. The play Donald had used as a training ground for me, the fall of 1983, just as our relationship was getting started. The play that had given us a pretext for spending time alone together, something I had needed so that I could pretend that it wasn't my attraction to Donald, or his to me, that brought us together. It was the play we had been working on just before the first time we'd had sex. The first time I'd ever had sex. With anyone.

I was barely able to focus on what Donald said next.

"Isn't it amazing? Ruth knows someone who's married to an agent, and the agent agreed to talk to me. He said he wasn't ready to offer me representation, but he'd just learned that the understudy for this show had to leave. Don't know why. Very mysterious. Very hush-hush. So he needed to find someone who already knew the play. He had me read for the director and the producer, and—Spencer, you won't believe this. They gave it to me on the spot!"

"Okay, now I'll say it again, this time with feeling: Congratulations! And break a leg. Donald, that's wonderful. I'm so happy for you." And I was. It almost surprised me how happy I was.

"Of course, I might not get to fill in more than a few times, but —Oh, my God, Spencer, it feels so fucking good to be part of the scene again."

"And it must be validating to have your talent appreciated so quickly, and to such an extent."

"Yes! But I would replace 'validating' with 'exhilarating.'"

I laughed again. "And that's exactly how you sound."

"And I'm not even acting!"

"Will you tell Jonathan?"

"At some point."

To fill the awkward silence that followed, I said, "I don't know whether he would have mentioned this, but Boyd Harper, who was so good with Kira, is hoping to work with Jonathan at Prospect House."

"Yeah, Jonathan did mention that they were talking. I hope that works out."

"So you and Jonathan have been in touch a few times then?" *And this is the first time you're calling me?*

Ugly, Spencer. Don't be ugly.

"Just once, actually."

Changing that subject, I asked, "So will you stay with Ruth, or will you get your own place?"

"Oh, I can't afford anything in the city at this point. Ruth's place on the upper West side is plenty big enough for now. I can come and go from the show at whatever hours I need to without disturbing them. She and Nelson have said I can stay as long as I need to."

"Donald, I have to say this is working out really well for you. It's like the Universe greased the skids, and you're sliding right along in the direction you want to go."

"It does seem like that, doesn't it?" We gave that some space, and then he said, "So what's going on in your neck of the woods?"

"The usual, really. Myra has adopted the collie who lost her leg to the coyote. And her relationship with Johnny Caldwell is continuing apace."

"Are you enjoying your Pagan god often enough to keep you happy?"

He would ask about that. I couldn't exactly say, *Adam has taken himself off the stage because he expects you to play that role now.*

"I have no complaints." Not exactly a lie. Not exactly the truth.

CHAPTER 25

Sunday evening, June tenth, Donald called again.

"You'll never guess!"

I paused long enough to imagine what might have happened for Donald to sound even more elated than the last time he'd phoned.

"Okay, I'll take a stab. You're not just the understudy now?"

Silence. Then, "Did Ruth call you?"

"I guessed it? Did I? No, she didn't call. Are you Milo for real, now?"

"I am! Justin broke his ankle. Something unmentionable that happened on his boyfriend's boat. I don't care. But this is so great for me! I still can't believe it. Spencer, I'm so fucking nervous!"

I laughed. "Well, this part is a far cry from Puck. But I have every confidence in your range. And I've heard you as Milo before."

"Will you come see me?"

"Oh, I—" *Would I do that? Would I be able to do that?*

His tone sounded like back-paddling. "Not right away, of course. I need to get my sea legs under me. But maybe in a few weeks?"

My head felt light, and I had to bring air into my lungs deliberately or I might have suffocated. I felt suddenly, inexorably, pulled toward Manhattan. My home town. A city I hadn't left until less than a year ago. A place that was the polar opposite of Assisi, other than being in the same country. A place where I used to go to plays and concerts and museums and restaurants and parks and—

"Spencer? You still there? Um, listen, if you can't get away, that's all right."

"No!" I found my voice at last. "No, that's not it. I was just taking a long trip down memory lane. Yes, of course I'll come see you. I would love that."

As I hung up the phone, I realized that this time, I had told the whole truth. I truly would love to see Donald play Milo Tindle.

It was only as I was getting ready for bed that I recalled something about the service that morning: Loraine had not been there.

Monday, a large piece of sky fell.

My phone rang before I'd finished breakfast. "Spencer Hill, here."

Silence, then a strangled noise that was trying not to be a sob.

"I'll be right there." I hung up, my mind in turmoil. I knew it was Loraine. It was the call I'd been waiting for with a dread I hadn't dared admit, let alone prepare for.

Loraine opened the door before I reached for the knocker, her face nearly quivering with pain, her eyes sunken and red. She threw herself at me, and although she sobbed, she seemed to struggle to be as quiet as possible.

Vanessa lay in the hospital bed that had essentially taken over the living room, her face nearly grey, her eyes at half-mast. So she was still with us, but clearly it wouldn't be for long.

Sheila, who'd been seeing to Vanessa's medical needs for months, stood in the doorway to the kitchen. She must have witnessed scenes like this before, but she seemed to shrink against the doorframe as though to be sure she had some kind of support.

Loraine stood on one side of the bed and held one of Vanessa's hands. I sat in the chair on the other side, searching mentally for anything to say, anything to help ease the heart of this wonderful woman as she left her tormented body. Since assuming this post last August, I had been present at four deaths. Each one had been wrenching, but each time I had been able to be present, to fulfill my role, and to fulfill it well.

This time, everything felt different.

Vanessa tried to smile and failed. "I'm ready," was all she managed to say.

"I'll stay here with you in silence, or I could talk. Which would you prefer?"

"Talk to me. About dying. No one else will."

I glanced up at Loraine, who was clearly trying to be calm. Tears clouded my vision as I looked back at Vanessa. I closed my eyes to let those tears escape, and I took a deep breath before I opened them again.

"I believe it was Rumi who said not to think of ourselves as drops in the ocean. Rather, each of us is the entire ocean in a drop."

I saw Vanessa's hand flutter toward me, and I took it in mine.

"You have ushered so many souls off of this plane of existence. You have sent them off with a love that carried them safely into the Love that awaits us all. That Love now reaches for you. It is where you belong, where you will be wrapped in a warmth that leaves no room for cold, or fear, or pain."

I paused, needing to collect myself.

"Vanessa Doyle, Rector Emerita, I have had the profound and humbling honor of lifting from you the mantle of leadership you carried so well for so long. You have entrusted me with the people you have served and loved. I pray that someday I will have earned at least some of the trust they placed in you, some of the love they feel for you."

Loraine let out a single sob and covered her mouth with her free hand. I squeezed another few tears from my eyes before continuing.

"The love you have given now returns to you, more than enough to carry you on its crest as you attain the peace that passes all understanding, as you live again in the Grace you came from, the Grace you now return to."

Vanessa closed her eyes and squeezed my hand gently. "Take care of them for me. Watch over them." Slowly, agonizingly slowly, she turned her head to look up at Loraine, and I saw her mouth twitch into the best smile she could manage. She closed her eyes.

Her hand in mine went limp. Loraine gasped out a gut-wrenching sob as she felt the life leave her wife. I laid the limp hand gently beside Vanessa's deserted body and went to Loraine, and we held each other with an intensity that seemed to be trying to deny what had happened. She let her tears fall as her body shook with sobs. I did the same.

And then I looked to where Sheila stood, her own face wet, and I reached out an arm. She nearly ran to be with us, to be included in the shared connection that was part love and part grief.

At Vanessa's funeral, three days later, the church was full to overflowing, and there was standing room only. There were people there I didn't recognize. There were people there I knew were parishioners under David Foster, and even some Catholics from Milton Bryant's congregation.

Vanessa Doyle had lived a life of love and service. And everyone knew it.

I allowed tears to stream down my face as I delivered a very short speech, stopping as necessary to collect myself.

"Assisi," I told people who hardly needed to hear it, "will never be the same. A guiding light, a strength of purpose, and a source of boundless love that we sometimes took for granted has taken on a new life. Vanessa Doyle's physical presence is no longer here. I could tell you that she no longer suffers, and perhaps we can find some solace for ourselves in that. I could tell you that she is not gone, but I suspect that truism will bring little or no comfort to us, accustomed as we are to having her with us, to having her wisdom and her heart guide us and sustain us."

I stopped to blow my nose, and many in the congregation took advantage of the pause to do the same.

"She would not want us to mourn, and yet we cannot avoid the pain we feel at her passing. If I look hard enough for comfort, here's what I know: As each of us reaches the point where we leave the physical world behind, the love that was and is Vanessa Doyle will be there to greet us."

I was glad I had not planned to speak for any longer. I barely made it to the end of what I did say. Besides, there were many people who also wanted to speak.

The reception in the function hall was, of course, a somber affair. There was food and drink, though at first not many mourners took anything.

David and Martha Foster were there, as well as Milton Bryant. I wasn't surprised to see Myra and Johnny. But I wasn't prepared for the number of Forest Dwellers I saw. Even Elaine Gault, who—as far as I knew—hadn't been in Assisi in years, except for the Beltane celebration, was there with a man I'd never met, but who appeared to be with her as a husband would. Erik Stillman was with a woman, probably his wife. Adam was there, as were several others whose faces I'd seen in The Forest at one point or another.

I nearly wept again, with a bittersweet joy, knowing that not so long ago, no one from The Forest would have considered attending her funeral.

After introducing me to Gregory Mann, her husband, Elaine took both my hands. "I had the honor of meeting Vanessa Doyle only once. I was impressed with her." She smiled. "You have large shoes to fill. And I think you're off to a very good start."

All I could do was bow my head and say, "Thank you."

Erik shook my hand next, after I greeted his wife, Carol Still-man. He said, "Because of you, I've come to realize how much your spirituality and mine are similar. If she was anything like you, I regret not having known your predecessor."

Again the bow, again the thanks, though I was barely able to speak.

Behind Erik, Adam waited. He wrapped his arms around me and held me for several seconds, not because he was sad, but because he knew I was.

Of all the people there, the one I was the most surprised to see was Jonathan Ehrlich. He must have been waiting for a break in the number of people who spoke to me, but finally he approached.

Our eyes met with a softness I would not have expected, and he reached his right hand toward me. He said, "I didn't really know Vanessa. But I keep hearing about her. I keep hearing what a generous spirit, what a loving person she was."

"Keep hearing? Where?"

He smiled. "Everywhere. She's known to many people in Newport. Even the contractor at Prospect House knew her. He's the one who told me she had passed."

"I had no idea. I mean, of course I knew how much she was cherished here." I smiled. "Perhaps I shouldn't be surprised."

"I thought you might like to know that I'll be naming the large meeting room at Prospect House after her. The Vanessa Doyle Memorial Hall. Probably shortened to Doyle Hall for everyday reference."

I reached out and grasped Jonathan's shoulder, and then— briefly but honestly—we hugged.

The only person I hadn't spoken to by this point was Loraine. She didn't seem to need me, though; she was surrounded by people every time I looked her way. I would visit her later and let her know about Doyle Hall.

~

When I finally made it home, late that afternoon, I was exhausted. I had hoped to stop in to see Loraine, but when I'd gone past the house she had shared with Vanessa, several cars were parked there already. She'd need me more, perhaps, tomorrow, and the day after, and the day after that.

I've heard that dogs sense things in ways we don't understand. And, indeed, when I got home, Klondike was lying quietly on his kitchen bed, head on his paws. He looked up at me without lifting his massive head, and I could have sworn he knew where I'd been, and why. After all, this was his loss, too.

Drained of energy and purpose though I was, I fetched Klondike's lead. We walked, and walked, and walked. It was a slow pace, a mourner's pace, and I felt certain the dog's mind was just as empty of any useful thoughts as mine was.

One coherent thought that I had made me laugh aloud. Jonathan was naming Doyle Hall after a woman he'd met only once, very briefly. I'd been glad to see him, and happy about the dedication. I still was, though what made me laugh now was recognizing the business acumen of Mr. Ehrlich. Conspicuously honoring someone as esteemed as Vanessa would bring respect to his project and, possibly, a few donations.

Back home I hugged the white, furry creature and wept into his fur. He had been Vanessa's dog. This had been Vanessa's congregation.

Both were now mine for real.

CHAPTER 26

The return address had no name, just an address in Burlington. It was handwritten, as was my name and address on the front of the white envelope. The paper was of very high quality; I could see the weave of linen in it.

Did I know anyone in Burlington? I wracked my brain and came up empty. And yet the handwriting seemed familiar in a way I couldn't identify.

Carefully I inserted into the envelope the letter opener my father had used for his correspondence, a beautiful thing made of something like rosewood, the handle worn from years of use. As thick as the paper was, it tore easily and cleanly. Inside was stationery of the same quality paper, also with hand-writing.

Dearest Spencer,

I heard myself gasp and then quickly scanned to the end for a signature:

Love, always.
Marshall

I was glad of the sturdy wooden chair supporting me and of the solid wooden desk I could lean on. The edges of my vision blurred, and I felt light-headed.

Marshall.

How many times—how many hours, in total—had I spent wondering where he was? *How* he was?

"Well, here's your answer," I said aloud. "Read it."

> Dearest Spencer,
> Surprise! Sorry. Couldn't resist. But knowing you, I believe you've wondered about me at least occasionally in the past few months. I pictured you reading the note I left for you, and I'm pretty sure you would have wept. Your heart is so warm, and your love so deep. It's deep for everyone in general, I know that. And it's especially deep for some. But I also know it wasn't deep enough for me, or not as deep as mine for you. This is not a complaint or a criticism. It's a fact, and it's a fact it took me almost until this moment to face. I knew it, I think, always, but I didn't want to see it.
> Now, looking back at our time together, what I see is my own reflection staring back at me from a glass window. I can see the beautiful diamond beyond, the diamond of your love—visible, close, but beyond reach. Surrounding it is fire. There was a time when I would willingly have reached into that fire, would have braved the burning agony of it. It would have been insanity, or at least I would have been dancing around the edges of insanity, to break that glass, to burn myself on a fire that wasn't burning for me.
> I almost don't want to tell you this. I know you will feel guilt that I don't want you to feel. I tell you because I need to assure you that I am undamaged, that my belief in

love is not diminished. I want you to know that I'm now content in the knowledge that the fire was not burning for me, and that I can say this without rancor: I envy the man for whom it will one day burn.

When I left Assisi, I headed for known territory, for a place where I'd once known happiness. For me, that's Burlington, and my alma mater UVM, because of Robert. You remember Robert, I'm sure. He's the music professor who gave me the medieval vielle, the man I was in love with, the man who died in the car crash, the man I almost followed into death. He had made me believe that there could be love for me.

I'm glad I didn't follow him, because of you. You, too, made me believe there could be love for me, and I will always be grateful to you for that.

So I'm back in my old stomping grounds, as it were, and I'm about to start another degree program (the first, of course, was my degree in education). This one is in creative writing. Perhaps I'll write the mythological Great American Novel. Perhaps I'll end up teaching creative writing. Perhaps both.

I don't expect you to write back. I don't expect you to want to stay in touch in any way. I merely offer you the option. For now, I send you —

Love, always.

Marshall

Something fell onto the paper, smudging the word "expect." Then another blurred "stay." I set the paper down where no more tears would obscure Marshall's message.

Not a complaint. Not a criticism. And yet I felt ribbons of

wounded, tortured flesh rise in welts across my back, and then across my heart.

So many times since he'd disappeared, I had tormented myself with imagined scenes that might have become real if I had admitted the truth to Marshall. I had known that he was emotionally fragile, and I had used that as an excuse to remain silent, to hide the truth from him. I'll never know whether silence was the better course. But at least now I knew that Marshall had survived, that he had weathered the storm that had threatened him here. It had been a storm of hatred from one direction, general love and acceptance from his church, and from me—what? I'd offered him nothing harmful, nothing toxic, and yet what I'd given him had been destructive in its emptiness. Or so I had thought.

It would have been destructive, except that Marshall had proven himself to be made of sterner stuff than I'd given him credit for. And now he was setting off in a new direction, putting his life onto a track that suited him so well I rejoiced in it.

I would write back. But not yet. I would re-read this letter, and again, and maybe again until I felt my response to him would be as truthful and as courageous as his letter to me.

The blotched spots dry, I folded the beautiful paper and tucked it back into its envelope.

I didn't get down to New York until the end of July, partly because I wanted the trip to last more than a few days. I hadn't had a vacation since I'd been Assisi's UU minister, just shy of a year. Plus I'd wanted to give Myra a chance to come up to speed as our newest lay minister before I left; in my absence, it would be too much to rely on Andrea and Jenny alone, especially since Jenny was standing in for me on the Sunday I'd still be gone.

Early on Tuesday the twenty-sixth I dropped Klondike off at Myra's. My dog and hers had, as the Little Boundary vet had hoped, become friends. I thought Myra had done a great job at rehabilitating Nellie, treating her as she'd been advised without expressing regret or sadness at the dog's injury. And Klondike didn't even seem to notice that his companion was handicapped.

My old copy of *Sleuth* packed safely in my luggage, I headed out on the four-plus-hour drive to New Haven, where I'd leave the Jeep, and then a couple more hours via train to Manhattan. The train from Montpelier to New York wouldn't have taken a lot longer, but I wanted some freedom on the return. I hadn't seen much of Vermont, and I might want to take a side trip or two.

As I drove, I pictured my planned visit. I wanted to make a few more decisions about what was still in storage from my parents' house, and there were some places I'd been especially fond of in the city that I wanted to revisit. The Cloisters was a big draw for me, as was MOMA, the Museum of Modern Art, which my parents had supported generously. Sunday I'd go to services at the church I'd grown up attending, but I also planned to spend some time with the minister at Ruth's UU church. Dr. Stein had been hugely influential in my decision to join the UU tradition, and I wanted to pick her brain now that I no longer had Vanessa to bounce ideas off of. Maybe I'd even visit General Theological Seminary, where I'd earned my Master of Divinity.

And I wanted to visit Green-Wood Cemetery in Brooklyn, where my parents' graves were.

I didn't know how much time Donald would have to spend with me. I wasn't sure how much time I even wanted to be with him, given how I felt about him.

The final show of *Sleuth* would be Saturday night, and Donald had told me my ticket, along with those of Ruth and Nelson, were for the Friday performance.

"Saturday the cast will be all, like, 'It's the last show! We're so sad! We're so happy!' I don't know how focused we'll be with our delivery."

It rained for most of the drive down, though it was mostly light showers except for a couple of times when it pelted down. At one point, Jeep or no Jeep, I pulled off to the side to wait for a particularly heavy downpour to pass.

Without the distraction of traffic, freed from the task of assessing the danger posed by the rain, my mind wandered. At first it traveled to New York. But within seconds, as though pulled by some strand of elastic, it leapt to Marshall's letter.

Some of the phrases danced inside my mind, but the one that appeared most often was this: *I envy the man for whom it will one day burn.*

In my effort to hide from Marshall the deficiency of my feelings for him, I'd never told him about Donald, except to say he was someone I'd been with in New York, years ago. And what Marshall hadn't known, what I knew now with a certainty that tore at my heart, was that that phrase—the man for whom it will burn—should not say "one day." That man was Donald. And it burned already.

Was this my punishment? That the fire Marshall couldn't or shouldn't reach for, was burning for someone who would never reach for it?

The rain pounded on the roof of my car and ran down the windows as though in substitution for tears I didn't shed, tears I couldn't shed. Tears were inadequate.

The train part of the journey was uneventful, though I surprised myself in Penn Station. At first it seemed overwhelming: all the people rushing around, the vendor carts everywhere, and every so often a police officer or two. But then something kicked in, and I felt like a New Yorker again, weaving and dodging despite my luggage, and standing in the line of people waiting for taxi cabs.

The sky here was grey, and the streets were wet and steaming, but the rain had passed. I was glad I'd chosen the same hotel where I'd stayed last October, when I'd been here for Ruth's wedding. It wasn't home, but it felt at least a little familiar.

Ruth and Nelson had invited me for dinner, but I'd begged off until Wednesday night. All I wanted to do after my long journey was enjoy a quiet meal alone in the elegant dining room and then turn in early.

Wednesday dawned bright and hot, and as I walked to MOMA I inhaled the familiar, faint smell of garbage, inescapable throughout the city on hot summer days.

After the museum, I wandered through the southern part of Central Park for a while and then took a raspberry snow cone to a bench in the shade, where I watched crowds of tourists parade by wearing brightly colored clothing, most of it damp with sweat, putting me in mind of the expression "air you can wear."

I took a luxurious shower and changed clothes before heading over to Ruth's. I was glad Donald would already be at the theatre by then; I wasn't ready to see him.

Ruth hugged me for nearly a minute when I arrived at the spacious penthouse apartment she shared with her husband, Nelson. He hugged me, too, and once more I was struck by his Nordic good looks. Nelson was a deprogrammer, a psychologist who worked with individuals who'd been swallowed up and brainwashed by cults. He didn't kidnap them, but he had connections to people who did. Nelson had deprogrammed Donald. I smiled inwardly at the idea that Nelson's attractiveness might have helped that work.

"Thank heaven you have the air conditioning on!" I said as I pulled the top button of my cotton shirt away from my body in a fanning motion.

"July in New York," Nelson agreed. "Every year I'm tempted to move to Alaska."

Ruth gave him a teasing scowl as she handed me a tall glass of refreshing iced tea. "You're welcome to something stronger when you're ready," she said, "but first, re-hydrate."

Ruth had me sit where I could look through the large living room window at the trees of Central Park waving to me gently with the light breezes that flirted with them. Or perhaps it was the leaves that were flirting. It was late afternoon, and the slanting rays of the sun on its way toward the horizon caused shadows on the leaves to dance—a gentle waltz perhaps, not a polka.

I could have sat for quite a while, saying nothing, doing nothing other than slowly reducing the amount of iced liquid in my cold glass. But I wanted even more to ask Nelson something that had occurred to me during the moments when I'd pulled over to wait out the heaviest rain.

I set my glass down and looked at Nelson where he sat, a little off to the side in an upholstered chair that matched the couch where I sat, the pattern in the fabric a subtle, almost subliminal pattern of vines and flowers in pastel shades on a cream background.

"There's something I'd love to know," I said to him, "though I'm not sure it's something you're ethically allowed to talk about."

"Color me intrigued," he said and set his own glass on the table beside him.

"I've talked with Donald about what it was that drew him toward the Risen Christ cult, though I don't fully understand how he became so subsumed. But what I'm curious about is how challenging it was for you to convince him it wasn't where he needed to be."

He gave me a coy look from under his blond eyebrows. "You want to know my secrets, do you?"

I laughed. "No. I leave them undisturbed. I'm thinking more about Donald in particular. Is there anything you can tell me about what convinced him to leave that group behind?"

Nelson took a deep breath, releasing it as he scanned the room with his eyes, more likely focusing on things inside his head than on anything around him. "I can tell you this much. People don't change their minds—or their hearts—because of facts. There is a deprogramming technique that depends on peppering the adherent with facts intended to dismantle the veracity of what the cult told them. That can be useful, and it's a tool I use judiciously. But the way I practice, getting the adherent to listen to me requires that I first listen to them. I need to get a sense of what it is in their lives they lack that they thought the cult fulfilled. Only then can I begin to introduce facts and logic that help them see they won't find what they seek within the cult." He chuckled. "Of course, really, the first thing is to get them to talk to me."

"How do you do that?"

"See? See? You *are* after my secrets!"

Ruth interrupted the exchange briefly to offer smoked salmon roulades with cream cheese and chives. I paused to admire the slivers of chive stuck into the rolls so that the slender green fragments stood straight up.

"Seriously, though," Nelson continued, "the best technique is silence. Most people don't deal well with silence, especially if they feel challenged. And, believe me, adherents newly escaped or removed from cults feel challenged."

Ruth asked me, "Are you considering a side hustle to augment your ministerial duties?"

I laughed. "Oh, there's no time for that." I described the progress of opening lines of communication between The Forest and Assisi, and how the effort was affecting even Little Boundary. When we moved to the table for the meal, I talked at length about the Beltane festival, including Kira Blake's surprise announcement.

Ruth and Nelson listened intently, interrupting rarely with a clarifying question, until I said, "I'm sorry. I've monopolized the conversation for too long."

Ruth set her wine glass down and shook her head. "No, we want to hear all this. We've had Donnie's version, in which you are the hero. Your version shines the light on other people's efforts and contributions, which," she grinned at me, "kind of makes you the hero as well."

"Oh, pish," I said. "There were so many heroes that day."

"He said you found a home for the transsexual girl whose father beat her?"

"Yes. A wonderful couple. She's a psychologist, so she already had some understanding of Kira's situation."

Nelson asked, "Do you find it difficult to use feminine pronouns for this child?"

"Child," I echoed. "Kira is fast becoming something other than a child. And no; no difficulty at all once I met her and witnessed her conviction."

I decided to venture into less than comfortable territory for me, and maybe for my hosts as well, given the breakup between Donald and Jonathan. "Situations like hers is something Jonathan Ehrlich hopes to be able to support with Prospect House."

"Yes," Ruth nodded. "And I'm so glad he and Donnie have worked out a few things."

A few things…. These would be "things" of which I was ignorant, "things" that would require more than a few conversations between them to "work out." I made my tone as casual as I could manage. "That sounds good. What kinds of things?"

"As you know, Donnie's always been interested in outreach. Working with schools, that sort of thing. And Jonathan asked if he'd be interested in grant writing, so now he's looking into that. He might even do some coursework on it."

"I'm glad they've been in touch."

I was tempted to ask if the two had patched things up to the extent that Donald would move north again, back with Jonathan. My brain couldn't wrap around what the relationship looked like at this point. Had Donald decided that working with Jonathan was a dream they shared after all? Had he had enough of acting already? Or was he going to do this work for Prospect House from New York, between acting gigs?

My mind froze. I enjoined my heart to do the same, but it was unruly. Unbiddable. It kept insisting that if Donald was going to move north, he should be with me, not with someone who hadn't proved he could see Donald as a whole person, not with someone who disapproved of Donald's crazy vocabulary while still preferring Donald's silly, whimsical side and ignoring the spiritual depth and intellect of my Puck.

I busied myself over-assiduously with the spaghetti carbonara on the plate in front of me, though in my peripheral vision I barely caught the look that Nelson and Ruth exchanged, a look that I interpreted as, *Should we not say any more about Donald?*

I changed the conversational topic by asking about Ruth's studies. She was in the process of becoming a psychologist, and I teased her about having quite a few of those among my family and friends.

Nelson narrowed his eyes at me. "And isn't that part of your own job, at least to some extent?"

"Busted."

I spent most of Thursday at The Cloisters. The cool of the stone walls, the shade of the central garden, and the dark rooms where the unicorn tapestries lived were calming. I sat wherever there were free benches and let the art and the antiquity wash over me, pacify my spirit, and appease my over-active mind with imaginings of what it would have been like to tread these stones in sandaled feet as a medieval-period monk, arising several times each night for various prayer rituals. They did this in all seasons. Perhaps the stones would be refreshing in summer, but in the dead of a European winter it might have tried their very souls.

I considered getting last-minute tickets to a Broadway show, but I'd have to go alone. Plus it might feel like a slap in the face, or at least a not-so-subtle put-down to Donald in his off-Broadway role. Off-Broadway was nothing to sneeze at, but it wasn't Broadway.

Alone again at my dinner table at the hotel, I indulged in something I loved doing at fine restaurants: making a meal out of appetizers. After placing my order I opened my copy of *Sleuth*. I had re-read the script at home a couple of days ago, but I couldn't resist revisiting Donald's character Milo and how he had turned the tables on the narcissistic, self-aggrandizing Andrew Wyke.

I had just finished my final appetizer of subtly-flavored meat dumplings when someone appeared on the other side of my table, standing beside the empty chair. I looked up to see a stunningly attractive man, perhaps in his early thirties. He was no one I'd seen before. His dark hair was just long enough to form a teasing wave over his forehead. Dark eyes framed in darker lashes gazed at me from beneath perfectly-shaped brows. The term "sculpted" came to me when I regarded his jaw, decorated by full, cleanly-defined lips.

I should say something, I thought. *I should speak*. Nothing came to me.

"May I join you for a drink?"

I tilted my head, which I did out of confusion but which he took for invitation. I didn't disabuse him.

He reached a hand out. "Ned Bennett," he said.

I gave him my hand. "Spencer Hill."

Ned pulled the chair out and sat in it, and a waiter brought him the half-bottle of wine and the glass Ned must have left at his own table, or perhaps at the bar.

"I saw you here Tuesday night," he opened. "Also alone. You're traveling?"

I closed my script and held the front so he could see it. "A friend has a leading role. I'm here to see him do what he does so well."

"*Sleuth*. Kind of a classic, I would say. What's his role?"

"Milo. Do you know the play?"

"Sort of. Where is your friend's production?"

"I don't know, actually. Another friend procured the tickets, and," I braced myself for my next words, which would not have applied to me for most of my life, "I'm not from New York."

"No? Where's home?"

"Northern Vermont." I could have said Assisi. I could have said I was a minister. I could have said any number of things that would have made it clear I was not available, even to this god of a man who, for some reason, had taken an interest in me.

"No? Something about you tells me you're quite comfortable here in the city."

No harm in talking, I decided, so I told him where I'd grown up, where I'd gone to school, how much I had enjoyed the culture of Manhattan, all the while answering questions he asked. I did my best to ask him similar questions, but he seemed more interested in hearing my stories.

We both ordered desserts and glasses of Armagnac, and then more Armagnac, and then he asked, "What took you to northern Vermont? Why did you leave the city?"

There was no point in obfuscation. "It's where I was sent. To the parish of Assisi. I'm a Unitarian Universalist minister."

One eyebrow rose. "Really. Well, now I'm even more intrigued." Then he said, "You have a room here in the hotel. Yes?"

"Yes." I knew he wanted me to say more. I wanted to say more. But I didn't.

"I'd love to see it."

Tempted. I was so tempted! But being back in New York had reminded me about the prevalence of HIV/AIDS. The idea of going through the process of assessing each other (whether he'd been tested, and having to admit that I had not done that recently, and figuring out who had condoms) when, really, there was only one man I wanted to bed, made me decide against what might have been a great night but would definitely have been a risky move.

Besides, he'd said he was here Tuesday. He'd seen me Tuesday. Did he come to the lounges of elegant hotels to look for action? If so, that was another reason to decline.

I set my empty glass down slowly. "I admit, I'd kind of like to show it to you. But I don't think so. No."

He threw me a look that was part puzzlement, part irritation, then nodded and left.

I watched his retreat, greedily admiring the way his ass filled out his slacks, imagining running my hands over those broad shoulders and giving a series of gentle pinches to his tits, almost feeling in real time the way my tongue would play with his.

Stop it, Spencer. Plenty of time for this upstairs, later.

I sighed and picked up the script once more, though my mind didn't register the words my eyes saw. I smiled, delighted that someone like Ned had seen me, even watched me to some extent, and had propositioned me. And, far from being put off by my profession, my calling, he had launched right into the suggestion of sex. I almost wanted to call him back, tell him I'd changed my mind.

Still staring sightlessly at the words on the page before me, a realization slammed into the side of my brain. Although when I'd been in New York as an out gay man, and although I'd become accustomed to precisely the kind of safety check I hadn't wanted to go into with Ned, nothing like that process had occurred to me in Assisi. It's true the only men I'd fucked there had been Marshall and then Adam, and it's true we had always used condoms. But it hadn't even occurred to me to talk with either of them about testing. It hadn't occurred to me to get tested. The threat of HIV/AIDS hadn't occurred to me at all since I'd left New York.

Foolish. I'd been foolish. Snow and ice and farmlands and mountains were no protection from this menace, this scourge. Convinced as I was that I was not in danger, I vowed to see a doctor as soon as I returned home.

And with that thought I took myself up to my lonely hotel room and imagined a sensual encounter with Ned. But before the consummation, Ned had disappeared.

I was having sex, for the first time in years, with Donald.

CHAPTER 27

When Donald and I had met, in that New School class on acting techniques, my delivery style had been so lackluster that my seminary advisor had insisted I enroll in exactly that kind of class. At Donald's suggestion we'd worked on *Sleuth* together, and he did manage to pull me out of my shell—in terms of delivery, that is, as well as in other ways. But we hadn't made it all the way through the script before I got cold feet, before I decided that in my chosen vocation, that of an Episcopal priest, I would be handicapped as a gay man.

I'd cut myself off from Donald. I'd tried going out with a beautiful, fascinating woman, also a candidate for the priesthood at General Theological Seminary. When that had failed, I'd considered celibacy.

Ha.

So I'd thought my life's goal, the only goal I'd ever had, was gone, and I'd thrown caution to the wind. I'd reconnected with Donald and dived headlong into a relationship with him. That had lasted until he'd dived headlong into the Risen Christ cult.

At some point I'd finished reading *Sleuth* and had even practiced some of the parts myself, in the privacy of my home. Years later, seeing it played out on stage by real people—with Donald as

Milo Tindale and an actor named William Baines as Andrew Wyke —was captivating.

I sat beside Ruth, Nelson on her other side, and forgot where I was. I nearly forgot *who* I was.

William was good. Donald was magnificent. And as the play continued, I became gradually more despondent. *This* was where Donald should be. *This* was his calling, as sure as the ministry was mine. He would never be my life partner, even if I were given a Manhattan post. And if, for one second, he made a move to be with Jonathan in Vermont again, I would hogtie him and bring him back to the city.

God, but my heart hurt! I think it was sitting there in the dark, watching Donald be the actor he was meant to be, that I finally acknowledged our separation, that I managed to slaughter any hope I'd harbored that maybe, just possibly, by some slender chance, we'd be together again.

I told myself it was better to know. I told myself to be happy for him, and in a way, I was. But in another way I was devastated.

Saturday I avoided seeing anyone. Donald called my room before I could escape and said we should "do something together," but I begged off. I needed to go through the storage rooms, I told him. At least I needed to whittle the mass down to two rooms, and I wanted to do that alone.

"So can we have a late dinner together?" he wanted to know.

"I'm not sure when I'll be finished, but I am sure I'll be an emotional wreck."

"Tomorrow, then?"

"Tomorrow I'm attending my old church, and then I'm going to visit my parents' graves."

I thought he might ask to come with me, but by then he must have picked up that I was deliberately making myself unavailable. All he said was, "When are you headed back?"

"Monday morning, unless I decide to leave Sunday afternoon."

There was silence on the line, and then, "Spencer, are you all right?"

"Me? Oh, sure. Just a little nostalgic, I think, being back more or less in my old stomping grounds."

More silence. "K, then. Bye for now."

~

Sifting through my parents' derelict belongings was about as unsettling as I'd expected. I didn't find anything like that box of love letters I'd discovered during my last excavation, but in my resolute state—brought on by my determination to exorcise Donald from my hopes and dreams for the last time—I was able to separate enough material to be donated or trashed that I did clear out one storage cell.

So that was good.

~

No one approached me over dinner Saturday. Not surprising; I must have had a figurative rain cloud hovering a few feet above my head.

I did manage to find some peace Sunday morning, sitting alone toward the back in my old church, Saint Ignatius of Antioch Episcopal. I even went up for communion, giving Father Fleming a bit of a shock when he saw me.

It was my intention to leave quickly, back out into the heat that was only partially mitigated by passing clouds. But before I could escape I was accosted by one of Father Fleming's minions, an African American altar boy who didn't introduce himself. He just said, "The Father would like you to see him in his office. Now."

A royal command. I couldn't exactly refuse. The man had supported me at a time when I'd desperately needed support.

He'd been the first to suggest that my ministry did not have to be in the Episcopal Church.

Father Fleming hugged me and then smiled broadly as he held my shoulders with his hands.

"Spencer Hill. The Reverend Spencer Hill. How absolutely delightful to see you!"

We sat in the two chairs in front of his desk, and he asked what had brought me to the city and why I hadn't told him I was coming.

I tried for nonchalance. "A good friend is in a play, and I decided to take a few days. See him perform. And visit my parents' graves."

At first he seemed to accept my act at face value, and we chatted about life in general for a few minutes. But then silence fell.

"You seem troubled, Spencer."

I looked down at my hands, fingers clasped in my lap. "It's an old story," I said, and I sat back in the chair as if it weren't really important. "I only just managed to convince myself that a relationship for which I'd been holding out vain hope will never be."

He nodded. "The actor friend?"

One side of my mouth lifted in a sardonic smile. "You're very good at your job, aren't you?"

"As are you, I'd wager. Don't talk about this disappointment if you don't want to, but if there's anything you'd like to say, I'm here to listen."

I shook my head. "No. It's just taken me some time to allow myself to face reality."

He chuckled. "I think it was Elwood P. Dowd in the film *Harvey* who said, 'I struggled with reality for thirty-four years, and I'm happy to say I finally won out over it.'"

"Okay, you got me to laugh. I only wish it were that easy."

"You aren't thirty-four yet. Give it time."

I hired a car for a round-trip to Brooklyn, to Green-Wood Cemetery. I wasn't sure I'd find the gravesite right away, but as soon as the car went through the front gate, it was as though something, someone, an angel perhaps, guided me. I had the driver wait nearby, just out of sight; I didn't want to be watched, and I didn't want to be concerned with the fact that someone was waiting for me to complete something that needed an unknown amount of time.

Bettina Maude Reed Hill. Joshua Samuel Hill. They lay side by side, and for the first time I saw that as it had truly been. That is, they had loved truly, deeply, in a way revealed to me only by the letters I had found.

I had imagined that what I wanted or needed to say to both of them would come to me as I stood here. Nothing came. Instead of words, I was consumed with emotions. There was confusion. Anger. Remorse. Frustration. All these and more tumbled over each other, twisting my heart, gripping my throat, and blurring my vision.

As if it came from someone else, I heard my strangled voice say, "I didn't know."

I didn't know how much you loved each other. Father, I didn't know you were capable of adoration or passion for another human being. I didn't know either of you had ever expressed yourself in such naked, vulnerable phrases as those you wrote in those letters.

"I never understood what each of you had given up for love."

And I, I was the product of their passion. I knew Mother had had three miscarriages before me and had been told not to try for a fourth pregnancy at serious risk of her health, even her life. But she did. She was willing to give up her life, if necessary, for me.

My breath caught in a sudden, anguished pain. She had not been alone. As much as he had adored my mother, Father had been willing to risk that love for a child. For me.

My knees buckled and the ground came up to meet me. I knelt there, at the feet of my dead parents, and wept.

∼

At some point, the sobs softened and my breathing evened out, with only the occasional painful catch in my chest. I sat there, grateful for the shade of the huge maple tree nearby but wrung out, unaware and uncaring of the passing of time. Eyes on the headstone my parents shared, my fingers pulled absently at grass blades until I became aware that I was not alone.

Donald sat beside me, close but not touching, facing the graves. I felt emotionally dead—so much so that his appearance did not cause any perceptible reaction.

Neither of us said anything for several minutes. I broke the silence.

"How did you get here?"

"Nelson drove me."

"How did you know where I was?"

"Ruth told me."

"Ruth?"

"She came with you one time, while she was staying with you. While you were still in seminary."

I nodded once, remembering that visit vaguely. Still not looking at Donald, I asked, "Why are you here?"

"If Mohammad won't come to the mountain…."

"What does the mountain want with Mohammad?"

"The mountain wants Mohammad to know how much it loves him."

I shook my head several times, not sure whether I was clearing my ears or denying what I'd heard. Emotion pushed aside the deadness I'd felt a minute ago, and it rose, zombie-like in its determination to live. I stood, and so did Donald.

"And how much is that?" I demanded. "Because however much it is, it's not enough." It could never be enough to be greater than his love for the stage.

He looked confused, hurt. "What's that supposed to mean?"

I fought to control my voice, to convince myself, as much as

Donald, that my desire for his happiness was greater than a desire for my own. "I watched you Friday night. I watched you on that stage, in your element. In your true element. You were where you belong. You came here to rediscover a life you'd left behind, and you've done that. You've found your calling again. And it's as important to you—"

"No!" His shout disturbed the silence of the graves around us. "No."

"No?" My voice began to get the better of me, and it sounded harsh. "So you're going back to Jonathan, to Prospect House?"

He scowled as though I'd spoken in a language he didn't understand. "To Jonathan? Where did you get that idea?"

"Ruth said you'd worked things out. That you'd be doing the work you'd planned."

He stared at me, clearly trying to work out a response. Angry, now, I didn't wait for him to come up with something.

"So which is it, Donald? Are you staying here, where you belong, or are you going back to someone who, you told me yourself, doesn't take you seriously?"

"Will you please let me tell you what I came here to say?"

I crossed my arms over my chest, a gesture that was both off-putting and protective. "Fine."

"I loved being in that play. I loved being back on stage. I loved the applause, the attention, the acknowledgement. The praise. The waves of love from audiences. And that was the problem."

He turned away for a moment, a hand clutching his hair.

"I don't understand," I said. "What was the problem?"

"The problem," he said as he turned back to face me, "is that the waves of love were impersonal. Those people loved what I gave them. They loved me for the part I was playing. They didn't know me at all. They aren't supposed to. And the praise? The attention? Oh, sure, it was great. While it lasted. Which wasn't very long. It's all temporary. And to get it, I have to keep earning it. Over and over and over."

We stared at each other as I tried to work out what he was telling me.

"Don't you see?" His voice begged me. "Acting is just my way of trying to fill the hole where my parents' love should have been. I was desperate for them to look at me. To see me. To really see *me*. They never did. And when I'm on that stage...."

He walked a few steps away, hands on his hips. When he turned back his voice was soft. Tender.

"When I'm on that stage I can almost believe in love. In love that's there for me. But it's a trap. It's not for me. Not really. The kind of love I need isn't something I can get on a stage. The kind of love I need, that I want, and that I want to give, isn't something that's earned." He stepped up close to me and added, "Whether Jonathan expected me to earn his love or not, it felt like that to me. It would always feel like that to me."

My brain tried desperately to take in all that he was saying, to make sense out of it, to understand what it meant, for him and for me and for us.

"Spencer, when I left Vermont, it wasn't just to see if I could make it as an actor. That was part of it, sure. At first. But what I really wanted to do, what I *needed* to do, was find my *self*. I believe I have. And it's not on a stage."

I took a step back, as though more space between us would help me see him better, understand his meaning better.

"And I think it was that play," he said, "that particular play, that helped me see myself more clearly."

"*Sleuth?*"

"*Sleuth*. Not because of the play itself, but because it had been *our* play. The play we worked on together. Oh, Spencer!" One hand clutched his hair again. "Every scene had you in it. You were everywhere. I could barely keep my mind on the script."

"But you were amazing! You were magnificent!"

He barked out a humorless laugh. "Because I was speaking to *you*."

I shook my head in confusion. Unable to form words, I just stared at him.

He threw back his head and laughed a real laugh, though it carried some combination of nervousness and unshed tears. "Here we are again. Back in 1983, with you not realizing that I'd followed you into that classroom." His smile was a little wobbly. "What happens next is up to you."

"Me?"

"You." When I didn't speak, he added, "I've told you I love you. I pray like hell that you love me. Because, Spencer, I don't belong here. I don't belong with Jonathan. The only place I feel like I belong, the only place I've ever felt loved for the ridiculous, impetuous, irrational person that I am, is with you. So, yeah, it's up to you."

What was he saying? What the *fuck* was he saying? "But—are you saying you'd want to be with me? A minister? Because that's nothing like how you've seen yourself. Not for years."

"I know that."

"Do you have any idea what it would be like for you? My time is not really my own. I might get called out at any time, day or night. My Sundays are always work days. My responsibilities—"

"Yes, yes, I know all that. I was up there long enough to see what your schedule is like. You know what would be harder for me? If you had a standard work schedule, tied to a rigid timeframe every weekday, anxious for the weekend by Friday afternoon, steeling yourself Sunday evening for the next five-day stint." He chuckled. "I'm better suited to the schedule of an actor. Or of a minister's partner."

"But—what would you do?"

"Oh, so many things! Jonathan still loves the idea of having me do outreach for Prospect House, like you had suggested. And I'll take a course in grant-writing so I can help with ongoing funding. And I'll support you, just like I did with the Beltane festival. Spencer, I loved—loved!—seeing you with all those people. I was moved to tears so many times while we were working on your surprise party. They adore you!"

He stepped closer to me. "And they accepted me, Spencer. I felt like I'd come home." He swiped at his eyes, a quick, almost irritable brush at the tears that had formed there. Then he threw an arm out sideways, a theatrical gesture gauged to call an audience's attention to him. "Besides, I never did get to visit The Forest."

And there he was. My Puck, punctuating an expression of deep feelings with a true if flippant assertion.

Even so, I struggled to believe what he was telling me. "You're serious."

He let out an exasperated breath. "Not unless you love me, you silly man. Not unless you can finally tell me something you've never actually said to me. Not unless you'll let me love you and all your slightly stuffy, somewhat snobbish, open-hearted—"

I didn't let him finish. I pressed our bodies and our faces and our mouths together as though the world was about to end, as though this was the last kiss anyone anywhere would ever give or get. When I came up for air, I caressed that sweet face with both hands, smoothing his hair, stroking his neck.

"Have I really never told you that I love you?"

"You have not."

"I love you. I love you so much I was willing to let you go, to return here, where I couldn't see you, or hear you, or hold you, or kiss you, because I believed it was what you needed, what you wanted."

He closed his eyes briefly and said, "So for love, you would have given up love. How like you. Truly. And it makes me love you even more."

I pulled him close again and just held him, basking in the warmth of his body, the warmth of his spirit, the warmth of what we shared, and the prospect of what we were going to share.

I held him away enough to see his face. "I want you to be really sure. Because I have no idea how long I'll be in Assisi. It could be years, or I could be asked to serve somewhere else. I might be called to someplace that you might not like. Are you prepared for that?"

"As long as it isn't someplace we can't be together." He shrugged. "And, maybe not, you know, North Dakota."

I resisted the urge to laugh for fear it would end up in tears of joy. "What about your relationship with Jonathan? Working with him again?"

"I always loved Jonathan's project. And what we've 'worked out,' as you put it, is that it should be easier for him to take me seriously if I'm not also his bedmate. For sure, it will be easier for me to insist that he does."

A blue jay called. I think I heard a wren. Then I said, "Are we really doing this?"

"We are. And it's about time."

We kissed again, a long, lingering, gentle kiss, and as I held Donald in my arms, a lightness came over me. Not a light-headed feeling. It was more as though some cage that had encircled my heart had opened, and as heavy pieces of it fell away, my heart fairly grew wings. As though I hadn't known they'd been constricted, my lungs felt suffused with air.

This might not work. I knew that. It might be too much for him. Hell, it might be too much for me. This was such a quick turn-around. But was it? It felt as though this decision had been hovering for a long time. For three years. So it looked quick, but was it really? No.

I turned toward my parents, my arm around Donald's shoulders, and I said something I'd never believed I could have said to them while they were alive. Now I knew better how very much they had loved me.

"Mother, Father, I want you to meet Donald Rainey. My partner."

As we walked toward my waiting car, Donald waved to another car, and it started up and drove away. Nelson, no doubt. I'd have to thank him later.

On the drive back to the city, Donald's hand in mine, we gazed foolishly at each other from time to time, and I thought, *I can't wait to tell Adam he was right.*

FOR LOVE

(*Blessed Be* Series, Book 3)

Robin Reardon

ABOUT THIS GUIDE

The suggested questions are included to enhance your group's
reading of Robin Reardon's novel, FOR LOVE,
Book 3 of the BLESSED BE series.

DISCUSSION QUESTIONS

Note: The questions in this guide contain spoiler information. It is recommended that you finish the book before reading the questions.

1. Do you have reason to think that you have a good idea of who your parents are, and who they were earlier in their lives, as people? Or is your perception of them defined by their role(s) in your life?

2. When Spencer asks Donald whether Jonathan plays piano, Donald answers, "Not as well as you." Did you interpret Donald's answer as referring to something in addition to piano playing? If so, did it surprise you that Donald would say that to Spencer, with Jonathan in the next room?

3. When Spencer meets Jonathan Ehrlich, his reaction is that he likes him. Did you? Why or why not?

4. David Foster asks Spencer to go with him to the hospital, where Ralph/Kira was sent. During the ride, Spencer reads from the DSM (*Diagnostic and Statistical Manual of Mental Disorders-III-R*, pub. 1987) about "transsexualism," which as how this phenomenon was

referred to in 1988. How differently do you see the phenomenon of transgender discussed today? Do you think society has made progress toward acceptance of transgender individuals?

5. After meeting Kira, Spencer wants very much to accept her as who she says she is. Even so, he admits that he struggles to look directly at the concept of "transsexualism," to see it for what it is, because it's so foreign to him. Can you imagine how that would feel?

6. At one point, Boyd Harper tells Jonathan Ehrlich that homosexuality and "transsexualism" are not the same, that one is who you sleep with and the other is who you sleep as. Does this distinction, simplistic though it is, make sense to you?

7. David Foster, Spencer, and then Boyd Harper each interact differently with Kira. Can you describe the differences?

8. Spencer tells Adam that the more secretive The Forest seems to people outside the community, the more intriguing it will be. Does Adam's reaction surprise you? Would you, like Spencer, have expected a more thoughtful reaction from Adam? Or was Adam's reaction understandable, given the history of the region?

9. A number of times, Spencer meets one-on-one with Donald. Each time Spencer feels a reconnection, which grows stronger with each meeting, although at one point he determines that anything rekindling their past relationship must stop. Did you believe his intention? Or was he fooling himself—and, if so, was he aware of it?

10. Before reading *For Love,* were you aware of how many traditions that are considered Christian today had their roots in Paganism? Can you name some of them?

11. In Chapter 18, Spencer tries to help Duncan understand that Kira is the same person she was when Duncan had thought she was "Ralph." Can you picture the metaphor

Spencer uses, about tables? Does that metaphor make sense to you?

12. As the Prospect House project begins in earnest, Donald tells Spencer that he and Jonathan have agreed that renovations will go more smoothly (in 1988, in northern New England) if the project's purpose, and Jonathan's sexual orientation, are not obvious. Can you see how that might be true? Do you think it was the right approach to leave Donald so much in the background, given the time and the place?

13. Spencer becomes convinced that the actor in Donald has meant that he tends to adjust the part he plays in a relationship to accommodate the person playing the other part. Many people make this kind of adjustment to some extent. Have you found yourself acting in different ways depending on whom you're with? Do you think Donald took it to an extreme so great as to jeopardize his relationship with Jonathan? Or did you see other reasons why that relationship failed?

14. Spencer was surprised, at first, when Myra Langtree said she was leaving The Forest and wanted to join the Unitarian Universalist congregation. There were some clues earlier in the story that might have given a sense of something about to change with Myra. Did you pick up on any of them?

15. What would you give up for love?

AUTHOR'S NOTE

[This material contains spoilers. It is recommended that readers finish the story before reading further.]

Each individual who writes has their own process for the work. Some authors of fiction won't write the words "Chapter One" until they have a complete outline, as well as character sketches of the most important characters. Other authors, like me, love a blank page; we write "Chapter One" and then we're off.

I'm far from the only author of fiction who feels more like a medium than a creator, in that my characters tell me the story and I write it down. Following this process, I'm frequently surprised by who the characters are, and by what they say and do. Here are some examples of surprises that *For Love* had for me, things I didn't know would happen until they did.

- Kira, named Ralph at birth, is transgender. I had thought "Ralph" would be gay.
- Spencer and David Foster, the Protestant minister, become good friends.
- Boyd Harper and Spencer do not end up having any kind of personal relationship. Boyd does not become a UU lay minister, and in fact he leaves Assisi to work with Jonathan Ehrlich at Prospect House.
- Myra Langtree's idea of combining Beltane and May Day into a festival for both Pagans and non-Pagans feels

to me like genius on *her* part. Almost everything about that festival surprised me.

- Klondike works with two border collies to protect a herd of sheep from coyotes.
- Spencer's congregation gives him a surprise birthday party. It surprised me, too.
- Adam foresees the change in the relationship between Spencer and Donald, and he plans his final intimacy with Spencer accordingly.
- Myra Langtree leaves The Forest and joins Spencer's UU congregation.
- Donald leaves Jonathan.
- Donald realizes that the love he receives from acting is not only temporary, but also that it must be earned over and over; he wants a life with Spencer, in which neither of them must earn love.
- Spencer comes to a realization about his parents that makes him understand how much they had loved each other, and how much they had loved him. He sees what they had given up for love.

If you enjoyed this book, please consider posting a review on the online sites of your choice. This is the best way to ensure that more titles by this author will become available.

If you would like to be notified with news about this author's work, including when new titles are released, you can sign up for Robin's mailing list at https://robinreardon.com/pages/contact.

ABOUT THE AUTHOR

Robin Reardon is an inveterate observer of human nature, and her primary writing goal is to create stories about all kinds of people whose destinies should not be determined solely by their sexual orientation or gender identity. Her secondary writing goal is to introduce readers to concepts and information they might not know very much about.

Robin's motto is this: The only thing wrong with being queer is how some people treat you when they find out.

Interests outside of writing include singing, nature photography, and the study of comparative religions. Robin writes in a butter yellow study with a view of the Boston, Massachusetts skyline.

Robin blogs (https://robinreardonwrites.substack.com/) about various subjects that influence her writing and her life.

Other Works by Robin Reardon

Novels
FOR LOVE OF GOD (Book 1 of the *Blessed Be* series)
FOR LOVE OF SELF (Book 2 of the Blessed Be series)
ON CHOCORUA (Book 1 of the *Trailblazer* series)
ON THE KALALAU TRAIL (Book 2 of the *Trailblazer* series)
ON THE PRECIPICE (Book 3 of the *Trailblazer* series)
AND IF I FALL
WAITING FOR WALKER
THROWING STONES
(Above titles published by **IAM Books**)

~

EDUCATING SIMON
THE EVOLUTION OF ETHAN POE
A QUESTION OF MANHOOD
THINKING STRAIGHT
A SECRET EDGE
(Above titles published by Kensington Publishing Corp.)

~

Short Stories
GIUSEPPE AND ME
(Published by **IAM Books**)

www.ingramcontent.com/pod-product-compliance
Lightning Source LLC
Chambersburg PA
CBHW072054190726
48294CB00005B/1506